# OKAY, CUPID

## MASON DEAVER

**PUSH**

ISBN 978-1-338-77770-3

10 9 8 7 6 5 4 3 2 1    25 26 27 28 29

Printed in the U.S.A.  40

This edition first printing 2025

Book design by Maeve Norton

THIS BOOK IS FOR HƯƠNG,
WHO IS STILL HERE.

# CHAPTER ONE

I've never understood why humans have to make it so difficult to fall in love.

A meet-cute, a little flirting, some hand-holding and dates, maybe a scary movie that causes some "accidental" physical contact. Then a walk home that ends with kisses stolen on the front steps as they say good night.

Or rivals in college, vying for that coveted position as . . . well, I haven't been to college, or really even high school, so I don't know what smart college students fight over, but maybe they want to be the professor's assistant or something? Maybe a couple broke up, one of them getting cold feet before they realize they *do* love the other person, and they were just afraid to give love a shot.

My favorites are childhood best friends—extra points if they grew up next to each other—whose stolen looks and unrealized feelings build to this crescendo of big emotions boiling over, realizing that the person that they wanted was right there beside them all along, and they just never saw it. But luckily, it wasn't too late.

Love is so magical.

Except humans are . . . well, complicated, to say the least. Always getting in their own way, letting their anxieties and fears distract them, never being bold enough to make that move.

Then again, I guess if humans knew everything about falling in love, I wouldn't have a job.

In my experience, few people actually want to run halfway across a city during rush hour or buy a ticket for a flight they'll never make just to catch the person they love moments before they board a plane to the other side of the country.

That's our responsibility, though. To push the humans toward something more, to urge them forward and break down the boundaries, to fight for their own love.

That's what we're here for.

That's what *I'm* here for.

Because I'm a Cupid. And a perfectly fine one too.

Today, being a perfectly fine Cupid means sneaking into the back of a local café. I grab a blue apron from the alcove near the exit and wipe the name Gary off its name tag, writing my own in its place in big white letters.

A quick little wave of my hand, and suddenly everyone who is either in this café or walks in will think I belong here, that I've worked here for months. And that way, no one will think I'm just some random kid who stumbled into the back of the café without permission. I can't afford to miss the couple that I'm here to help.

Richard's voice echoes in my ears. I can imagine the expression on his face once I've done my job, that look of pride that's mostly hidden by the beard, but I can still tell when he's making it. It's the look that tells me he doesn't believe he wasted sixteen years of his and Leah's lives training me to be a Cupid, that I am actually worth his time and energy, and that he hasn't screwed up by giving me a second chance. I have to ignore the voice in the back of my head that's telling me I'm the one who's going to screw up. Again. Even though I've done this dozens of times before, and I've only ever fucked up once. And okay, maybe it was a *huge* fuckup, the worst fuckup I ever could've made. But if the nerves get to me now, I can kiss this all goodbye.

Ugh, kiss.

I nod to one of the guys washing the dishes, doing my best to make it seem like I belong here. Because my magic is only half the performance.

The rest is all me.

Fixing the cap to my head, squashing down my hair so it'll fit, I walk through the door to the front of the shop, which is right where I need to be.

I'm the background character, the cardboard cutout tree, unnoticed. Invisible.

"Hey, Jude!" Another coworker steals a sip of water from a transparent plastic cup hidden under the counter. "Hope you're ready for the rush."

"Right, yeah," I tell her, because my mouth is about a mile behind my brain in terms of functioning right now. There's a lot to take in, from all the coffee dispensers and flavor options to the menu to the line that's stretching toward the door.

At least I know the disguise is working.

"Okay, Jude, we're busy today, no messing around!" My brand-new manager, Ray, stomps right up to me without giving me a second to breathe. He looks like the kind of guy who might keel over at any moment, his poor heart giving out. I step in behind him, double-checking the crowd so I know for a fact I haven't missed who I'm here for. "I need you on register. *Now.*"

Register, directly in front of all the customers.

There's no chance I'll miss Claire and Henry as they come through the front doors for their morning orders.

There was a time I loved being in the middle of the action, getting to be the center of attention. I'd go up to adults when I was younger and use my cuteness to my advantage. Richard and Leah always told me I was meant to be a Cupid, that it was evident from a young age. Leah loves telling the story of the time I pretended I was lost in a park and got these two best friends stuck in a perpetual will-they-won't-they situation to finally admit their feelings for each other while they helped me find her.

I'm still pretty proud of that one.

That was a long time ago, though, and this is my first time out in the field in months. I'm wondering if Leah was right when she said it's too soon after . . . everything that happened.

*It's not like you can lose your touch,* I remind myself. *This is what you were born to do. You're good at being a Cupid.*

I take a breath and pull out my customer-service voice. A little rusty, but it's still there.

One thing Cupid training can't prepare you for, though?

How to work a register.

My first customer of the day just wants a tall black coffee, and that's easy enough—there's even a button just for that, though he says something about dark roast and I have no idea what that means. The guy behind him wants a white mocha with three shots of caramel. I barely know what a mocha is, let alone a white mocha, and it takes me several seconds to find where the shot buttons are hidden. He gets irritated with me, snatching the receipt out of my hand when I give it to him, but I try to brush him off.

I'm here for one thing, and one thing only.

Next is a customer who wants a fully customized drink with chocolate drizzle, medium ice, extra whipped cream, cinnamon, and nutmeg, with ten pumps of hazelnut and three pumps of mocha powder, and no actual coffee in sight.

"It is eight in the morning," I whisper to myself as I manage to charge the customer for only about half the order.

I keep looking up toward the door when I hear the bell ring as customers walk in, adding to the line that's already forming in front of me.

If all my info was correct, Claire and Henry should be here any moment now.

There are many things our magic can't do for us, many things that leave us to our own devices. Like researching the people we're meant to help.

Richard was nice enough to send me an email with the need-to-know details: Claire and Henry are coworkers, their cubicles on opposite sides of the office, both of them pretty addicted to their work and trapped in the office during and after work hours, so they haven't had much time for love lives. But there's something between the two of them, something the universe has deemed worth my attention.

Stolen peeks when the other isn't looking, awkward breakroom conversations, second-guessing the wording of emails, but not a word exchanged between them.

You'd think there were scarier things in the world than a conversation.

But I can also sympathize.

I decided to take things out of the office in the hope of having a more chill environment. Thankfully, it was easy to determine that they both come to the same café every morning, after I faked being a delivery person and noticed the cups on their desks as I delivered flowers to Henry.

Another sneaky little move to inspire a little jealousy, taking a bouquet of flowers in and asking Claire if she knew where Henry's desk was. She'd pointed me right to him, and I could hear the hesitation in her voice, the curiosity over who just might've sent him flowers.

Being a Cupid means being a little conniving.

After a few too-early mornings of camping out in the café, I had everything ready to go. It was that first day, though, that I snatched my ace in the hole, the finest little detail that would pull them together:

They both order the same thing.

Iced chai, shot of espresso, oat milk.

Once I had that, the rest of the pieces clicked into place. I'd take their orders, make just one of them, and avoid calling out their names. That way, they'd go for the drink at the same time, their hands meeting, fireworks going off as they finally, finally noticed each other outside passing glances in the hallway or in meetings . . .

"Jude! What are you doing just standing there?" Manager Ray glares at me, his brows furrowed together.

I'm stuck there, staring at the screen, wondering how I make sure the coffee order is made to the incredibly specific temperature the customer has requested. "Yes, sir. Sorry, I just . . . don't remember the steps to the order."

He rolls his eyes and takes the cup away from me. "Just take the next one and hand the cups off to me."

I shake off the sinking feeling as best I can and get back to the register. I'm not here to make coffee; I'm here to help Henry and Claire. I only have to survive until they get here, and then I can abandon this post, go back home, tell Richard about my success, and prove to Leah that it was the right move to let me take an assignment.

"Go grab the cold brew from the fridge. We need to refill the dispenser," Ray tells me as he prepares another drink I don't know the recipe for.

"Sure, yeah." I peer over the display case of baked goods that blocks my view of the front door, cursing my five-foot-five stature. I'm not too eager to step away from the register, but Claire and Henry haven't made their pre-work appearances yet.

"Jude, what are you doing? Stop standing around. Come on, you're not new at this!"

I catch the awkward glances of some of the customers, unsure what to do when a manager shouts at an employee.

"Right!" I rush to the fridge, looking for the large vats of black coffee that I can only assume are the cold brew I'm supposed to find. I pour quickly, managing to spill only a few splashes on Gary's apron and my shoes before it's ready to go. By that time, the line at the cash register is stretching toward the door once again, and I'm shoving croissants and bagels into the oven and accidentally burning a few when my attention gets pulled elsewhere.

My heart goes out to baristas everywhere.

Between the heat of the ovens, the smell of coffee that I'm sure I'll never scrub away, and the old people yelling at me because there's too much caramel or not enough sugar or they're sure that I gave them decaf instead of regular, it's almost enough to get me to walk out of here.

The bell rings again, and when my eyes shoot toward the door, I see Henry walking in, holding the door for Claire as she comes in behind him. There's this moment of cute but awkward hesitation, and for a second, I think that my job here might be done without me having to do a thing. It's rare, but it happens sometimes. But Claire's on her phone, Henry forgotten, and he's content to watch her from afar.

So there's still work to be done.

I make a rush for the register, making sure I'll be the one who takes their orders.

"Good morning, what can I get started for you?"

Henry's a pretty handsome guy in that classic sense, looking strong in a button-down that might tear if he flexes the right way. His glasses complete the Clark Kent of it all.

"Large dirty iced chai, please. With an extra shot. Oat milk too, please." It's cute that he repeats his "please."

"Coming right up." I tap the screen on the register.

Claire comes next. She seems a little frazzled this morning, a wilder look in her eyes as she wraps up whatever memo she had to write.

"Hi, how are you?" I ask her, but she doesn't hear me at first. Or she does and her mind is racing too fast to register what I've said.

"Sorry?"

"How are you?" I repeat.

"Oh." She laughs awkwardly. "I'm just . . . my boss, he's . . . you know."

I steal a look at Ray, who is currently passive-aggressively chewing out another barista for the amount of "cookie crumble" being used in our new drink. "Yeah, I know," I say. I take her familiar order and get right to work.

Now's the moment, my time to shine.

The two of them stand at the end of the counter, waiting to pick up their orders. Claire is staring at Henry, watching as he does a crossword on his phone. I can tell Claire finds this endearing; I've caught her smiling, and she even offered an answer once, which Henry thankfully thought was charming instead of intrusive. These kinds of things can always go either way.

"Jude, register," Ray tells me while I'm making Henry's drink. "Abby's taking over the drinks."

"But I—" I have to make sure only one of the drinks makes it to the end of the counter. I have to make sure they both reach for it so their hands will meet and sparks will fly! I have a plan; I don't have time to adapt.

"Jude, did I stutter?"

"No." I duck my head to hide my shame. I nearly trip over myself as I make my way back to the register and try to keep an eye out for Claire's and Henry's drinks.

It's not like I have to be in front of them for the magic to work, and I didn't write their names on the cups, so it should be okay. Yes. Direct intervention isn't always needed; sometimes it's enough for us to line up all the details where they need to be, and they can be carried through on their own.

But part of me wanted to see it happen, to watch it all come together.

I tap the register to wake the screen up. "Good morning, what can I get—"

And I freeze.

Staring at me from the other side of the counter is the cutest boy I've ever seen in my entire life. His deep brown eyes gaze into mine, accompanied by a wide smile that still seems so small, and a dotting of freckles against soft brown skin. His hair is mostly covered by a beanie, but the ends that escape are curly and untamed.

It's a face I know well, unfortunately.

Because I've kissed that face.

I can't even fathom what the chances of this reunion are. There are literally hundreds of thousands of people in this city, more arriving and leaving every single day. And there are hundreds, if not thousands, of coffee shops.

And Leo Dawson just had to walk into mine.

A million different feelings try to drown me all at once. But only one thought comes to the forefront.

*Why?*

Just . . . *why?*

"Hi there." He smiles again, and I notice that gap between his two front teeth that first made my heart rumble. He hasn't changed much since last summer, when I went over to Oakland every single weekday as a counselor for this day camp because two of my fellow counselors had crushes on one another.

I hadn't meant for it to happen, but Leo . . . the way he smiled at me, the way he looked at me with those warm brown eyes, the way he tapped his fingers on his knees when he was nervous, the thick sound of his quiet voice, the way that he loved helping the kids out, lifting them into the air or racing them around on his shoulders . . .

It made me fall.

All of it.

I made the mistake of letting a human get close, letting things get personal. I let the situation go somewhere it never should have gone. I thought it would be okay. I thought being so far away from the city, from Leah and Richard and Cal and everyone else, would make things okay. I sat next to him, I texted him, I held his hand, I whispered sweet things in his ear, and I let him do the same to me. I knew that it wasn't allowed, that it could never go anywhere. Humans are too messy, too emotional, too unpredictable. We're meant to help them as much as we can, and then leave them to their own devices.

But I liked him.

A lot.

And I thought . . .

I don't really know what I thought, actually. Even now, I don't know what to think. The expression on his face is plain; there's no magic in his eyes, no familiarity. When I kissed him, when I let that happen, my powers poisoned him like a venom. I watched as each and every memory he had of me vanished from his mind, erased second by second until there was nothing of me left in him.

It was awkward, to say the least. He stared at me, and he asked with a heartbreaking curiosity in his voice, "Who are you?" My hands still cupped his cheeks. I could only stare at him, dumbfounded, scared, wondering what I'd done to get that reaction out of him.

It's one thing to know what will happen when you break a rule, and quite another to experience the punishment.

"It's me," I tried. "It's Jude?"

"Sorry, uh . . . Jude . . . were we making out?"

For a moment, I hoped it was some cruel joke, that he was just messing with me. But in the weeks that I'd known him, I'd learned that there wasn't a cruel bone in Leo's body.

What the Cupids had warned was true: He'd forgotten all about me. In the span of minutes, the time we'd spent together was gone, and there was no getting it back.

I arrived at my apartment with tears in my eyes, feeling like the only way to feel better was to crawl through my skin and do whatever I had to in order to stop feeling things. That pain lingered with me for a while, and now, seeing him again, I'm realizing that it never really went away.

I just got better at burying it.

"Did you catch that?" he asks, the drawl of his voice luring me in all over again.

"Oh, um . . . I'm sorry." I hesitate, turning to the register. "Can you repeat your order?"

He peers at the menu, rocking on his heels as he tucks his hands into the pockets of his hoodie. "Iced Americano. Venti, please. I need the caffeine."

"Lots of studying?" I ask without meaning to. The quick math in my head tells me that he's a senior now. I wonder if he's still planning to go into childhood development. He was so passionate about working with kids, about volunteering at camps and hospitals. "I mean, were you up late? Studying or, like . . . something?"

I shouldn't be having a conversation with him. He's the reason I'm on probation. Which makes him the easiest possible way to get into more trouble.

He's still smiling, though. "You could say that."

"I, uh . . ." My words are lost the moment they leave my lips. "Sorry."

"You're good. I can imagine your brain gets pretty fried dealing with these people."

"Yeah, it's been a rough one," I tell him.

"Well, if there's anything I could do to make your afternoon more relaxing, I'd be happy to help."

No.

Nope, no. I can't do this. I'm going to combust, right here, right now, in front of this entire café. That will be my lasting legacy. I need to end this; I need to get away from him. Because my heart can't take this. Half a year ago, I felt like I knew this boy better than I knew myself. We shared music and touches and truths—well, all truths but the big one. Right now, looking at him hurts. And part of me can't help but wonder if he recognizes me at all. Am I a phantom to him? Does he even remember those precious awkward seconds after our kiss, after I lost him? My hair was shorter, and I didn't wear makeup because of the heat. But . . . am I still in there? Deep down?

"Sorry, I'm too much of a flirt," he says. "My moms say it'll get me in trouble one day."

"No, it's fine. I, uh . . ." My mouth has gone dry. "I'm sorry, what was it that you ordered?"

He laughs, that soft sound that became music to my ears. "Iced Americano, remember?"

"Yes! Right!"

God, I should never work in customer service.

Ever again.

I grab the cup and my marker, putting the order into the computer.

"What's your name?" I have to ask so I don't raise suspicion.

"Leo."

"Like the constellation." It just slips out. Just like it did the first time he told me his name.

"More like the astrological sign. My moms set me up to be self-centered."

"Yeah . . ." The computer flashes, prompting me to finish the transaction. "Oh, do you need a receipt?"

"Only if it has your number on it."

I understand that he doesn't know what he's doing, that every word he says to me is torture. None of it was his fault, not an ounce of it. He didn't know; he didn't realize what would happen, that we couldn't love each other.

"I, uh . . . uh . . . um . . ." I stammer for a bit. Every word I've ever known has suddenly left my brain.

"You okay?" he asks me, his voice slow. I can't tell if it's his actual accent or if I just can't process anything right now.

"Jude! Get it moving!" Ray shouts from the entrance to the back kitchen.

"Sorry," I spurt out to Leo, writing his name on the cup and finishing the transaction, printing out the receipt and handing it to him in record time before I have to step away from the register, grabbing the cup I've prepared. "I can't do this."

He looks at me in confusion for a moment before I walk away from him. Ray calls out my name, but I don't turn. I just pull the hat off my curls and untie the apron, everything forgotten. Claire, Henry, Ray, Leo. I can't do this. I'm not prepared.

Whatever is going on, I can't deal with it.

"Jude, get the cash register!" Ray shouts over the rush one last time. I feel bad leaving my coworkers here to deal with the slammed line alone.

But I have to leave.

I walk back through the kitchen where my coworkers are racing around. I'm not fit to be a barista anyway. I remember I'm still holding Leo's cup and I drop it like it's burning me. I untie the apron, leaving everything behind for Gary and his shift tomorrow. When I close my eyes, I can still remember the confusion on Leo's face that night, the way his brows knitted together, the blacks of his eyes blown out.

And here I am, six months later, doing the exact same thing I did that night.

Leaving.

Abandoning my post, leaving a job undone. Leah's going to be so pissed at me, and I can imagine the disappointment on Richard's face so easily.

I just . . . I can't.

I stand behind the café, and with a series of gestures, everyone who dared enter that café in the last hour has forgotten about me. It's not necessarily a full erasure of the mind—what good would that do any of us, if we erased the minds of the humans we'd just gotten to fall in love? Instead, the spell works on their memories of me, casting me as a shadow, filling in the spaces where I might've been present.

Even Leo.

For the second time.

I don't like doing this. I don't like worming my way into the minds of other people and taking something that isn't mine. But it's necessary. Part of the job.

I'm back at the starting line all over again. If I'm lucky, my probation will only be extended, extra weeks of training and conditioning.

Because of the same boy.

All for a boy.

A weakness that we're expected to exploit in humans but suppress in ourselves. Because we're above that. At least, we're meant to be.

I walk down to the bus stop, reaching into my pockets to pull out my headphones, pulling up Spotify and pressing play on the first Sufjan Stevens song that comes up on the front page because why not amplify the emotional torture?

The bus arrives a second later, and I stare at the open doors, wondering if I should actually get on and go home, or find another bus to carry me farther south until I reach Los Angeles or something.

But no. This is my life, and I have to deal with what I've done.

I've failed again.

Just like last time.

All over some boy.

# CHAPTER TWO

I don't know how to feel when I get back to the apartment and it's totally empty.

I almost wish Leah were here, so I could go ahead and tell her that I messed up, that she was right all along and maybe I need some extra time and practice. I lock the gate behind me, the draft from the wind nearly snatching our front door out of my hands and slamming it hard. The third-floor walk-up takes the breath right out of me; when I get inside, I slump toward my bedroom and fall face-first into my pillows.

I let out the deepest, ugliest groan that I can muster. I thought I was over this, I thought I was done. Leo wasn't the piece in a puzzle. He didn't fit anywhere; he wasn't meant to.

I'm *supposed* to be over this.

But even now it's so easy to remember the chlorine smell that stuck to his skin after the days at the pool. The way his hair felt in my hands. The moments he'd stretch his arms into the air, giving me that glimpse of his stomach just above the waistline. A sight that drove me wild.

I roll over and stare up at the ceiling, my eyes finding the cracks that sit right above my bed because this building is so old and we've never bothered to do anything about them.

I'm over him. That's what I told Leah and Richard. And I wasn't lying; I truly thought that I'd gotten over him. That I'd managed to throw him away.

Because I am never one to pass up the chance to make a bad situation worse, I make my way to Instagram. Leah and Richard aren't that fond of me having an account. But Cal and I and some of the other Cupid kids convinced them it was necessary. We just have to keep the accounts private.

Leo's profile isn't in my recent searches. Nothing is. The phone was taken away during my probation period because I wasn't going on assignments. But his username has been committed to my memory. There are so many pictures since the last time I saw this profile, stretches of time where he's with friends, family. A day at the beach, a picture from a flea market where he holds up a ceramic cup with fish painted on it. His family went down to Anaheim, to Disney, where he got to make a lightsaber at the Star Wars park.

There's a gap in the pictures as I scroll back, though, a week that's missing that I know was once there. Our magic is nothing if not thorough. Every second of our time together has been scrubbed clean, at least on his end. I still have a picture, though, in my hidden folder, the only picture that sits there. My head on his shoulders, the two of us as close as we could possibly be.

It hurts to look at it now.

It hurts so much.

I close my eyes, wanting nothing more than to open my window and throw my phone out into the backyard, where it'd soar three stories down to the hard concrete and shatter into a billion little unrepairable pieces.

But I don't.

Because I need this thing.

I exit out, going to my text messages, where just three names stare back at me. Richard and Leah, of course. And Cal, the name at the top of my list because he's the person who I talk to the most often.

It feels terrible to say that Cal is my friend by default, because I do genuinely like Cal. He's smart, a great Cupid, and funny. I feel like my day is always better when we get the chance to hang out. But we only know each other because we were trained at the same time, because Richard picked both of us to take as his students. When we got older and I went to go live with Leah, Cal and I still helped each other out and practiced how to use our powers together.

He's the one person who might understand what I'm feeling. And even if he doesn't, because these feelings are supposed to be so foreign for Cupids, then he'll at least pretend for my benefit. He did once before.

ME: are you busy?

His reply comes moments later.

CAL: nope! whatcha need judy jude?
ME: come with me to royal grounds?
CAL: i can be there in ten
ME: thanks.

I manage to sit up, feeling terrible and looking worse. I slip onto the floor in front of the mirror that hangs on my closet door, taking in the damage I've done to my makeup. I only have the energy to wipe away the NYX Light Ivory because I don't feel like hiding behind anything anymore, even the thing that makes me feel the most like myself. Grabbing my bag and slipping my shoes back on, I stomp down the stairs. Once I'm on the street, I try my best to fake any emotion other than the heartache that's settled in my stomach.

The café is closer to me than it is to Cal, so he isn't there when I walk in. I order an iced mocha, but even as I sit there, staring at the cup with the condensation gathering on the glass, the paper straw disintegrating, I can't bring myself to drink it. The thought of coffee, the smell of it even, it's almost enough to make me sick.

As a Cupid, I'm expected to be a master of emotions, both in maintaining my own and understanding just how humans' work. I'm supposed to understand their body language, their movements, their words and tone. I've spent hours analyzing them, trying to get an understanding of how their brains work.

But if humans were simple, easy to understand, then we wouldn't need to intervene the way that we do. If they were honest and forthright with each other, we wouldn't have to make friends with them, influence their lives, convince them to make the right move at the right time.

Then again, I suppose leading a life where you know every correct step and word would be pretty boring.

I turn to a couple in the corner. All they're doing is sharing the same side of a booth, both on their laptops, working on something. One girl looks away, stretching her neck, relaxing into her seat and putting her head on the other girl's shoulder, closing her eyes as if she could fall asleep right there, right now. The other girl smiles, and their hands meet underneath the table, tightening.

I feel myself looking at the two of them, wondering just what their story might be, what they mean to each other.

There's something so soft about love, about allowing yourself to fall for this other person so hard that your brain can't comprehend anything other than being around them for hours at a time, so unwilling to let go of them when the time comes.

But then I hurt my own feelings all over again, conjuring images of that time I spent with Leo and wondering what I'd do to get that back.

I sit there and try to figure out for the millionth time if I was actually in love with him. Leah promised me that I wasn't, that I'm a teenager, that it's so easy for me to get my emotions all mixed together, that I'd make it to the other side glad I didn't do something that I'd regret.

Well . . . look at me now.

I made it to the other side, and I still regret what I did. The problem is . . .

I don't really know which part I regret.

When I was with Leo, things just made sense. They added up. Around Leo, I never felt that urge to second-guess myself or what I was letting happen. Even if the voice in my head never let me forget how wrong it was *supposed* to feel, it never actually felt that way.

He made me feel like I belonged somewhere. He made me feel like I had a place where I was welcome. He made me feel like . . . me. For the first time I felt like myself.

The evolution of me finding my fit began when I grew out my hair and liked the way it looked, when I "borrowed" some clothing and makeup from Leah and did some of the worst things I've ever done to my skin, thinking I was already an expert. I'd grown up just assuming that I was a boy. It's not that the label was forced on me or anything; when I told Leah and

Richard and Cal I felt I was more of a they/them than a he/him, they understood and changed to my correct pronouns without incident. It wasn't even that I felt nonbinary outside the rules that I'd grown up around. I guess agender is a better word. I just didn't care about it at all. I wanted to feel like *me*. I wanted to dress and look how Jude looked and felt, how this version of me that I actually liked would be. And I think I found them, eventually.

But that doesn't mean there wasn't a battle to fight on the inside, wondering how I might want to present myself, thinking of how I wanted to dress, figuring out how things fit me and how I wanted them to look. It was a journey, one that I'm still on in a lot of ways. There are times when I'm doing my makeup that I wish my cheeks were sharper or wonder what I might look like if my body shape were more of an hourglass. Wearing dresses seems like so much fun, but I despise the way I look in them. I mostly go for skirts, tighter pants, baggy jeans, and the oversized-sweater look. Things that help me hide my body, that force me to not have to think about it while also feeling the most comfortable.

"Judy Jude!" As usual, I can hear Cal coming from a mile away. He slips into the seat right across from me, leaving his bag to dangle off the back. "Is this for me?" He grabs the iced mocha.

"Sure, I'm not going to drink it." I just hope coffee isn't ruined for me forever.

"Mhmm!" Cal sticks the straw in his mouth, obviously perturbed by how the structural integrity of the straw has been compromised. "How did things go! You were supposed to seal the deal today, right?"

I look around us for any prying ears. Despite the privacy of our work, Cal's always been pretty cavalier about being a Cupid. He bursts with a confidence in his job that I envy more than anything.

"It, um . . ." I grab the paper wrapper of the straw, balling it up as small as I can get it. "I messed up."

Cal realizes in an instant that this is a serious situation. He puts the coffee down and leans forward in his seat. "Okay, okay . . . Do you actually want to talk about it? Or do you want me to help get your mind off it?"

I bite at my bottom lip. "I wish I knew."

"What about Leah?"

I shake my head. "She's out right now, haven't told her. Though Richard will probably know by now."

Cal bites the end of his straw. "You can't hide much from him."

I let out a long sigh, dropping the wrapper and covering my face with my hands. "Cal! What the hell am I going to do? I was supposed to be able to do this! It was so simple, and I still fucked everything up!"

"Hey, hey." Cal reaches over, pulling my hands away. "It's all right, Jude."

"Is it, though?"

He stares, his gaze comforting. Cal and I might not have that much in common beyond being Cupids. He doesn't engage much in "human" activities like watching movies or reading books. Music is probably his biggest vice; he's always making Spotify playlists and sending them to me because he wants me to expand my musical horizons.

"We've literally all messed up, Jude. All of us. You're not any different."

"I'm supposed to be better than this, though," I tell him. "I . . . just . . . I . . ." I don't know what to say. It almost feels like I'm running out of air, but that I'm breathing too much at the same time. "Leo was there," I finally admit.

"Oh, wow. *Leo.*" Cal pauses, and for once I wish our powers included mind reading. I'd love to know what's going on in there, what he's thinking right now.

I told him about Leo the night before the kiss happened. I said, "I think I have a crush on a human, and I don't want to talk about it right now but I just wanted someone to know and I know that you're not going to judge me." It all came out in a single breath.

Cal accepted this information and kept it to himself.

Now I tell him, "He was there, at the coffee place. I had everything set up, ready to go. Henry and Claire were seconds away from their meet-cute moment. But when I saw him, when I realized that there was nothing of me left in his memory, I couldn't handle that."

"I know what you're feeling . . ." Cal says.

I have to resist the urge to tell him that he doesn't. Cal's a picture-perfect Cupid. There's no mark on his record that'll be there forever. He's never been stupid enough to fall for a human.

He continues, ". . . and I know that whole situation hurt you a lot."

"I thought that I was over it. I thought I'd gotten past it. I'm over him, I am!" It sounds like a lie even to my own ears.

"Jude, you and I both know it's not that easy." He sips more of his drink. "But that's why we're Cupids. 'Cause we're better than humans. We know our emotions better."

Pfft. Right.

"Maybe it's normal that you're still feeling these feelings," Cal says to me.

"You think so?"

"It's been . . . what? Six months? I've got this guy I'm supposed to help out—he and his girlfriend broke up a year ago and he's still stranded in his feelings about it. Which helps because I'm supposed to be helping them get back together, but whatever. You have to get over him. He's just some lousy human, after all. You can do better with your life."

I wish more than anything that I could pop up on the other side of whatever "getting over him" looks like. Because I'd love to know.

Usually hanging out with Cal is an instant mood booster. We understand each other in ways that I don't think even other Cupids are lucky enough to get. I suppose that's natural when you've known each other as long as we have. I've spent many nights venting my frustrations to Cal, and he's done the same to me.

Right now, though, I just want to crawl away into a deep dark hole and sit there with my amateur feelings. I know that isn't the best response, but it feels like my only option.

"Oh, speaking of which. I'm supposed to meet Mr. I-Can't-Live-Without-Her downtown. He needs new clothes and the ex just happens to work at the place where ninety-six percent of his fairly disposable wardrobe comes from. Want to join me?"

I hesitate for a moment and can tell that Cal sees the answer clearly on my face.

I pick up the straw wrapper again. "I think I just want to go back home."

"I know you're just going to go back to the apartment,

sink onto that couch, and wallow in your feelings with one of those godawful movies you call 'rom-coms' that you've seen a thousand times while you have an anxiety attack about Leah coming home."

"Technically *The Devil Wears Prada* isn't a rom-com," I clarify.

Cal stands up, snatching the empty glass off the table and dumping the contents into a bin near the trash can before he leaves it at the counter nearby; then he waves over to me, smile bright on his face. "Are you coming or not? We're going to the Uuuuuuuuuuuuuniqlo." He sings it like he knows the key to my heart.

I feel so tired and energized at the same time. Cal's infectious, even when I don't want him to be. So, really . . . I can't say no.

"I'm looking for a new skirt anyway." I stand, grabbing my own bag.

"Atta they-them!" Cal wraps his arm around my neck and pulls me in close. "See? Things aren't so bad."

# CHAPTER THREE

We take the 38R all the way downtown, where Cal is meeting this boy after school. I insist that I can hang out at the food court until Cal is done, working on what I'm going to say to Leah and Richard, but Cal is insistent.

"I could use your help here," he tells me.

So before this boy gets to the Uniqlo where they're meant to meet, I'm supposed to go in, browse, and find the girl that we're here for. Cal doesn't give me directions; he simply tells me to improvise.

"Cal, I don't know about this," I tell him as we pretend to look through the table filled with oversized T-shirts at the front of the store. If I mess up Cal's assignment, I don't know what I'll do.

"Please, Jude. You've got to get back out there one way or another." He holds a black shirt up to me before deciding that he doesn't like it. "Plus, you're obligated to help me, remember?"

Yeah, didn't need that reminder.

It's been a part of my probation, to be partnered with Cal on multiple assignments of his. Richard thought it would be good for me.

Cal nudges me when the guy approaches. He's tall and broad, built like a football player, with closely cropped hair. You'd never imagine that someone like Cal would ever be friends with a guy like him. Cal stands only a few inches taller than me—though he'll never let me forget those few inches—and since he's more of a fan of the sun than I am, he's more tan, with thick-rimmed black glasses and a nest of hair on top of his head. He's very Peter Parker in his charms. The Andrew Garfield one.

"What am I supposed to do?" I ask him.

"Come on, Jude. It's not your first rodeo." Cal walks away, pretending that he wasn't just talking to me as he goes up to the guy. The two do some weird secret handshake, and the taller guy wraps an arm around Cal's shoulder. It's almost like Cal is a different person. He's always been better at the acting than me.

I move into the store behind them, going for the girl. Her shiny black hair is done up in a ponytail as she makes sure blouses are properly folded. She looks strong, and when she puts the blouses away, I can read the letters on the front of her styled sweatshirt that spell out O'CONNELL HIGH WRESTLING TEAM.

The nerves are back, my hands getting sweaty.

Why did Cal trust me with this?

I spy two girls walking in with drinks from the smoothie shop in the food court, and a plan begins to form. A little dangerous, sure. But what's love without the risk of a few broken vertebrae?

I chew on my bottom lip, scooting closer to the girls, waiting for the magical moment when one of them might set their drink down. Cal reads my mind, our eyes meeting as his friend checks out some Uniqlo anime collaboration. We'll need to get the pieces just right here. A girl is walking toward this section, then stops and puts down her smoothie to check something out. Which means it's time.

I nod at Cal, and he and the boy start walking toward me. I slip into the aisle, ducking down so I can take the lid off the smoothie and tip it over without anyone noticing. Cal's keeping our guy's attention, so he doesn't notice when an entire strawberry-and-mango puddle spills out onto the floor in front of him. His eyes meet the girl's just as his feet are stepping into the smoothie.

The floor is pulled out from underneath him, his shoes sliding on the already too-slick surface.

The rest of the exchange plays out in slow motion. Cal hangs back as his friend flies into the air. For a moment, I'm worried that I might've just ruined someone's life. Back injuries are no joke, and landing on this hard floor will undoubtedly do damage. I ready myself, just in case I need to intervene.

But our girl is quick. The blouse in her hand falls to the floor, now stained with strawberry smoothie as she reacts quickly, holding out her arms and grabbing on to her ex-boyfriend, her arms strong enough to support him. In an instant, both of them are standing there, her staring down at him, him staring up at her as he almost floats in her embrace. There's this beat of shock where neither of them is really sure what to do next. Their gazes linger.

"I slipped," he eventually says.

She lets out this exasperated but happy breath, a smile on her face. "I can see that."

"I, uh . . . Thanks." Finally standing on his own two feet.

"Just watch out for hazardous smoothie spills in the future," she says to him. The moment is awkward, but it's clear from the look on Cal's face that this is the scene he's been waiting for. It's hard to describe when we know we've finished our job. There are no actual fireworks or sparks that go off, no message above their heads that reads MISSION COMPLETE.

It's something internal, unexplainable.

It's the moment that a manager makes an appearance to check on everyone, asking if anyone was hurt, if everyone is okay. The two of them look at each other, their gazes lingering as if they're the only two people in this entire store.

"Yeah," she starts to say. "We're okay."

Cal and I steal another glance at each other and nod, knowing that we've done our job.

Well, Cal did his job. I just helped.

My eyes go back to the lingering stare that the boy and the girl have for each other, the way their cheeks are flushing. They don't even notice that their hands are less than an inch away from each other, but it's like their bodies do, almost as if their fingers are reaching for each other by themselves.

I feel so much worse so suddenly that it hurts.

Because I had that.

I need to stop these thoughts in their tracks. It's no use dwelling on them. Because it's a dangerous path, and if it happens again, there's a worse fate than just probation waiting for me.

I feel a warm hand, fingers intertwining into mine. I finally look away from the couple and their renewed love to see Cal looking at me. He must've snuck around the other side of the aisle.

"Come on," he tells me. "They've already forgotten all about us."

I don't say a word as he leads me away. I think he can tell that something's off again. He's always been too good at reading me. I appreciate the feeling of him against my palm, the knowledge that he's there, that I'm grounded in something other than my own mind.

"You did great," he tells me.

I pause, swallowing hard. "Should we head back?"

"We could . . ." Cal half sings. "Or . . ." He looks past me, and I follow his stare toward the large H&M that takes up a whole corner of this mall. "Maybe a little retail therapy?"

I look back at him, smiling. "You read my mind."

There's an odd sense of guilt that washes over me as I enter the apartment later that day, coming up the stairs with Cal right behind me, each of us with a bag in hand. I was proud to find a new skirt, and a cute T-shirt with a weird advertisement for an apple orchard that was obviously meant to look like it was some stolen prize out of a thrift store but instead sat on a row with twenty other identical shirts.

"Ah, and our two students return!" Richard turns to face us as we walk through the doorway. He's a tall Black man with a short goatee. You'd think he's a good three decades older than any of us with the way he dresses, but he's only a few years Leah's senior. He has the look of a professor, with wire-rimmed glasses, and he's almost always in a tweed jacket, complete with those little elbow patches. And his favorite dress shoes, of course. Cal and I have teased him endlessly about finding him a better fashion sense. "Get some shopping done?" He steals a glance at the bags, and suddenly I feel my face getting warmer.

"We were celebrating." Cal steps in. "On a job well done!"

"Really?" Leah leans in.

"Yep, I asked Jude for their help on a job. They were all too happy to give me a hand!"

Richard smiles. "That's commendable, Jude! Well done."

"Yes, well done." Leah's voice is quieter, more mellow. It

31

usually is, but right now, more than anything, it tells me that she knows what I wish she didn't. But maybe it's better that I didn't have to tell her that I botched my entire morning. She's always felt like an older sister to me; it's believable enough when we needed to use the disguise for our job. We both have the same curly brunette hair, the same pale skin, same green eyes even.

I'll never forget that look on her face as she realized what happened last summer, that dawning, that understanding. She seemed to grow so angry, only to quell it in an instant.

"Well, I'm glad you're home now, Jude." Richard motions to the chair next to him, and I take it, Cal doing the same with the seat next to me.

"Richard?" Leah looks at him expectantly. "Are we going to discuss what happened?"

"Yes, Leah. I was just about to bring it up. Thank you."

"I don't see the point in beating around the bush," she tells him.

"I was giving Jude a chance to tell me themself. We would've gotten there."

Leah ignores this and asks me, point blank, "Is there something you need to tell us, Jude?"

"Right . . . yeah. About that, I—"

Richard looks at me, his gaze both comforting and judgmental. And Leah . . . I know that she loves me, she's never really made me question that. But she takes her duty as a Cupid seriously. When I told her what happened with Leo, it was like I broke her heart.

"I was there, I was doing my job. I had everything set up." I look down at the table because I can no longer handle looking at either of them. I wipe my hands on my skirt, my palms getting sweaty again. "And, well . . . someone was there."

"This person being . . ." Richard prompts.

I gnaw at my bottom lip, pulling the skin with my teeth before I curse myself. I pay too much money for my favorite moisturizer to be chewing my lips to shreds.

The name finally slips out. "It was Leo."

Neither of their expressions change, confirming that they both already knew. Cal reaches over slowly, his hand on my back simply to remind me that he's there.

"I didn't mean for it to happen; I didn't expect him to be there. But he was, and it threw me off. I just . . . I couldn't be there anymore."

"Jude, I thought that we'd worked past—" Leah begins to say, but Richard holds his hand out to stop her.

"So, you now see the full consequences of getting so close to a human?" he asks.

I nod.

"We are meant to help the humans, and then walk away. That's all."

"I know."

"Good." Richard clears his throat. "Our emotions can run rampant if not controlled. Sometimes, they can control us. We're meant to be better than that."

"I know," I repeat.

"And yes, you succeeded at what you were tasked with, but at the expense of your emotions."

"I kno—" I start to say again because these are the words he wants to hear. But then his words click. "Wait. What did you say?"

"That you succeeded?" Richard smiles. "Caught that, did you?"

"Seriously?"

"Despite you leaving early, Claire and Henry still reached for their drink at the same time, just as you intended. I've always liked that idea; it's a classic." Richard smiles softly. "They had a spirited conversation afterward. They're meeting up after work for drinks."

"Jude!" Cal reacts before I have the time to. "You did it!"

"I did it?" The words are still coming slow. "I actually did it?"

"We still need to work on how you control your emotions, Jude," Leah reminds me. "If you're still this raw even after all this time, then perhaps it's for the best that we pull you back in. Additional training, maybe even relocation so the chances of you seeing this boy go from minuscule to impossible."

Relocation? I've heard the word thrown around every few years. It makes sense; we're needed at different places. But Leah always argued that giving a Cupid a place to call home was better than shifting us around for our entire adolescences. I've lived in the Bay Area for my entire life, and the idea of living anywhere else, or being somewhere without Cal . . .

I don't want to think about that.

"Relocation isn't necessary," Richard tells all of us, and I wish it didn't feel like there's still a ball that's about to drop. "I believe in Jude and their abilities."

Leah doesn't say anything, though I know she wants to.

"Look," Cal says, "Jude was able to get not one but two couples together in the same day. Shouldn't that mean they're off probation?"

"Well," Richard says, "I will admit that it could've been cleaner. And Leah isn't wrong; it's clear that Jude is still working through something here. But they *were* successful, I can't deny that. And, perhaps more importantly, they won the bet for me." Richard steals a look at Leah. "You owe me twenty dollars."

"I'll pay you later," she grumbles.

"You bet *against* me?" I can't believe it.

"It wasn't that I didn't believe you could do it," she explains. "I just wanted Richard to be wrong."

"Which I never am," he says with too much pride in his voice. "Regardless. I still want to keep a close eye on you, Jude."

"It isn't going to happen again. I promise the both of you. And I'm going to work on controlling myself. We don't have to move."

"I'd like to believe that. I'd hate to lose the two of you," Richard says. "And I want to trust you. It won't happen again because it *can't*."

Because kissing a human costs them their memories. It's meant to be a teaching moment, to show us that we can never have what we want. That second kiss, though? It costs us everything. Our powers, our memories, our lives as Cupids.

Gone. Just like that.

All because of a kiss.

I look at Leah again, and she looks away, unable to meet my eyes. I can tell that she's still wary, and I wish I didn't understand why, but I do. "So, if I passed today, if I'm ready . . . what's next?"

"Is Jude getting back out there?" Cal asks before I can. I'm glad he does, though. I'm not sure I could've been as direct.

"Well, Leah and I spoke to other Cupids, and we came to a decision. Well, less of a decision, and more of a test, really."

I don't like the sound of this. "A test?"

"Something tougher than your normal assignments," Leah says. "Something longer term."

"Really?" I look over at Cal, who seems to have excitement in his eyes as he looks back at me.

Leah continues, "Two teenagers who live in the area. There's history there—it's messy. You both know how teenagers are. But deep down, the two of them still harbor feelings for each other. We want you to go into their school, get ingrained in their lives, and then do what you have to do to enable them to fall in love again."

"High school?" I've never actually been to human high school before, not in any regular way. All my assignments lasted a week at the most, and they usually involved adults, though I've had to sneak onto campuses once or twice. Usually all I've had to do in the past is steal a job, pretend to be an intern or something. "What do you mean by 'longer term'?"

"This assignment will be more involved," Richard says. "You'll have to do a lot of the work for yourself. So, we're giving you a month."

"A month?"

When I say it out loud, it somehow sounds like too much time, and not nearly enough. A month of public school, of being around other kids my age. I'll go to classes, do homework, maybe some sports games, all while I get to know these two strangers. If the high school rom-coms I've seen are anything to go off, high school is a totally different animal. Social hierarchies, drama, hormones running rampant.

Richard continues, "I know it's a big ask. But this will be a real test of what you can do, your capabilities. You up for it?"

I mean, what could my answer be other than yes?

# CHAPTER FOUR

I can hardly sleep the night leading up to my first day of school.

I feel giddy just thinking it. My first day of *school*.

For an hour, I roll around in bed before I realize that I'm not going to get any rest at all, so I grab my headphones and my laptop and find *Enchanted* in my digital movie catalog. Every month we're given an allowance for food, clothes, groceries, household stuff, and I'm not ashamed to admit how much of my money goes toward my ever-growing rom-com collection.

Okay, maybe I'm a *little* ashamed.

I have to scroll through my movies to make a decision, wondering if I'm in a *You've Got Mail* or *Nick & Norah's Infinite Playlist* mood. Maybe I want something newer, a *Crush* or *Fire Island*, though I do always love a good *Pride and Prejudice* retelling.

Leah doesn't like just how much time I've spent investing in the human world, in their stories. But I think that by watching and reading the things they create, we can get insight into how their minds work, into the stories that they want to tell and how they tell them, their emotions, and the wish fulfillment they craft into the story.

It's a pretty bogus lie. But I mean, I'm not *wrong*.

Tonight, though, I don't even really watch the movie. No, instead I take my phone, going to Instagram. Leo's username sits there right at the top of my list, tempting me to tap on it. But I avoid it, typing in the name *Huy Trinh* letter by letter. That's one of the people I need to set up—Huy Trinh and Thanh Tran, who also goes by the name Alice. Since all the research is my responsibility, I've got next to nothing on Huy or Alice other than their names, addresses, and some pictures Richard has sent me.

The problem is that Instagram is a big website, and simply typing in their names doesn't really lead me anywhere. So, I go to the Hearst High School website—there obviously isn't some free database of student names for me to look through, but it certainly doesn't hurt to look. And my gut feeling is proven right when I get to the page on Hearst's sports teams, and there, in the lineup of the soccer team, is Huy Trinh. He even has a little *Captain* in parentheses next to his name.

The picture is obviously different from the school record photo Richard provided. That one looks like it was taken freshman year, when he had a rounder face and shorter hair. He looks thinner here, taller, his hair more grown out. His skin has softened, but there are still pockmarks. I take a shot in the dark back on Instagram, trying out a few different names.

*Huy Trinh Soccer*

*Huy Trinh Hearst High School*

*Huy Trinh Hearst Soccer Team*

It's only that last one that leads me anywhere. To an account named *__huytrn__*

Unfortunately, it's locked. I can only see 0 posts, 323 followers, and 409 following. Plus, a bio that reads *hearst soccer captain* and then his class year.

Alice is tougher to find, and ends up being the same way:

private profile, with a bio that just reads *weeb, but not the cringe kind.*

I lie there on the bed, watching the movie in the soft glow of my room. I close my eyes for just a moment. And when I open them again, my phone alarm is blaring in my ears.

"Jude!" Leah is knocking on my door.

I wake up in a daze, feeling like I'm not in my own body, my cheek hurting from where it was planted against my arm for the last six hours.

Another knock comes, Leah's voice coming through the door. "Go ahead and get up, you'll be late for your first day."

School!

I pull my comforter off me, then shower in record time. Thankfully, I was picturing my first day outfit all weekend. There's this netted olive-green sweater where the sleeves hang down past my arms. It's annoying to constantly have to fix them as I do my makeup, but it's also my favorite sweater, despite how the way it's made means that its one purpose as a sweater is completely undone.

Whatever. I put on an undershirt and tan pants that hang a little loosely around my ankles. I look at myself in the mirror, feeling proud of how I look. It took me months of trying out different things, going to different stores and wondering what I thought I looked good in. There was a point when I was afraid to shop in the women's section, when I was worried that I was being judged, standing there, pretending like I was shopping for a friend's birthday present or something just so employees that I'd never see again for the rest of my life would think I was a cis boy.

It's almost hilarious to think about now.

Almost.

I wanted to go all out with the makeup today too, hearts painted around my eyes with a vibrant blush on my cheeks. And now, when I look at myself in the mirror, I feel pride. I feel pride in my clothing choices and how I style them, how my makeup skills have improved. I like myself.

And it feels good.

"Jude!" Leah calls out again. "Come eat something, you'll be late!"

"Coming!" I grab the backpack that we bought this weekend because none of my purses or other bags were nearly big enough to handle the books I'll be expected to carry around.

"You're going to miss your bus," she tells me. The judgment is dripping from her voice, and the way she's leaning against the kitchen counter with a cup of coffee in her hand certainly isn't helping.

"I know, I know. I'm going." I reach up, having to jump to reach the top shelf of the pantry so I can grab a breakfast bar. I'd love coffee too, but I don't have the time to go anywhere. "Are you busy today?"

"I have a shift as a waiter tonight. I'm going to spill wine on this couple, make them cut the dinner short and go back to one of their apartments. So, I'll probably be late. You're on your own for dinner."

"That's okay." I stand in front of the doorway to the kitchen, holding my arms out. "How do I look for my first day?"

Leah seems to think for a moment, taking a sip of her drink. "It's cold out. Is that sweater doing anything for you?"

"That's not the point," I tell her. "It's fashionable."

"Whatever you say!" she sings. "I just don't get you young kids and how you want to dress."

"You're eleven years older than me."

"Which is basically fifty years."

"Whatever," I tell her, adjusting my bag around my shoulder. "Wish me luck!"

"Good luck!" she calls out.

Because it would be too confusing to just show up at a new school out of the blue, Leah and I went in last week to register me for classes. We re-created our usual schtick of her pretending to be my older sister because there's no way anyone would believe she's my mom.

We'd worked on our backstory, our history, changing things up to have our parents die in some tragic accident. According to Leah, there's nothing humans love more than a sob story, especially when you give them the chance to be the hero.

Hearst High is right on Geary, meaning I only have to walk two blocks to the bus stop to catch the 38R just as it's stopping to hop on for a few stops. The bus is nearly empty, with only two older ladies talking to each other near the front. It's easy to slide my bigger headphones on, pick a playlist, and relax on the twenty-minute drive. The closer we get, though, the more excited I become. It's slow, and then all at once I feel like I'm going to be sick, like I'm going to throw up out of excitement.

I look at the older ladies at the front of the bus; one of them is knitting something, showing the other. And they both smile at each other, a special kind of joy in their eyes. The one who isn't knitting kisses the other tenderly on the cheek. It feels private, like I shouldn't be looking at them in this moment.

I shouldn't, because the longer I watch them, the more this odd feeling settles deep in my stomach, dragging, pulling me further. I want to meet someone and know that I'm meant to be with them. I want to hold their hand, to kiss them. I want to be taken out on dates and take bad pictures. I want to get caught in the rain and steal a kiss. I want to watch bad movies and take the bus down to Ulta because I'm out of my favorite moisturizer.

I shouldn't chase these thoughts; they'll only lead somewhere I don't want to be.

Luckily it's not long before the bus pulls up to the stop in front of Hearst, and I and several other kids around my age hop off the bus, stepping out onto the sidewalk and crossing the green lawn to the front steps of the school.

This is my place for the next month. Or, with any luck, just for a few weeks. It's bold, but I want to beat my own deadline. That'll *really* impress Richard and prove to Leah that I know just what I'm doing.

The school almost looks like a castle or an old church, with these high brick walls and steep roofs. There's even a bell tower! And the interior is just as fancy, the hardwood floors shining, lockers lining each of the walls, tall windows letting in plenty of light. Kids walk around in the early morning, either heading to their classrooms, hanging out in the hallways, or grabbing breakfast from the cafeteria. One kid zips by on a skateboard, a teacher shouting for him to stop, but he just keeps skating by.

I steal a moment to take it all in. I've only ever gotten to see high school through the movies, where homework doesn't seem to really exist, and kids have too long between classes to have their emotionally fraught conversations. But now I'm in a *real* school, surrounded by real teenagers.

It's so chaotic.

And I already love it.

I catch a few stares and wonder if the kids are looking at me simply because I'm an unfamiliar face, or if there's something more malicious to their glares. I'm not going to hide myself; I won't be someone who I'm not.

I wish it wasn't such an exciting feeling to see all these new faces, all these kids my own age. But the truth is, it is. There's something so magical about feeling like I blend in, like I'm being perceived as a normal, everyday teenager. None of these kids have any reason to suspect that I'm not actually human.

I stop by the guidance office to grab my finalized schedule—a little Cupid magic ensuring that I share a fair amount of periods with both Huy and Alice—and the lock for my locker, following the map to the box the counselor highlighted for me.

I look over the papers in my hand. My locker assignment, the campus map, my schedule, which at first seems to be standard fare. English 3, algebra 2, biology.

It's the other three that get me. Culinary arts, orchestra, and last and certainly least, physical education and weight lifting.

"Weight lifting?" I whisper to myself. "Orchestra?"

I don't know how to play an instrument, and I've never even dared to try to lift weights, but I can imagine my arms snapping like toothpicks the second I try to pick up one of those dumbbells.

If I had to guess from the photos I've seen, Alice is a band kid, meaning I could get some great one-on-one time with her in class if I play my cards right. I could totally fake an instrument! Give me a triangle or drumsticks and I can pretend all class period long. And cooking—well, I can barely boil water, but it can't be *that* hard.

Weight lifting, though? Yikes.

I follow the map to the little highlighted box toward the center of the school, counting the lockers as I pass by them to the only one that seems to sit unused, without a lock on the door. I triple-check the number to make sure I'm using the right one before I slam the door shut, fixing the lock and making sure I have the combination copied in my notes app. Out of the corner of my eye, I spy a girl. Around the same height as me, Black, with long, large box braids. Her attention is fixed on a mirror that hangs on the inside of her locker; she's pulled the skin around her eye in an attempt to get her eyeliner to work, but based on the R-rated words she's whispering under her breath, I feel like it isn't going well.

*"Shit,"* she hisses, grabbing a makeup wipe from her locker to clean up the failed attempt.

My first instinct is to leave her alone. I'm a stranger, after all. But Leah's lessons come back to me. She and Richard always warned me about forming connections to humans, getting too close. But they also told me how important it can be to get closer to the people I'm meant to help. How to use humans to our advantage.

"It's a balance," Leah told me once. "You have to find it, be aware of it."

It's just my luck that there, on this girl's mirror, is a picture of Alice. Even from a few feet away, I can tell it's her. And when I look a bit further, I see more pictures of this girl with Alice,

44

hugging, kissing each other's cheeks. The girl's locker is pretty eclectic—for every picture of Alice there's another of John Boyega and another of Pedro Pascal, so it's hard to see if I'm missing any other evidence.

So, this girl and Alice are friends. Best friends, maybe? It feels like best friend behavior to have pictures of someone in your locker.

"Hey," I say, stepping behind her. This makes her (a) jump and (b) only ruin her makeup attempt further. I wince. "Sorry."

"No, it's fine." She grabs another wipe, cleaning up her face. "It was going poorly anyway."

"I, uh . . . I can do makeup," I tell her, turning my cheeks so she can see the hearts and clouds painted around my eyes. I don't want to toot my own horn, but I've put hours of work into this face. "Do you want some help?"

She seems a little wary, which is fair. "You did all of that?" She inspects my face more closely.

"All me!"

Evidence of my ability outweighs her hesitation. She hands me the pen without a word.

"Look up for me." I balance my hand carefully. It's a different game having to worry about someone other than yourself. The last thing I want to do is poke this poor girl in the eye. What a terrible first impression that would be.

My hand is steady, despite the nerves, and in one solid motion, the dark line around her eye makes the soft brown color of her iris that much more pronounced. I do the other eye with ease as well.

She turns toward the mirror to check my work. "God, you're a lifesaver."

"You're very welcome." I hand the pen back to her, hoping this moment isn't done. "My name is Jude, by the way." I hold my hand out for her to shake before I realize how unbelievably dorky that is.

Still, she takes it. "I'm Neve. Are you new?"

"Yep, brand spankin' new!" *Why* did I just say that? I need to chill.

Neve gives me an awkward look, but the kind that tells me she finds me at least a little endearing. "Need help finding your classes?"

"Well . . ." I was sort of just going to go for it on my own, but as I pull my schedule and the map out together, I see this is an amazing chance to make a useful friend.

The fact that she knows Alice doesn't hurt either.

"Here, I owe you one now anyway." Neve grabs my schedule. "Oh, we've got the same algebra class second period. Got your things? Follow me!"

Neve's an excellent tour guide. She leads me through the hallways, showing me each of my classrooms, the gym, and the cafeteria, all before she leads me back to my first-period English 3 classroom. She's a little surprised when I tell her that I'm from the Bay, that I've lived in SF all my life, and that I was homeschooled before this.

"So, you just decided public school was the move?" she asks.

"Yeah, my sister thought it'd be good for me."

"Sister?"

"She's my guardian. My parents disappeared in a plane flying over the Atlantic." The aforementioned tragedy that we decided on. Maybe a bit dramatic, but I thought it was a solid choice.

The shock registers on her face *just* as the bell rings. "Shit!" Her voice is quiet. "Okay, well . . . we're going to talk about this later."

"Fair."

"I'll save you a seat next period!" Neve walks backward, adjusting her backpack as she makes her way back down the hallway. I wave at her, then walk into the classroom. Some kids have taken their seats, some are still talking, a few are reading. The walls are decorated with those motivational-style posters, like a cat trying to do a pull-up.

"Can I help you?" I hear a voice ask me. When I turn, I can see my English teacher waiting for me.

I have to double-check my schedule quickly to remember his name: Mr. Benson.

"Hi, I'm Jude Ricci."

"Oh, Jude!" Mr. Benson moves to hide the crumbly breakfast bar he'd been eating in a desk drawer. "It's nice to meet you. I'm sorry, this is the only chance I get to eat." He brushes the crumbs off his hands. "The class is arranged in alphabetical order, but most of the kids are already used to their spot, so you can take the desk in the corner there." He points before leaning back over and diving into another drawer. "We started *The Crucible* last week, are you familiar?"

"A bit."

"You covered it at your old school?" he asks.

"Uh . . . no . . ." *Think of a lie, Jude. Come on. Get it together.* "I mean, yeah. Yes!"

Smooth.

Mr. Benson smiles at me, skipping right past any awkwardness. "Hopefully it won't bore you too much to go over it again."

**47**

I give a quick thanks to Mr. Benson and navigate my way to my new desk. I keep watching for Huy or Alice, but neither of them makes an appearance, even when the bell rings.

Then, just as Mr. Benson is shutting the door, a tall Vietnamese boy who seems to ooze charm just by moving his body stops the door from shutting by almost slamming into it.

"Sorry, Mr. Benson!" he exclaims, sounding out of breath.

"Ah, Huy, nice of you to join us."

I readjust in my seat, suddenly sitting with my back totally straight. He's right there, right in front of me. Is this what meeting a celebrity feels like? Huy's cheeks are flushed as he says, "Sorry, Mr. Benson. Car trouble."

"It's okay, Huy, just take your seat."

There are some things you can't plan for, being a Cupid; some things just happen naturally, almost as if the universe is working alongside us. That's what Richard thinks anyway, that the world knows what we're out here to do, and lends a hand every now and then.

I figure I must've done something to make the universe work in my favor, because Huy walks down the same aisle of desks I did, sitting down at the only empty one.

Which just so happens to be in front of me.

He doesn't pay me any mind as he lets his backpack drop to the floor, reaching down to pull a notebook out of his bag. His hair is shaggy, falling around his ears in loose curls, with sparse hairs coming down the back of his neck. He even has a mole back there, right under his left ear.

It's a weird angle, the back of someone's head. It feels like something you should never see, like we totally forget that it's even a thing until we're faced with it for an hour and a half.

Mr. Benson takes attendance, and we're forced to sit through fifteen minutes of the student news that plays on a television hooked up in the corner of the classroom.

Then we finally get to the class discussion of *The Crucible*, and Mr. Benson goes over homework that I haven't done. For that entire time, I try to think up a way to get Huy's attention. I don't think I can just interrupt all the talk of puritanical gossiping to tap on his shoulder and say, "Hi, I'm Jude! You're Huy, right?"

I need to be Huy's friend, to get in close with him so I can learn more about his and Alice's relationship, why they fell apart, and why they're destined to be together.

"Okay, everyone." Mr. Benson goes for his desk, grabbing a stack of worksheets. "Here are a few questions about what we just covered. I want you to think about what we read, examine the themes present in the play."

Huy turns toward me for a split second to pass back the worksheet, but I don't earn an ounce of his attention.

So I go for the classic.

I reach over, tapping on his hunched shoulders, waiting for him to patiently turn.

"Yeah?" he asks.

"Hey, sorry," I say. "I don't have a pen—can I borrow one?"

There's the slightest hint of a smile, almost like he's a cat or something. Huy turns back, reaching into the front pocket of his backpack and searching for a bit before he pulls out a black ballpoint pen and hands it to me.

"Thanks."

"No problem."

Perfect.

Sure, he's only said three words to me. One of which is *Yeah?* But that's more than I had before. It's a start.

The period ends without much more progress, and I follow my memory of Neve's instructions toward algebra 2, where Mrs. Henry gives me a textbook and I take everything in.

On the plus side, Huy and Alice are *both* in this class. It's just that whatever their preexisting drama is was clearly bad enough for them to want to sit as far away from each other as humanly possible. Which will make things tough. There will be no pen borrowing to fix things this period. I try to watch their body language before class begins, but they don't interact. Huy's busy talking to his friends, who all seem to have the same golden-retriever vibe.

Alice is alone, near the back of the classroom, phone in hand as she scrolls quickly through whatever it is that she's reading. There's something about her body language that sends a chill down my spine. Like I definitely shouldn't bother her.

But then my decision is made for me as Neve comes up behind me.

"Got your seat yet?" she asks.

"Not yet."

"Good, you're sitting with us." She leads me toward the back of the classroom and Alice's desk, which I sit behind.

"You survived English?" Neve asks me.

"Oh, well . . . you know, it was . . . English."

"Mr. Benson's pretty chill. By the way, the very rude young lady ignoring you is Alice."

"Hey," I say. I try to play it cool as a cucumber. But the fact that I even had that *thought* proves I'm not cool.

"Hmm." She nods, her eyes never darting away from her phone.

"Forgive her," Neve says. "She's not used to being outside."

I stare at Alice's screen, and that's when I spot the comic panels that she's scrolling through.

"What are you reading?" I ask.

"Manga." She doesn't bother to look at me.

Well, I can see that. "What's it called?"

"*Summertime After You.*" Again, her words come without even a glance in my direction. She's a very pretty girl who accents her entire look with pink. Rose-colored phone case and backpack, a soft pink denim jacket over her outfit, pink peach earrings. Which is all hilarious considering how icy she's being.

"Oh, nice . . . what's it about?" Come on, give me anything to work with here. A conversation that lasts for more than five seconds.

"People."

Right.

"When she's like this, she barely hears a word you say. Look." Neve nods in Alice's direction. "Alice, they're discontinuing the tropical Hi-Chews! Starbucks isn't going to do the pink drink anymore! SZA said she's done making music."

Neve turns back to me when none of the threats get a reaction out of Alice.

"See, all of that should've devastated her. But she'll have to talk to us sometime."

"No, I won't," Alice remarks before she *finally* looks up at the both of us. "You fixed your eyeliner?"

"All Jude here." Neve smiles. The two of them get lost in

their own conversation about their weekend plans, which somehow ends with me being invited to go to the downtown Ulta with them.

"I don't know, I—" I start to say before Neve stops me.

"Jude, please. I'm desperate, none of those people know my colors," Neve pleads. "The last time someone did my makeup they told me I'm a winter."

"Oof." I don't have to think at all to know that Neve is an autumn. Her skin tone lends itself so well to vibrant yellows and oranges.

"Good, and we can figure out Alice's colors while we're at it."

"Don't press your luck," Alice says without looking up.

Mrs. Henry starts class, and Neve leans over and whispers, "I'll message you. What's your Insta?" Her phone is out, under her desk.

Oh boy. Here's the true test. How will Neve react when she sees my private Instagram, with a single follower thanks to Cal? There used to be more. Leo and the other counselors from the camp, but Cupid magic is nothing if not thorough.

I give Neve my username, and watch as she types it in.

"Oh wow, off the grid, huh?"

"My sister makes me keep it locked," I tell her.

At least there are actual posts up there. I learned to keep pictures consistent for moments like this. I watch Neve hit "Request to Follow" before she slips her phone back into her pocket just as Mrs. Henry clears her throat and tells us to pay attention.

"Okay, so I want to take the time to go over last week's exam." Mrs. Henry taps on the SMART Board she's standing in front of. "You all did well, but the last three questions stumped more than half of you, so we're going to review." She taps on the board again and an equation pops up.

There are a few groans.

I write down the formula in my notebook: $x^2 + 9x + 16$.

Then I stare at the numbers and letters. What the fuck does any of this mean?

"Who can tell me what we do next?" Mrs. Henry asks. "We're looking to determine whether this problem is a perfect square."

Not a single hand goes up, not at first at least.

"Come on, guys. We've been over this before."

Alice raises her hand.

"Yes, finally. Alice."

"Factoring the 16, you'll find that it isn't a perfect square because 9x isn't equal to 2(x × 4)," she recites, which is extra impressive because she's got her phone out again and has gone back to secretly reading her manga.

I can admire the dedication.

"That's correct!" Mrs. Henry grins and turns to the board. "We're going to go through what Alice just explained, step by step."

It's only then that I notice Huy out of the corner of my eye, his shoulders hunched and eyes close to his notebook like he can't see or something. He turns, and I think he's staring at Alice, looking right at her.

It's enough for me to sense that spark. So much can be said with just a look.

Then he notices that I'm staring at his staring, and I panic and look away. I can just play it off, can't I? Except our eyes most definitely met. I sit there, counting the seconds in my head until I think it might be safe enough to look back in his direction.

One. Two. Three.

Are three seconds enough? Well, now it's been four, and now five. So, five has to be enough, right? He's not looking at me anymore. What am I up to now? Ten? It's got to be at least ten seconds.

Maybe I'm up to twelve now?

I'll give it fifteen.

I'll look back at fifteen seconds; surely, he won't still be looking at me.

I glance in his direction one last time, just to make sure he doesn't seem weirded out or annoyed, that he doesn't think I'm a weirdo for staring at him. I was just trying to get a read on his body language, see how he was doing. I didn't mean to stare.

Except he isn't looking my way anymore. He's focused on the board, taking his notes, brushing his hair out of his face when it falls free of where he's tucked it behind his ears.

Alice is a lucky girl, to be tied to this boy by some invisible string, her fate decided by the universe.

I just need to pull it in the right way, bring them back to each other.

This should be easy. At least, that's what I keep telling myself.

# CHAPTER FIVE

At lunch, Neve, bless her heart, helps me avoid the cliché that haunts many a coming-of-age movie: grabbing my tray and wandering aimlessly around the cafeteria, waiting for an empty seat at an unclaimed table to be freed up before I just go eat in a nasty bathroom stall.

She calls me over to where she and Alice are sitting next to each other in the middle of the cafeteria, a table entirely to themselves. It's nice, comforting almost, to know that I already have someone who's looking out for me.

"Neve was telling me you're one of the homeschool weirdos?" Alice's voice shocks me, and Neve looks at me with pure mortification.

"Alice!" Neve elbows her in the gut.

"What?"

"I didn't say 'weirdo,' I swear." Neve turns back to me. "I was just telling her you were homeschooled."

"How is it?" Alice asks. "It's different, right?"

"Yeah, you could say that. I'm used to just sitting at our dining room table."

"Sounds really boring."

"Alice!" Neve groans.

"Curiosity is never a bad thing," Alice argues.

"With you it definitely is." Neve apologizes on her behalf again.

"Oh," I say, "that's . . . okay? What about you?" I look to Alice, going for broke. "What's your story?" I need to get some info.

"What kind of a question is that?" she replies, grabbing a Starburst candy and unwrapping it carefully until the wrapper is a perfect square. Then she lays it on top of the other wrappers she's gathered.

There's something about her stare that makes me hesitant to answer. "I was just . . . you know. I got to know Neve, and I thought maybe I could . . . and you were asking me all those questions."

"So that gave you the right to ask about me?"

Her face is a flat line for another full second before she cracks, finally smiling and letting out this soft laugh. Then I realize that she's been messing with me.

"Alice, please don't scare Jude. It's their first day." Neve steals some of Alice's candy.

"But it's fun!" she mock whines, picking up another piece for herself.

"For you," Neve tells her. "Everyone else thinks you're one tragic radioactive-waste bath away from becoming a supervillain."

"I would rule fairly," Alice says.

Neve shakes her head. "See, I know you, and I know for a fact that's not true."

"Not my fault you don't believe me."

Neve scoffs. "Feel free to ignore her."

"I'm trying."

"Ohh . . ." Alice eyes me. "They *can* talk!"

I glance over my shoulder as a nearby table erupts in booming laughter. It doesn't take much to realize the source of the sound was Huy, seated with many of the same boys from alge-bra, laughing about something while the two of them flick a Cheez-It like it's a paper football. Huy ducks his head low over the finger goalposts, catching the Cheez-It in his mouth and cheering himself on with the rest of the boys.

I turn to Alice just quickly enough to see her switching her attention back to her candy.

"What's next for you?" Neve asks.

"Band," I say.

"Orchestra," Alice corrects me, but it's clear I've got her attention back. "What do you play?"

"I, uh . . ." Her stare sends another shiver straight down my spine. "Nothing."

"You signed up for band but don't play an instrument?" Neve asks, holding up her hand to stop Alice from correcting her. "You signed up for *orchestra* but don't play an instrument?"

I *really* should've paid attention to what classes I was giving myself. To be fair, I was in a rush. So really, can I be blamed? "All the other electives were full."

"You should've asked for study hall," Alice says sourly.

That's when a Cheez-It sails across the table over me, land-ing right square between the three of us. We all turn over our shoulders, glaring at the table of boys, who seem to be pretend-ing that they don't know what happened. All of them except for Huy, who gives me an apologetic shrug.

My eyes follow his to Alice's, who's staring at him harder than I've seen her stare at anyone before.

"Ignore him," Neve sings, grabbing the Cheez-It and hiding it on her lunch tray.

Easier said than done, Neve.

• • •

Unfortunately, being in orchestra means *actually* having to be a part of Hearst's orchestra. Who'da thought? Mr. Lawson just sort of stares at me when he asks what instrument I play, and I tell him I don't.

"Don't play what?" he asks.

"Anything?" It comes out more of a question than I mean for it to.

"You're serious?"

I shrug.

"Are you sure that you're supposed to be in this class?"

I unfold my schedule from my pocket. "Orchestra, fourth period."

He eyes the schedule over his glasses. "But you didn't take orchestra at your old school?"

"This was the only elective left, that's what Principal Kurt told me." Another lie to add to the list.

Mr. Lawson lets out a frustrated sigh. "Okay, okay." He moves his glasses, slipping them all the way to his forehead when he goes to pinch the bridge of his nose. "Let me think for a moment."

I just get to stand there awkwardly while he tries to come up with whatever idea will save him the most pain. That's when Alice walks in and I see his eyes go wide.

"Alice! Get over here!"

She doesn't look too thrilled to have the attention called to her, but she steps in next to me.

"Georgia still has that parasite?" he asks.

"Yeah, she's getting treatment for it." Alice says it like this is a totally normal conversation.

"Okay, good. Because Jude is going to be your alternate."

Alice looks at me and scoffs. "Jude doesn't play any instruments."

"And you've never given me a reason to put in your alternate. But you need someone to turn your music, and Landon has to get back on the xylophone."

Alice groans.

"Alice, please don't argue. I've got to find a place to fit Jude in."

I don't appreciate being talked about like I'm not here.

"Fine." She nudges me.

"Thank you," Mr. Lawson says with relief in his voice. "Show Jude the ropes. It'll be easy."

Alice nods toward the chairs where kids are putting their things away and readying their instruments. "Come with me."

"What's an alternate?" I ask her as I follow her toward the large drum set tucked off to the side.

"Normally, we'd have two drum players, in case something goes wrong," Alice tells me. "But also, I need someone to turn my sheet music. I can't exactly do it myself." She picks up the drumsticks.

It's embarrassing to admit that's when I realize that, yeah, a drummer can't exactly turn their own sheet music. I guess I just never thought of it before.

"So that's your job now."

"Do orchestras usually have drum sets?" I ask her. I feel like my impressions of orchestras usually have that one huge drum with the big sticks. But Alice takes a seat in front of a full set, like one a band might use.

"It's a jazz orchestra, so yeah, we have a drum set." Alice pulls a stool around and points. "You'll sit here and read the sheet music." Then she pauses. "You can read sheet music, right?"

"Oh, totally, yep!" I nod.

"Okay, good."

Except I absolutely cannot read sheet music. I can't even make it through one full round of practice without revealing myself either. The song comes to an end and Alice grabs on to her cymbals to stop them.

"What was that?" she asks.

"I thought that . . . I don't—"

"You were all over the place, dude." At least she keeps her voice down to limit the shame I feel.

"I'm sorry. I thought I knew what I was doing."

"Yeah, clearly you don't."

"I'm sorry," I repeat.

"Just turn when I tell you to turn, okay?"

I don't say another word for fear of making the situation worse. I hate to admit that I feel like crying, but the way she talks to me stings. For the first time I consider going to Richard and begging him for a different assignment, a new couple to help. Because I have zero clue how I'm supposed to help this girl fall back in love.

No wonder Huy dumped her.

At least, I'm assuming he was the dumper.

I close my eyes, breathing carefully. No, this isn't fair to her. I *did* fuck up, and I did lie. I just have to try harder next time.

And I guess learn how to read sheet music.

Next comes the class that I've been dreading the most. I can fake it in English, and try my best in math. I've even already bookmarked YouTube videos about learning to read sheet music and various kitchen safety techniques I was told to learn in culinary arts.

But PE?

Weight lifting?

Yeah, no.

Coach Thompson calls me toward him when I walk in, picking me right out of the students as the unfamiliar face. He gives me a whole speech, assuring me that I'm not the only nonbinary or trans student in the period, and that the locker rooms are coed with privacy curtains for those who prefer to use them. And he seems genuinely proud of the steps the school takes to ensure inclusion, which is honestly pretty admirable.

"Oh, that's great. Um . . . do you have any clothes I can change into?" I ask.

He gives me a look similar to the one that Mr. Lawson gave me.

. "You didn't bring a change of clothes?" Thompson kind of has that stereotypical gym-teacher thing going on, bushy mustache and a nylon jacket and pants that swish every time he moves.

"Well, I . . ."

Thompson straightens, shouting across the gym at Huy just as he's pulling his gym bag out of his backpack. "Trinh!" He waves at Huy and we stand there and watch as he jogs over. "You got extra clothes?"

"Yes, sir!" Huy says cheerfully. "In my bag."

"Mind giving a set to Jude here?"

I don't even have to try on Huy's clothes to know that he's a good two sizes larger than me, but I guess if he's the only one with extra clothes, I don't have many options.

"Come on." Huy steals a glance at me before he pats my shoulder, and there's nothing left for me to do except follow him through to the locker room, trying my best to ignore the crowd of half-naked students surrounding me.

Huy leads me to his locker and pulls out a fresh shirt and shorts for me to wear. "Here you go."

"Thanks." I check the sizes. Thankfully, the shorts have drawstrings, so there's no risk of me flashing my classmates my underwear.

"No problem, just give them back at the end of the period."

"Yeah, sure." Since the locker room lockers aren't assigned, I can pick any one of them to leave my stuff in, so I pick the one next to Huy, figuring this might give me an opening. And even though I'd much rather change behind one of the privacy curtains, I start to slip my shirt off in front of everyone.

"Thanks again." I turn back toward Huy just as he's slipping his own shirt off, and that's when I see the pieces of tape affixed to the spaces just under his armpit, stretching to cover his nipples, pulling his breasts down to flatten them. "You're trans?" My voice carries louder in the locker room than I mean it to, echoing off the walls.

Huy stares at me, his shirt half off, as do half the kids in the locker room.

Shit.

"Yeah." He turns back toward his locker. "That a problem?"

"No, no, I just . . . I'm trans," I tell him. "Sorry, I didn't mean to blurt that out."

He gives me the barest hint of an awkward smile. Great, I made him uncomfortable. "It's not like it's a secret."

"No, yeah. That's not what I—" Jeez, Jude, how's that foot in

**62**

your mouth taste? "I meant that it was a surprise." God, that still sounds wrong. I just don't know that many trans people, even living in the Bay. Sure, I've come across some for work, and after I came out to Richard and Leah, I snuck off to a teen support group in the Castro.

But some part of me still felt fake, like I didn't belong. A lot of people have these backward ideas, that nonbinary people don't "count" as trans, or that you can't be trans without body dysmorphia or getting surgery and shots so you can "pass." As if the only way to be trans is to fit into the binary narrative. Back then, I just . . . I felt like I wasn't trans enough when I was literally surrounded by other trans people. It was frustrating because I was the only one making me feel that way.

Huy's brows furrow. "Why was it such a surprise?"

"I don't know." I hate that there's still a novelty to meeting another trans person. And I also think that maybe this is something I could've been told. Maybe they didn't know. "It's cool," I assure Huy. "I'm cool with it."

"Oh, whew. Thank God. If a total stranger approves of my identity, then all those doctor's appointments haven't been a waste."

"I'm sorry," I apologize. I'm batting great with these two so far.

"Relax," he tells me, shutting the door to his locker. "I'm just messing with you."

Except I *do* feel bad for what I said. "Sorry, I haven't met that many trans people. It's one of the reasons my sister wanted to put me in public school. So I could meet more kids." There, if I play up the "woe is me" angle, then maybe I'll get a bit of sympathy.

"Understandable. We do live in the shadows," he whispers like it's a secret, a sweet smile forming on his lips. "Always watching, waiting for our moment to strike."

"So that's the trans agenda?"

"You didn't get the pamphlet when you came out?"

I shake my head. "Must've gotten lost in the mail."

He laughs; it's a soft sound. "I'm Huy, by the way."

"Yeah, I know."

"You know?"

Dammit.

"I mean, I, uh . . . I heard Coach say your name." Even though I think he only called Huy by his last name. Still, he doesn't seem to notice.

"Right, right." He crosses his arms, leaning against the cool metal of the locker.

"I'm Jude."

"I know," he says with a smile. "I heard Coach say your name."

"I *am* sorry," I say. "For what it's worth. Which might not be much."

"I'll have to talk to my accountant, but I think we're square." He smiles at me again, the look on his face so tender.

I can't stop the blush that creeps up on my cheek. Huy pats me on the shoulder as he walks past me and out of the locker room. My eyes follow him, watching him until he vanishes around the corner.

And, for some reason, I can't stop myself from smiling.

There is pride on Cal's face as I recount my entire day to him.

He hangs on to every single word as I convey every detail to him. He'd been texting me all day, but after I saw a girl get her phone taken in algebra, I decided against checking it entirely. So I couldn't reply to any questions he had until I was on the bus back home, and by that point, we just decided to go to NaYa, this delicious Thai dessert café on Geary.

Cal was all too happy to accept the invite.

"And they really use lockers!" I tell him. "I thought that was just a thing for movies or whatever. But no, they actually use them!"

He sips on his yuzu soda. "Wow. And you just, like, went to class and sat there?"

I nod, stealing the soda from him. "It's weird, but, like . . . I guess it's okay. I have to run to my last period, though. And I have *so much* homework."

"But it went well? Like actually talking to the two of them?"

"Yeah, I think so. Alice is kind of . . . difficult? She's got some walls up. And Huy . . ." I pause, wondering what words might come next.

"Yeah?"

"I don't know, actually." I play with the straw. "He's trans."

"That's cool." Cal hesitates. "Right?"

I love Cal, and, yeah, he's queer, but he's a very cis brand of queer. He doesn't get the idea that even just meeting another trans person can be an *experience*.

"He's nice," I say. "Let me borrow his gym clothes."

"Gym? So that explains your plain face."

"It's fine—we just ran a lot today." I slide the soda back toward him. "Talk to me after we get to the weight-lifting part."

"You're seriously going to do it?"

"What choice do I have? I just want to do a good job."

"It sounds like you took some great first steps."

"But did I do enough?" I want to pull at my hair, but I settle on brushing it away from my face.

"Do you want me to tell you that you did?"

"Only if you actually believe that."

"Then you did enough," Cal says to me. "You're being too rough on yourself. It was your first real day back out there. Relax, take a deep breath. Finish off this soda."

I do like I'm told, drinking from the cup until the slurping sounds fill the restaurant.

"Good." Cal rubs the top of my hand softly. "You've done this before. You've done it since you were literally a child. Over a decade of helping people get together. You can handle two teenagers."

I sigh. "Alice is a tough cookie, not very social. Right now, the best bet is to make friends with her, figure out what happened, and then I'm thinking about re-creating the moment they fell in love the first time."

"Nothing screams romance like eighth grade."

"You think?"

"I think you should go for something more original. Something more epic. We can brainstorm this weekend. Maybe watch a few of those movies you like."

"I can't Saturday," I tell him. "I'm going to the mall with Alice and Neve."

"Ditching me already?" Cal puts a hand over his heart. "I'm wounded."

"It's a chance to get to know Alice," I tell him, trying not to feel guilty, even though I know he's kidding.

"I guess I can forgive you this time," he says, leaning closer and putting his head on my shoulder. That's when our waitress brings our food. I've gone with my classic, pieces of white bread cubed and toasted with egg custard in a bowl made out of a hollowed loaf. Cal adores chocolate, so he's gone with a bingsu, covered in Ovaltine powder and Frosted Flakes.

"Anything interesting happen with your day?" I ask him. "All we've done is talk about me."

"Oh, you know . . . the usual." He picks at the bingsu.

"What's wrong?"

"Nothing, I promise," he says. "I just realized how much I missed hanging out with you."

"Please." I brush him off. "It's been half a day."

"Don't laugh!" he says with a smile that tells me it's okay. "We've basically spent every hour together for the last half a year. I miss it."

"We only had to do that because I couldn't keep my lips to myself." I try to joke, but there's a subtle bitterness to the words.

"I *knowwwwww*," Cal whines. He keeps his head on my shoulder, and even though I'd never admit it to him, the weight is a comfort. I feel like it keeps me grounded, and his warmth is nice too.

We both hear the bell for the door ring, but it's the rush of voices that really draws our attention. A group of boys, all dressed similarly in dark shirts and gym shorts and muddy tennis shoes. A regular stampede of teenage hormones strong enough to make me feel sorry for the single waitress working the entire restaurant.

And right in the middle of this crowd of boys is Huy Trinh, looking marginally sweatier than when I last saw him. Which is saying something, since I last saw him before his shower after gym.

He sees me right away, like he's looking for me, which isn't even possible. Our eyes meet for a moment, and instead of going over to his friends, sitting between them, he walks right over like he's sitting with me and Cal.

"Jude!"

I decide to settle on the idea that I didn't notice him walking in. "Huy, what's up?" I feel a little heat in my cheeks, straightening so that Cal has to sit up.

He looks at my bowl. "Grabbing some egg custard? Nice choice."

"Yeah, totally . . ."

We sit there in an awkward silence, the sound of the Thai pop music playing through the speakers.

Cal clears his throat.

"Oh, uh, Huy! This is Cal."

"Nice to meet you, Cal." Huy holds out his hand, and Cal's all too happy to take it.

"Jude was just telling me about their first day at Hearst," Cal says, and I'm relieved when he leaves it at that.

"Recounting the saga of the forgotten gym clothes?" Huy asks with a raised eyebrow.

"I didn't mean to forget them," I promise him.

"The gym clothes I can forgive." He smiles. "It's the not bringing a pen to your first day that left me scratching my head. You really should be more prepared, Jude."

"I'll try harder in the future to make you proud." I try not to roll my eyes, but, you know, in an endearing way. "What were you up to?"

"Oh, just the soccer crew. It's off season, so we play in Golden Gate Park most nights."

"Sounds like fun!"

He shrugs. "Sometimes."

More awkward silence as he looks at me and only me. Then he lets out this laugh, our staring contest finally breaking.

I won.

Huy says, "I, uh . . . I guess I'll let you two get back to your thing."

"Oh, okay."

"It was nice to meet you," Cal says.

"You too. See you later, Jude."

I watch him as he makes his way to the table where his friends are waiting for him. I can't help but notice how nice his butt looks in his shorts.

"So that's the boy?" Cal asks, his voice quieter once again.

"Yeah."

"He seems friendly. And very cute."

"I think he is." I pause. "Friendly, that is."

Cal just looks at me, and doesn't say a word.

# CHAPTER SIX

The next morning, I make sure I have my gym clothes packed. And I go lighter on the makeup, especially if all my hard work is only going to last a few hours before sweat ruins it.

The moment I walk into English, Huy is at his desk. I guess he was spared the car troubles this morning.

"Here you go." I zip open my backpack, grabbing the shirt from the top of my stuff. "Sorry again."

"It's okay."

"I made sure to wash it so it wouldn't be all sweaty." I had zero idea I could get that gross from simply doing jumping jacks and running laps around the gym floor.

"Thanks." Huy grabs his own backpack, slipping the shirt in. "I was surprised to see you yesterday."

"I try not to make a habit of going outside," I tell him. "Defeats the whole 'we operate in the shadows' idea." I give him a smile so he knows that I'm just messing with him.

It takes Huy a moment, but he grins right back. "Your, uh . . ." He pauses for a moment. "Your friend Cal seemed nice."

"Yeah, he really is."

"Are you two . . . close?"

"Yeah, you could say that."

"Nice."

"Is it?"

"Hey, um . . . are you doing anything Saturday?" He breezes past my question as if I didn't ask it.

"I have plans. Why?"

"Oh, my friends and I are playing soccer again. Thought you might want to watch?"

"Just watch? You mean you don't trust my soccer-playing abilities?"

He chuckles. "I wasn't going to say anything. But you were wheezing after one lap yesterday."

"It's a big gym!" I argue. "But I can't on Saturday, I'm already hanging out with Alice, actually."

"I saw you two at lunch yesterday."

"When you threw a Cheez-It at me?"

He smiles softly. "Right, sorry about that."

I smile back at him. "I forgive you."

"You know, Cheez-It injuries aren't something to joke about. Did you see a doctor?"

"I did, actually. The doctor said there was some damage, but I should heal fine. So long as I don't take any more Cheez-Its to the head."

Huy laughs at that, an excited sound, like everything he hears might be the funniest thing he's ever been told. I like it. I like people with good laughs. The bell rings, and Mr. Benson wastes no time in getting the classroom door shut, telling us to grab our copies of *The Crucible*.

"Maybe next Saturday? You can come watch us play."

"Yeah, sounds like fun."

Huy steals one last look at me before he turns in his seat, digging around for his paperback. My eyes find the back of his head again. I feel like this is going to become a familiar sight.

And you know what?

As far as views go, it's not half bad.

I'm learning the ins and outs of navigating Hearst, and the studying I did on how to read sheet music is paying off already. Alice still doesn't seem pleased, but I'd rather have a neutral Alice than an upset one.

"All right, everyone, sounding good. We're getting where we need to be for the showcase," Mr. Lawson says as he leans against his desk.

"Showcase?" I whisper to Alice.

"Rising eighth graders from the district come and visit as an early welcome thing. Mr. Lawson uses it to convince kids to join the orchestra. He needs the numbers to keep up funding."

Mr. Lawson continues, "I want to make sure you're all practicing in and out of class; it's an important night for us. Take five, and we're going to jump back into it, okay?"

My classmates set their instruments down, some of them leaving to go get water, others stretching or going about cleaning their instruments.

"You've been studying," Alice says, picking up her soft pink water bottle.

"A bit. Have I improved?"

"Not really. You're still late."

"It's hard to keep track, you all move so quickly."

"You'll develop an ear for it," she says reassuringly, and it's a pleasant surprise to hear something nice from her. "Either that, or you'll memorize the patterns. It's not as hard as it seems once you've found a groove."

"Yeah, yeah . . . sure." I hesitate, reading over the complicated sheet music. "Why'd you pick drums?"

"Is that so weird?"

"I guess not, it's just . . . unexpected?" Watching Alice play for only two days now, she's like a different person with the sticks in her hands. Her movements are loose, wild, and calculated at the same time.

"I just like the drums, plus my dad used to play with a jazz group. He'd take me to his practices when I was young."

"Oh, that's cool."

"Yeah." Suddenly, she goes cold again. Then she turns back to me, sizing me up. "Let me ask you a question."

"Um . . . okay?" Though it very much wasn't a request.

"Are you really going to stay in orchestra?"

"I don't see how I have a choice," I tell her.

She eyes me warily, then sighs. "I guess I can see that. It's why Neve picked art. The girl can't draw a stick figure to save her life."

"You two seem close," I say, unlocking the case for the triangle in my lap.

"She's my best friend, if that's what you mean."

"Makes sense. Neve's pretty friendly, huh?"

"You're saying I'm not?" Alice asks with a slyness that tells me—at least I hope it's telling me—that she's joking. "You couldn't tell by the way she basically adopted you on your first day?"

"If it weren't for her, I'd probably still be getting lost in the hallway."

"She has a habit of doing that." Alice begins to inspect her drum kit, noticing something that I don't and reaching to fix it, twisting a knob. "It's like she has a radar for pathetic people who need help."

Then she realizes what she said.

"I meant the 'pathetic' about me, not you."

"Noted." I feel a bit of relief. "How did you two—" I start to ask, but Mr. Lawson claps his hands together, drawing our attention back to the front of the classroom.

"Okay, everyone. Positions!"

My classmates all rush to their seats and Alice straightens on her stool. Mr. Lawson readies his hands in the air, bouncing them softly, and we begin to play again.

My worst fears come true as I make my way into PE at the end of the day.

After we've changed and I've wiped away my makeup from this morning, Coach Thompson tells us all to gather around. We go through the normal stretches that we went through the previous day, but then he corrals us all together and leads us to this much smaller room just outside the gym.

A room with the floor covered with soft black padding, various benches, racks of weights. Along one wall is a row of treadmills, and along the other wall are dead-lift setups and squat racks. At least, that's what Huy calls them as he shows me each piece of equipment. And because we're standing next to each other in the lineup, we're named spotting partners.

Which *definitely* wasn't on purpose.

Wink wink.

"Have you ever lifted before?" he asks.

I show him my bare arms. "Oh yeah. Can't you tell?"

"Come on, it's not that hard." He steadies a metal bar on the weight bench.

"No weights?" I ask.

"You've never done this before," he says to me. "So yes, no weights."

"I thought you said it wasn't that hard." I straddle the bench, falling back until I'm face-to-face with Huy's crotch.

Wonderful.

You know, is it any wonder that playing sports became associated with being heterosexual and a "manly" man? A bunch of hot sweaty bodies colliding with each other, getting all dirty, taking any excuse at all to wear tights, weight rooms spilling over with homoeroticism, all the "friendly" slaps to the ass.

Definitely straight.

"All right, keep your feet behind your knees and flat on the floor, and your hands here," Huy runs his hands along the bar, pointing to these two textured grip sections. "Keep your back arched slightly."

I ready my arms on the bar and take a deep breath. I heave and grunt as I lift the bar in the air . . . and it almost comes right back down. Huy's literally the only thing keeping me from dying the most embarrassing death imaginable. (Picture it. *High school junior's chest crushed by naked weight bar.*)

"Whoa, it's okay. Arch the bar. Don't let it come straight down." He keeps his hand lightly on the bar, helping me lift it up. "Just do five. Think you can?"

I press again, pushing my arms out and stretching them into the air.

"How much do these things weigh?" I grunt through gritted teeth as I continue to try and pump up and down.

"Forty-five pounds."

"You're joking!"

"No, my name's Huy. Nice try, though."

I groan again, but this time, it's not from the weights. "That was terrible."

"Well, that's the last time I try my material out on you."

"Thank you."

"And that's five!" he says out of nowhere, leading the bar back to where it normally sits.

"Are you serious?"

"Yep, five reps. Congratulations, you've done one full set. For you, at least."

I sit up, my arms aching. "I feel stronger already."

"Mind helping me put on more?" he asks. "Grab those." Huy points to the twenty-five-pound weights. I think I can handle those, though it's tough to line them up at first. Once the weights lock in place, it's Huy's turn to sit in front of *my* crotch. Never have I ever prayed harder for a boner not to strike.

Last summer when Leo held my hand for the first time, I had to use my shirt to hide my crotch.

Because *hand-holding* gave me a boner.

Leo just laughed at me, but not in a mean way. That sweet sound floating through the summer air, carried toward the ocean on the soft breeze. No, I can't think of Leo right now, boner or not.

It's not good for me or my anti-boner agenda.

Huy does his ten reps, and after a short break, he does ten more, and then another ten. Leaving me totally in the dust when it comes to exercises done today.

"Is there anything more appropriate for someone like me?" I stand in front of him as he wipes the bench off. Five foot five and barely able to lift forty-five pounds above my head, I doubt there's much. But the last thing I want to do is fail gym of all classes.

Huy smiles up at me, his forehead a little sweaty. "Yeah, how do you feel about leg presses?"

I don't know what those are, but as Huy leads me over to a machine that I think more closely resembles a medieval torture device, I suspect that I don't like them.

"Sit like this," Huy directs, his shorts riding up his thighs as he takes a seat. "Put your legs up like this, and *push*!" He does exactly that, pushing this large metal platform in the air as the weights on the machine are lifted off with ease.

He has really good legs, and huge calves, which I guess makes sense, being that he's the soccer captain. I'd imagine there are a lot of leg days in his schedule.

He stands just as quickly as he sat down. "Think you can do that?"

"Maybe." I do just like he did, pulling out this little metal rod in the weights to go for something much lighter. "You're a lot better at this than I am," I say as I struggle, though I'll admit that it's easier to do this than it is lifting the weights. I guess growing up in a walkable city gave me something to work with.

"When you're the team captain you can't get caught slacking."

"Is that fun?" I ask. "Playing soccer?"

"Is it fun?" He raises a brow. "What kind of question is that?"

"I'm just making conversation," I tell him, almost out of breath. "Work with me here."

I guess working out has its perks. There's no need for beating around the bush.

"It's fun, yeah. We made it to the championships last year, but San Jose beat us."

"Oh, that's a bummer."

"Yeah." He taps on his water bottle. "We played hard; it just wasn't enough."

"You sound like you blame yourself." Okay, maybe I should beat around the bush *a little*. "Sorry, I didn't want to say it like that."

"I mean, you're not wrong. I'm the captain, I could've played better."

"But it's a team sport."

He laughs at that, a low sound that lasts for half a second but lingers in the air. "Fair enough."

I think that maybe he wants to say something else, but he doesn't. Not until he tells me that I'm done with my sets. My legs feel like Jell-O as I stand. I take Huy's hand when it's offered to me; his palm is a little sweaty, pretty warm.

"You shouldn't blame yourself," I tell him as we switch positions. He moves the metal rod in the weights closer to the top, his thigh muscles constricting as he readies himself.

"It just makes me nervous for what's to come." He hoists the metal plate into the air. "Coaches were at those games; they were there to watch me. And I lost. It might've cost me scholarships."

"Well . . . you don't want to go to those schools anyway," I say, hoping that'll make him feel better.

"Trust me, I do."

Right. Bad advice.

"Do you think that's a possibility?" I ask.

"No idea. I guess we'll see. The last thing my parents need is to be proven right."

"They don't like you to play soccer?"

"They think it's too dangerous, that I'll hurt myself."

"You don't have to listen to them."

He huffs. "Yeah, try being Vietnamese and not listening to your parents. See how well that goes."

It's easy for me to forget that other kids actually have relationships with their parents. It's a part of the community aspect, for us to be raised by other Cupids. Besides, most of the time, the Cupids who give birth are too busy to give up eighteen years of their lives to raise and train a child. That's why we're given to people like Richard and Leah, who have the time and the skill to teach.

"I'm sure it'll be okay," I try to reassure him. "You love doing it, so that has to mean something."

"Right, yeah." I can tell that I'm sinking Huy's mood. "Hey," he says, "what time are you hanging out with Alice on Saturday?"

"No idea, probably the afternoon, why?"

"My family is going to be at the farmers' market in the Sunset. You should come by."

"Why are you at a farmers' market?"

"Our donut shop. We have a trailer we set up." He turns to me. "I'll even hook you up with free donuts."

"Oh, well . . . sure!"

"It starts at eight, so you'll have plenty of time to stop by before you head downtown."

"One question before I say yes."

"Hmm?"

"Will there be chocolate?"

Huy smiles, his teeth bright and pearly, showing off dimples as he laughs. "I'll save a chocolate just for you, Jude."

"Then it's a deal."

# CHAPTER SEVEN

"And what are we doing here again?" Cal asks as I lead him off the bus on Saturday morning.

"Farmers' market," I remind him for about the thousandth time. I think he's just cranky over being pulled out of bed so early in the morning. Last night, we decided to have one of our sleepovers because Leah had to go down to Santa Cruz for a "work event."

We ordered pizzas, did face masks, watched movies. I even did Cal's nails. It took all of five seconds for him to chip his left pinkie.

"It's cold," he whines, bundling into his hoodie.

The farmers' market is deep in the Sunset, just a few precious blocks away from the beach. Anywhere else in California, that might mean a nice breeze and some good sun to keep you warm, but here in the Bay, it means you can't see more than a mile past the shoreline, and the wind being carried by the ocean will chill you right to the bone.

Which is only made worse during the tail end of January.

The last few days have been uneventful. Alice missed a whole day because of a dentist appointment, but when she returned, I caught Huy staring at her from across the algebra classroom. Then, during culinary arts, he asked if she was okay.

Alice, on the other hand, seems totally unbothered by the potential of Huy. I want to urge her into talking about him more, but I don't want to press my luck. All my relationships to these kids are still new, and expecting them to unpack all their trauma over the course of a single week would be overkill.

"Come on, you agreed to help me." I take Cal's hand. "We'll get you coffee."

The farmers' market is split into two camps that each take up about a block. On one side, there's the homegrown and homemade goods. A candle company, fresh veggies and fruit, a woodworking stall, and a pottery studio showing off hand-made ceramics. The other side is all food, the smell of coffee and sizzling bacon going right to my stomach.

As eager as I am to find Huy, Cal's no good to me in the state he's in. So, we join a long line where we eventually get to order our breakfast sandwiches and large coffees.

"Oh God." I watch as Cal opens the paper container his food sits in. The sandwich is almost comically stacked, like a cartoon. "It's like I've died and gone to heaven."

"There, are you happy?"

"Ecstatic!" Cal says with a mouthful of breakfast sandwich. "Do you see Huy?"

"Not yet. We'll just have to walk around."

"How's all that going?"

"It's fine. I'm making progress."

"No, I mean—" Cal pauses to swallow his food finally. "School. How is school going?"

"Oh, well . . ."

To be frank, it's kicking my ass. Because I'm keeping an eye on Huy and Alice at all times, I find it hard to keep track of my notes in class. Yesterday, we had a quiz in algebra and I'm 100 percent sure I absolutely bombed it because I have zero idea what any of it meant.

"It's fine," I finally tell Cal.

"So, you're failing already?"

"I didn't say that."

"You didn't have to." He takes another bite with a satisfied smirk on his lips. "You touch your face when you lie."

"I do not!" Do I?

"Totally do. Done it for as long as I've known you."

"You're serious?"

"Have you never noticed?"

"No!"

"Well, it's your tell."

I pause, the realization dawning on me. "Is that how you always figure out what I get you for your birthday?"

His only answer is a sly smile, yellow stains on his cheek from the egg.

"Ugh, you're disgusting." I take a napkin and wipe away the mess.

"Thank you!"

"What would you do without me?"

"Hmmm . . . probably not sit through as many terrible rom-coms."

"You're not allowed to call *Princess Diaries* bad."

"Geriatric isn't even a real country!" he argues, his point null and void because he can't even get the name of the country Anne Hathaway rules over correct. "And you're telling me no one told her that she was a princess? I'm not buying it."

His hair is getting long, curling at the ends where it falls over the tops of his ears. I know he hates it, but I think Cal looks cuter with the shaggier look. There's something more relaxed about him that way. Then again, I'm a sucker for a boy with long hair. Leo's hair was nice, soft, and smelled sweet, just like him.

I sigh, my appetite no longer a concern, so I let Cal eat while the coffee warms us up. I'm usually against hot coffees, but given the temperature right now, I need it.

"You ready to get to work?" Cal asks, wiping his greasy hands on his pants.

"Sure, but I'm finding you a bathroom first."

"Yes, Mom." Cal groans, following me toward the empty intersection where the two parts of the farmers' market meet. A row of porta potties and freestanding portable sinks waits for anyone to use. "I'm gonna pee, actually."

"Okay, I'll be here." I stand among the crowd, looking around as Cal disappears inside.

My eye settles on the nearest donut stall. It's pink, very small, and easy to miss. Huy is hanging his head out the window, looking down at people as they give their order, pointing to the display case built into the side of the trailer that shows off all the flavors. He's dressed in short sleeves despite the cool air, showing off his broad shoulders. An apron that matches the pink of the trailer is wrapped around his neck and tied against his waist. The real kicker is realizing that he's wearing a hair band that pulls his hair free of his face, giving it this almost wildly windblown look.

I leave the porta potties, knowing that Cal will be able to find me easily as I make my way to the end of the donut line. Huy moves quickly, heating the preprepared donuts with ease and handing them back to customers in paper wrappers. The line moves, and the closer I get to the front, the tighter my stomach feels. I'm not sure why I'm nervous. I suppose this is the first time I'm hanging out with Huy outside school. Without the context of being classmates, will things be the same?

What am I saying? He invited me out here.

Eventually, I make it to the front of the line, watching the trailer as Huy ducks down to grab something. I don't even think he's noticed that I'm here yet.

"Welcome to Trinh's Donuts, what can I get started—" He pauses when he finally looks my way.

"Hi there, I believe I was promised free donuts by one of your employees."

He leans down with his arms crossed on the counter. "Now who would do that?"

"I'm not sure what his name was. Tall, sort of curly hair. Though he wasn't wearing a pink apron."

"I'll have to launch an investigation," he tells me. "We typically have a staunch 'no free donuts' policy."

"Like I said, I was guaranteed free donuts. So what do you plan to do about it?"

"Well, I suppose I can honor that promise just once." Huy's smile is wide. "But we'd better not make this a regular thing."

"No, I'm sure they wouldn't dream of it."

"Now . . . what flavor might be drawing your eye?"

I step back, taking a look at the display case. There are ten flavors, ranging from taro to strawberry to Fruity Pebbles to pandan. "Well, these all look fantastic, but I believe I was promised chocolate."

I watch his shoulders slump. "Bad news. That was today's most popular flavor."

"All gone?"

He nods.

"Hmm . . . I'm not sure how to take that since I was *promised* chocolate by this employee. But I suppose I'll settle for a . . ." I take another look at the flavors. "Blueberry?"

"You're in luck." Huy dips down for a moment, grabbing tongs. "Warmed?"

"Naturally." I nod.

"So!" Huy turns, slipping the donut into the small oven that sits behind him. No wonder he's in short sleeves; I can feel the heat radiating from the trailer from here. "How are you enjoying the Sunset Market's fine items and freshly grown produce?"

"It's nice, I've never been down here before."

"Seriously?"

"Nope." I shake my head. Maybe it's weird to have lived here my entire life and never gone to certain areas or neighborhoods. But it's just never happened; I've never had a reason to come down to the Sunset. "Never been across the Golden Gate Bridge either."

"Okay, I *definitely* don't believe it."

I shake my head. "Promise. I've seen it when I go down to Baker Beach. But I've never been across it."

"You're serious?"

"It'd be pretty sad if I felt like that was an interesting lie."

"That's the messed-up part, it sounds like you're telling the truth."

I shrug. "It's a bridge."

"Can't argue with that. The view isn't much to brag about when you're *on* the bridge. I'm more concerned about the practicality of it." Huy sighs. "There's some good hiking on the other side."

"Yeah, you've seen how well I do in weight training. You really want to put me on a hiking trail?"

"I think it'd be funny."

"So, you *want* to watch me struggle," I say, feigning offense.

"I've gotten plenty of that this week. Not sure I need more."

"You're not funny."

He grins at me, like he's so proud of himself.

"So is the shop just this trailer?" I ask, desperate for a change of topic that doesn't involve discussing how weak I am.

"It's a few blocks down. On Rivera."

"I'll have to come by sometime, get the real deal."

Huy turns when the oven beeps. "I can assure you that my trailer donuts are just as good, if not better."

"I'll be the judge of that." I just have to stand there while he wraps my donut up for me.

I like talking to Huy. Compared with Alice, he's a walk in the park. It's easy to slip into this mode where we find a rhythm, which isn't as common as you might think. Being a Cupid, you have to be adaptive, a skill I'm not sure I ever quite mastered.

"One blueberry donut." Huy hands me the bag, the warmth radiating through my hands.

Then I notice the shape. "Squares?"

That's exactly what it is. Fried dough with blueberries mixed in, drizzled in a frosting that's almost more purple than it is blue. And it's in the shape of a square.

"What's wrong with squares?"

"Nothing," I promise. "Just . . . unexpected."

"My mom thinks it sets us apart from everyone else. 'No one else does square donuts!'"

"Are you sure I can't pay for it?" I reach for my phone. "I can."

"Nope." Huy even grabs the little card reader that sits on the counter and turns it off. "Your money isn't good here."

"Well . . . thanks."

"Consider it a 'Welcome to Hearst' present."

I steal a glance behind me, wondering if I've been holding people up while I stand here. But miraculously, there's not a soul waiting.

"Thanks," I say to him. "Again."

"Don't worry about it." He waves me off without a second thought. "Speaking of Hearst . . . how are you liking it?"

Jeez, can't I get away from school talk for a single day? "It's fine. That algebra quiz was brutal."

"You're telling me; I was cramming all night Thursday. Thankfully, the shop was dead." Huy rubs the back of his neck. "Might be worth it to get a tutor."

I raise an eyebrow. "Are you offering?"

"You seriously don't want me tutoring you. But, you know, Alice is good at math, and you two seem to be getting along. Which is no small achievement, since she's so . . . Alice-y." He lets out a tired sound, halfway between a sigh and a laugh. "That's the only word I could ever think to describe her with."

"She's certainly unique," I tell him. "She actually brought you up the other day."

A total lie. But it hasn't even been a week since I started this endeavor, and I need to make some serious progress. I can't get them together romantically if I can't mend their friendship first.

"Oh, well." Huy shuffles on his feet.

I think, *Come on, ask! Ask me why she was talking about you.*

"What?" I say.

"Nothing." He grabs a rag, pretending to wipe the counter down.

"Is there a history between the two of you?"

"You could say that."

"Can I ask about it?" It's a bold move, direct. Not really my style, according to Leah, which frustrates her sometimes. "She seems . . . I dunno, angry with you."

"Yeah, maybe . . ." His voice goes low, as if he's ashamed.

"Are you angry at her?"

"No," he says a little *too* quickly before he pauses, not meeting my eyes. Huy lets out a huff before he continues. "It's nothing. Stupid teenager drama bullshit."

"Right." But how stupid? Was something said? Done? Feelings were obviously hurt. But before I can press further, I feel a hand wrap tightly around mine, another body pulling itself in close.

"There you are—I was looking for you!" Cal sings in my ear. "Oh, Huy!" Cal pretends to be surprised. "You're here!"

"Yep." Huy sighs. "Couldn't think of a better way to spend my Saturday morning."

"What were you two talking about?" Cal asks.

"We were just—" I start to say, but another voice interrupts me.

"Are you still open?" A woman with her child in a stroller pushes through.

In an instant, Huy's voice changes from his normal speaking voice to what I'd call a customer-service voice. "Yes, ma'am, we sure are."

"Oh, great. My kids have been begging me for these donuts."

Huy gives me a sympathetic look, and it only takes another second or two for the line to grow behind the woman, as if it's a sign from the universe that our magical moment has ended.

"Hey, Jude, do you have Instagram or something?" he asks me as he sets another donut in the oven.

"Oh, uh . . . yeah! I do."

He grabs his notepad and writes down his username for me.

"Find me," he says. "I'll see you at school Monday?"

"Oh, yeah. I'll see you then." And with that, I'm completely shut out.

Ugh.

I lead Cal away from the crowd, walking hand in hand.

"How'd it go?" he asks once we're away from any prying ears.

"I almost had something," I tell him. I don't want to blame him coming in, but I think Huy would've been more open to sharing if he hadn't appeared.

Cal can read as much from my tone.

"I'm sorry," he says to me. "I didn't realize."

"It's fine. Any progress at all is good progress."

But I can't help but think of the countdown, of the invisible clock ticking away, minute by minute, hour by precious hour.

After I say goodbye to Cal, I take the bus downtown to the Westfield Centre, where I'm supposed to meet Neve and Alice.

I follow the directory to the H&M where they tell me they're currently trying on clothes, walking toward the back of the store until I meet them near the changing rooms.

"What do you think, Jude?" Alice asks me, spinning in a skirt. "My style?"

"*You* want *my* opinion?" I ask.

"Shocking, right? But I guess you have a good fashion sense or whatever. So . . . thoughts?"

"I think it's cute," I tell her. "Do you have any top ideas?"

"This one?" She reaches back into the changing room she's been using, grabbing a flowy blouse with cute puffy sleeves and an open neckline. "I'm worried it'll make my legs look short." She spins back toward the mirror. It's a fair concern; Alice is maybe four inches shorter than me.

"I like it," I tell her. "I think it makes your legs look fine."

"Jude?" I hear Neve call out from behind a changing room door. "You're here."

"I am!"

I hear a door unlocking and she steps out in a black-and-white sweater, patterned in zigzags and diamond shapes, that hangs oversized on her. "Thoughts?"

"You . . ." I stare at the outfit. Maybe it's the jeans she's wearing that don't make it work, or maybe patterns just aren't Neve's style. Come to think of it, I don't think I've seen her wear anything patterned since we met. I let my sentence die.

If I can't say anything nice, don't say anything at all.

"I look like a zebra, don't I?" She holds her arms out. The sleeves are too droopy.

"Little bit."

"Ugh!"

"Having trouble?" I lean against the doorframe, turning away so they can both change in their respective dressing rooms. As if me facing the other direction does anything when they're still hidden behind doors.

"She's hated everything she's tried on," Alice tells me. She comes out a moment later dressed in what I'm guessing are the clothes she arrived in. "I keep giving her outfits and she keeps turning me down."

"Pick better outfits!" Neve adds.

"Want me to try, Neve?" I offer.

"Please?" she begs.

"So, *Jude* is good enough to pick out clothes for you?" Alice asks in mock offense.

"You literally picked out that ugly sweater," Neve points out.

"Fair."

That's when I choose to dip out to avoid getting caught in the middle. I like color blocking for Neve, solids that match well with her dark brown skin. I grab a few patterns just to see if we can find anything that works—I think stripes might be a good choice. I come back to the dressing room with too many options. Through the door, I avoid peeping in on Neve as I hand her the clothes.

"Oh wow, this is a lot."

"Got a little carried away." I grin sheepishly.

"No, no, I like the options. Thank you. You're saving my life again."

"I'll go wait with Alice."

Who just so happens to be waiting on a bench outside the changing rooms, looking at something on her phone like always.

"How's she doing?" Alice asks, scrolling.

"Good . . . I think." I take a seat next to her.

Alice lets out a little huff and shakes her head. Then she looks at my hand. "What's that?"

It's probably irresponsible to have held on to a donut for as long as I have. I should've just thrown the thing away. I don't want to carry the bag around all day, and I'm not hungry, not anymore. But it was a gift. I don't want to disrespect that.

"Oh, it's a donut."

"From the mochi donut place downstairs?" She perks up like she *wants* that to be my answer.

"Trinh's," I tell her. "I was at the farmers' market this morning."

"Huh." Almost immediately she shuts down.

"Yep. Huy was there."

"So?"

"What?"

"Nothing. It's just weird that you'd bring him up. I don't care if he was there or not."

"And it's weird that you'd have this reaction over a person you say you don't care about."

"Whatever." She crosses her legs tightly and folds her arms, almost as if she's physically putting the wall back up. But I catch her eyeing the donut bag before she faces forward again.

Okay, it's time to go for broke.

"There's something between you two, isn't there?" I venture.

"No, there's not," she answers too quickly.

"Well, I mean, he mentioned something earlier today. And you seem weird any time that you're around him."

"So he's talking about me?"

"Does that bother you?"

"No."

"I just get the vibe that there's a story there. And your behavior right now isn't really contradicting that. So why are you avoiding the question?"

"I'm not."

"You are."

"Did it ever strike you that I don't want to talk about him?"

"You could've said that," I tell her.

"I'm saying it now." Alice pauses. "I don't want to talk about him."

"Okay." Fantastic, Jude. Absolutely fantastic. "I'm sorry." Just like that, I've effectively undone whatever work I've managed to accomplish over the past week. Alice leans forward, resting her hands on her chin.

Okay, okay. I need to play this carefully. Alice and I might not have that much in common on the surface, but there is one thing we share with each other.

Hearts were broken.

It's a dirty trick, to maneuver closer to her, to pull out my phone and go to Leo's Instagram, scrolling back and forth and letting out a deep, melancholic sigh, laying on the drama to get her attention.

Humans all like to think that they aren't nosy, that they don't engage with other people's "private matters" or whatever. But when push comes to shove, they all love a good, juicy story.

"Who is that?" Alice asks after I linger on Leo's most recent picture, out at the beach with his sister.

"My . . . ex."

"Oh. He's cute."

"Yeah."

"What happened?" she asks because she just can't help herself.

"And *I'm* the invasive one."

"Sorry." She holds her hand out. "Forget I said anything."

"No, it's fine. Probably good to talk about it." I can make up

93

any story I want. Because what can she do about it? It's not like she can fact-check me. I think, given the circumstances, I can come up with something that'll remind her of Huy. "We were both counselors at this camp last summer, and we started dating. He was my first real boyfriend."

Alice turns toward me ever so slightly, tucking one leg under the other.

I go on. "It's so dumb, but I, like . . . I pictured this life together and getting married. Which is so cheesy, but . . . I don't know. I thought he was . . ."

"The one?" she finishes for me, just like I wanted.

"Yeah, I guess so."

"What happened?"

"Camp ended, and we kept seeing each other over the last few weeks of summer. Then he literally tells me he's not actually from the Bay. That he lives in . . . Oregon. And that he's leaving the *next* day."

"Jesus."

"Right? Totally caught me off guard."

"Did you ever consider dating long-distance?"

I shake my head. "He said he doesn't believe in it or whatever." I don't like mocking Leo, especially when he's literally never done anything wrong to me. But it's for the story. He'll just have to forgive me in another life.

"Wow, major dick behavior."

"Yeah." I add a little wetness behind the eyes, just to sell the story. "Sorry, I didn't mean to ruin the mood or whatever. I guess I'm still hung up on him."

"No, you're good." She puts a hand on my knee. "Trust me, you're not the only one who's been through that."

Bingo.

"Boys really fucking suck sometimes." I sniffle, wiping at my nose with my sleeve, and Alice laughs. Another crack in the wall.

"Preaching to the choir, Jude."

"I'm guessing that you and Huy . . . ?" I pause, letting her take it from here.

"Yeah, kind of. In that way that you 'date' during eighth grade. Like kisses on the cheek, holding hands in the hallway. But I thought I was in love with him." She huffs. "And then, over the summer, he basically disappeared. When I saw him again, he was totally different. He'd come out, started dressing differently, binding his chest, and he cut his hair. Which is fine, it's great. He didn't owe me a coming out, but I just felt . . . I dunno, blindsided."

Then she laughs.

"And I'm sure I'm getting all the sympathy in the world from you right now. Poor little cis girl whines about her trans friend coming out because *I'm* the center of attention, right?"

"Well, you wouldn't be the first," I say. But at least she's self-aware. I get it; these feelings are complicated to say the least.

"As I said, he didn't owe me anything, but I thought we were closer than that. But . . . I wasn't angry at him. I was happy, despite it all. Still, he totally ghosted me, ignored my texts and calls for *weeks*. And one time when I went to the Trinhs' shop to confront him, he just hid in the back."

"Ouch."

"He was still posting on Instagram and TikTok, and I saw him making new friends. It made me realize that I'm not good enough for him. At least, from his perspective."

I don't know what to say to any of this. I'm shocked that someone who seems as nice as Huy could do that to her. Then again, I've known Huy for a week, and she's known him for years.

"I'm sorry, Alice."

"It would've been easier if we'd had a fight," she says sadly. "If one of us had done something to make us hate the other. But it just *happened*." There's a quiet to her voice. "It's so stupid too because it was middle school. Like no relationship in middle school is real."

I can't really attest to that.

"But he was my best friend. We literally met in kindergarten. We went to the same church. Our families always celebrated Tết together, and Christmas, and suffered through those all-day Masses that we had to drive all the way down to San Jose to attend."

"I know that advice might not be what you're looking for right now, but can I say something?"

"Sure, go for it." Alice relaxes, falling back toward me. Our shoulders touch, but since she doesn't move, I assume it's okay.

"Did you ever talk to him about it?"

"No," she tells me. "And the funny thing is, I don't really know what I'd ask him. Or how I'd ask it."

"He might've had a reason for everything. Not that it makes it better, but . . ."

"I know it was a hard time for him, with everything going on. I just wish he'd been honest." She starts to pick at the holes in her jeans, pulling the light blue thread of denim free and balling it between her fingers. "Sorry, I didn't mean to dump this all on you."

"No, no. It's okay," I promise her. "I guess we're both not over it."

"Boys fucking suck." Alice stands, wiping at her eyes.

"Where are you going?"

"Bathroom." She looks at me, and then at the bag in my hand. "Are you going to eat that?"

"The donut?"

"Huy's parents make the best donuts in the city. I haven't had one in, like, three years."

"Oh, sure." I hand her the bag. "All yours."

"Thanks. I'll be back."

I watch as she strolls out of the store, taking a sharp right toward the bathrooms.

There's something there in Alice, feelings that linger for Huy. Because she never truly got over him. I can see it because I know those feelings. Because as badly as I want to believe it, I'm not over Leo. If I was, last week wouldn't have happened.

I wonder if it's possible to ever get over your first love like that. That first person you choose to give your heart to. There are people in the world lucky enough to be with that first crush forever, to get to fall in love with their best friend, to share their first kiss and so much more with the person they feel closest to. But what about the rest of us, who give everything we have to a person only for it to mean nothing in the end?

I can't change what happened to me, but I can change what happened between Huy and Alice. I can help to fix Huy's mistake, set them both on the path to something more with each other, to repairing that relationship.

"Where'd Alice go?" Neve asks, stepping out with the pile of clothes that I delivered to her.

"Bathroom. Anything good in there?"

"You've got an eye for colors, Jude." She smiles at me. "I like the stripes, and I'm sticking with this yellow sweater." Both of the tops she shows off were my favorites.

Neve hands the things she isn't taking to the guy operating the changing rooms.

"Shall we go find her?"

"Yes," I say, standing quickly.

I have work to do.

# CHAPTER EIGHT

"You never messaged me."

These are the first words Huy says when he sits down in front of me in English on Monday morning. I literally stared at his profile all weekend, wondering when the right moment to send my follow request might be.

"I, uh . . . had a busy weekend. I wasn't on my phone."

A complete lie. Leah even called me out for not taking my eyes off the thing all yesterday. She had to save me from walking into traffic when we went out for groceries.

"Come on, I don't bite." Huy leans in, his voice going low. Like this is a secret. "Can I see?" Huy holds out his hand, and it takes me a second to register that he's asking for my phone.

"Oh, uh . . . sure?" I reach into my pocket and hand it to him. Huy holds it up in front of my face, unlocking it in an instant, and only then do I realize how monumentally stupid I have been to do this. There are countless texts between me, Cal, Leah, Richard, talking about Cupid stuff. There are pictures, and . . . well . . . you know, websites that I've been to.

Huy keeps the screen in my line of sight, though. Almost as if he's making sure I know he's not doing anything weird. He goes to Instagram, where a post from this cute actor I follow pops up. Huy's fingers instantly go to the explore page, to the search bar, where he types his handle.

"There, request sent." Then he pulls out his own phone. "Oh, and what's that? I have a request from one Jude Ricci? What are the odds?"

And then he does the unthinkable. He opens my Spotify.

"What are you doing?" I ask him.

"Just checking out your music taste."

"Hey—" I want to yank my phone away.

"Uh-huh . . . I see . . ." He swipes up, tapping on something. I can see him stall on a playlist called "Cal's Music," which contains all the songs Cal has shown me, since my taste in music used to begin and end at Ed Sheeran.

*Ed Sheeran.*

"Do I pass your inspection?" I ask him.

"You really love Conan Gray, huh?" he asks with a mischievous look on his face.

"Stop!" I reach to pull my phone away, and he lets me take it. "I just like that one album."

"And the other album, and his EP, and a bunch of his singles that are already on the albums you downloaded, and his Spotify sessions . . ."

"It's good music."

"I never denied that."

"Then let's see *your* music picks, since you're such a musical connoisseur."

"Fine." Huy's smile turns lopsided as he hands me his phone and clicks on Spotify. There's a lot of stuff here. I mean a lot. I'm talking 9,000 liked songs, 523 liked albums, at least 70 different playlists.

"Wow."

"I need to organize it," he tells me.

There's a wide variety here. Phoebe Bridgers and Seventeen

and Kate Bush and Lady Gaga and Perfume Genius are the names I recognize. He's got playlists dedicated to Vietnamese pop songs and ballads, a few styled for different workouts, and one made of film scores that he's labeled *study music*.

"You listen to a lot of stuff. Like a *lot*."

"Is that a bad thing?"

"No, no!" I reassure him, handing back the phone.

"Are you doing anything after school?"

"Uh . . . not that I can think of?" I tell him, though I'd planned to worm my way into whatever plans Neve and Alice potentially had.

"Want to go somewhere?"

"Well, I, uh . . ."

"Come on," Huy whines. "All my friends are ditching me and it's like my first night off in weeks. I don't want to stay cooped up in my room."

"Fine, fine, yes. Where are we going?" The interaction happens so quickly I almost feel like I've developed whiplash from it.

"It's a surprise," Huy says with a satisfied smile, taking his phone back as Mr. Benson calls for our attention. The television in the corner of the room turns on automatically, and the student news begins to play.

I don't pay attention until I hear the word *dance*.

"Tickets will go on sale at the start of next week for the annual Valentine's Day dance. The front office is currently taking suggestions for songs, but asks that students please not send any Lil Jon tracks."

A Valentine's Day dance? That's just a few days before my deadline. I can see it now. Convincing Huy and Alice to go to the dance, their friendship fixed. Maybe I could sneak back-stage and take control of the lights or something, push them together during a couple's dance. A slow song will play, maybe something cheesy and sweet. They'll look at each other, and it'll all click. Huy will probably go in for the kiss first, since he seems like the bolder of the two.

And then . . . I'll be done. I can't help but smile at the idea of this grand finale.

At lunch, I watch for Alice's eyes to catch Huy. There's a moment when she's rolling a loose grape between her fingers while Neve tells us about this horror movie that her parents are design-ing the killer's costume and gore effects for. Alice hasn't said a word in ten whole minutes, which maybe wouldn't be that weird for her, but then I catch her eyeing the soccer team's table. Specifically, the head of said table, where Huy is sitting.

He must feel her stare, because he turns to look at her, his smile cracking before our eyes meet instead. He gives me this nod, and I give him a nod in return.

"You two are getting chummy," Neve says as she palms the grape out of Alice's hand, crunching into it.

"I don't get what you mean," I tell her.

"I saw that look." Neve's own look is a sly one, but she's still smiling at me. Alice, on the other hand, keeps her expression blank. I knew I should've played this more carefully.

"He's just being friendly," I tell them both. "We're in a few classes together."

"Mhmmm," Neve hums, and I look to Alice, but she doesn't say a word. Not even some biting remark under her breath like I'm used to. She looks back at Huy, but his attention is focused elsewhere, on a conversation he's having with one of his boys. But then, a moment later, our eyes meet again.

Just for a moment.

Huy's waiting for me as PE wraps up.

I dared to take a shower today despite how open and weird it felt because I figured I wouldn't be going home first thing.

"You ready?" he asks, throwing his backpack over his shoulder.

"As I'll ever be." My still-damp hair covers my forehead.

"You wound me." Huy puts his hand over his heart. "You're not excited to spend your afternoon with me?"

I look up at him. "That all depends on where you're taking me."

"I think that you'll like it." Huy points to his temple. "I've got a seventh sense for these kinds of things."

"Seventh? What's your sixth sense?"

"The sense to have great calves." As if to prove his point, Huy lunges forward, still in his gym shorts, so they ride up his thighs as he squats down.

"Ew, don't do that."

"Come on, Jude." He wraps his arm around my shoulder, pulling me in close. "We're going to miss the bus."

"I thought you drove."

"My truck is . . . currently indisposed."

"I was starting to wonder why you were on time the last few days."

"Oh!" Huy cries out. "Okay, okay!"

I can't help myself from laughing along with him. We walk out the front steps of the school, joining some of our classmates on the 38R and riding until the herd is thinned out quite a bit. Finally, we're the last two left in the back half of the bus.

"Here." Huy offers me an earbud, and I take it, the sound of a soft ballad playing through while we ride the next few stops to our destination. Huy gets us off in a familiar spot, and as we walk a block back toward where we just came from, I realize where he's taking me.

"NaYa?" I stand there in front of the café. "This is the surprise?"

"I've got a craving for egg custard," he says, holding the door open for me.

And you know what? Who am I to complain?

Thankfully, the café isn't too busy.

"You want to go ahead and get a soda, Jude?" Sammi, our waitress, asks me. I'm not sure what it says about me that I come here so frequently with Cal and Leah that I'm on a first-name basis with most of the employees.

"Yes, please."

"You want a bingsu this time too? Or are we trying something different?"

We hand the menus back without actually looking at them. "Actually, I think we want the salted egg custard, toasted, please."

"Come here often?" Huy asks once she's gone.

"Kind of." I rub my hands on my knees. "Cal and I love this place."

"I can tell." Huy hunches over the table, something left unsaid.

I try to ignore that stirring. "He took me here opening day, actually."

"You've known each other long?"

"Our families lived in the same building; our moms got

pregnant around the same time. We've kind of been friends since we were born, basically." It's a story Cal and I are both familiar with telling.

"That's nice."

"Yeah. He'd pretty much do anything for me. He was the first person I came out to. I couldn't imagine trusting that to anyone else. Not when we're as close as we are."

I hate using what I know about Huy against him, but this is a part of the job. I just have to tell myself that. I want to trigger a familiarity, something similar to the story that Alice told me. It's not even a total lie—Cal *was* the first person I came out to. And he told me he was queer in the same conversation.

"Wow, that's . . ." Huy pauses, looking down at the table. "Really sweet. You weren't worried about his reaction?"

Bingo.

"I mean, yeah . . . I think that's normal. But I knew that Cal loves me for me, no matter who I am. I mean, you're pretty much out to everyone, right?"

"Yeah. My parents are . . . my parents. They try, and that's what's important. The team?" Huy shakes his head as he laughs at his own private joke. "They're almost *too* supportive."

"Is there such a thing?" I ask.

"You'd think there wouldn't be. I know they're in my corner, even when I don't need them. Just like I'm in theirs." His smile fades. "Last year when the season started, another school petitioned to have our matches canceled because of me."

"Oh, fuck . . ."

"Yeah, the school board sided with us, and all the guys wanted to go down to their school. Teach them a 'lesson.' Whatever that means. Thompson stopped them, promised us the best thing we could do was beat them. Plus, I think he saw how weird it made me feel."

"They meant the best, but it still made you uncomfortable."

"It's a hard thing to put into words," he says. "But I don't want being trans to make me different from anyone else. Like . . . I just wanted to be treated like a normal, regular boy. Because that's what I am. But at the same time, I'm proud of who I am, my trans body."

"Sometimes being trans means being a walking contradiction of yourself," I offer.

"It feels like that a lot sometimes. Like I'm *proud* that I'm the first openly trans captain at Hearst, and that I'm the first trans captain to lead their team to the state championship. But at the same time, I hate that I'm the first, that even just walking around means I have to be some symbol for something."

"As much as we might not like it or want to admit it, being out and proud is an act of defiance," I say. "Especially in sports, with how many states and countries want to prevent trans kids from simply playing the sport they like."

"I know. Sometimes I just wish I could be a normal teenager, not a 'hero' or whatever people wanna make me."

"I understand what you mean. Sometimes it seems like cis people are prouder of my transness than I am."

"That's a good way to put it."

"Like at the end of the day," I say to him. "I don't actually think about my gender all that much. And I know it's because I'm comfortable with where I am, who I am. But cis people, they always want to be understanding, to be the ally, to overcorrect when they misgender. It's weird. It makes me feel more alien than if they were just straight-up transphobic."

Huy lets out a chuckle.

"What?"

"Nothing." He looks down at the table. "It's just funny how cis people managed to turn being supportive into some weirdo mentality. They forget that we just want to be treated like people." Then he laughs again, covering his face.

"What?"

"It's nothing, I promise. I'm just sorry for getting too deep."

"Don't," I tell him. "It wasn't a lie, what I said to you in the locker room that first day. I haven't really met that many trans people in my life."

"Seriously?"

I nod. "I went to a few groups. It didn't work out."

"My doctor made me go to a support group before he'd seriously consider me as a patient."

I blurt out, "That's fucked."

"Right? I survived, though. It was worth it."

It hits me that I've strayed too far away from the subject of Alice. Time to get back on course. "So, if you were out before you met your team, was there anyone else who was there?"

"My parents, of course. They were super supportive. Dad let me borrow his clothes until we could actually go shopping. My mom helped me cut my hair. My sister even stole my school ID and Sharpied over my deadname. Problem was I didn't have 'Huy' figured out, so she didn't have anything else to write."

"That's cute," I tell him. "Can I ask where 'Huy' came from?"

"I wish there was a better story. But my mom just insisted that I have a 'name that looks good' if I was going to change it. So, I asked her for a list, and it stuck out to me."

"I think that's a fantastic story. Like being trans turned into a group project."

He laughs. "What about you? Is Jude your birth name?"

"Yeah. It's not from anything special, as far as I know. I've thought about changing it, but . . . I don't know. It's mine. I like it. When I look at myself in the mirror, I feel like it belongs to me."

Once again, the conversation has gotten away from where I'm trying to direct it. Bringing up Alice right now might be too weird.

It's been so easy to slip into these conversations, to forget what I'm here to do. I like being around Huy. And around Alice and Neve too.

It's nice to have friends who aren't Cupids. Who worry about random teenager things like acne and homework and not about helping keep the balance of the universe or whatever by getting people to fall in love.

Too bad there isn't a world where I can have both.

"What?" Huy asks me, and suddenly I'm sitting in front of him again.

"What?" I parrot.

"You were just sitting there, like you were lost." He stares at me so intently. "Where'd you go?"

"Oh, uh . . ." I feel a heat creeping up in my cheeks. "I was just thinking."

"About?" he asks.

"Nothing in particular," I tell him. I feel like an alarm is going off in my head, warning me that I'm in danger. "Tell me about your car. Truck!"

"Truck?"

"What's wrong with it?"

"It'd be easier to tell you what *isn't* wrong with it. The headlights work, that's pretty much the only consistent." He laughs, pulling out his phone to show me pictures. "My mom gave it to me; it was hers in the eighties."

"The eighties?" I can't hide my shock. "No wonder it doesn't work, that's ancient."

"Hey, it works when it needs to. And I'm not going to pressure it."

"You'd think you'd want something more reliable, though."

"It has character," he says. "Besides, it's from my mom. That makes it extra special."

"Fair enough."

Our dessert is delivered, the waitress dropping off a mouthwatering dish, a large square-shaped loaf of bread, the inside hollowed out and the pieces piled inside, toasted to perfection, with egg custard dripping all over them.

"Do you want to see it?" Huy asks.

"Your truck?" I don't wait for him—I grab my fork, stuffing my mouth full of the dessert.

"Yeah, we could go after we leave here."

What answer can I give but yes?

I go with Huy to his family's house, which isn't too far from NaYa, so the bus ride is short. He pauses at the front of the building, taking a set of keys off the belt loop of his pants and messing with the lock on the garage door before it finally releases, and he slips it off, squatting down to lift the door into the air without much effort.

It's nicely built, a work area off to the side with toolboxes and kits lying around. It's gotten a lot darker, but when Huy flips the light switch, I can see some appliances toward the back, and something that looks like a deep fryer that I can only imagine used to be a part of the donut shop.

Sitting front and center is the truck. Huy digs the same keys from his pocket and walks over to the driver's side, unlocking both sides of the car.

"Climb in."

I do as I'm told, climbing into the passenger seat, trying my best to relax for a bit as I watch him insert the key into the ignition. There's a hesitation, and Huy closes his eyes, almost like he's praying or something.

Then he turns the key, and the car roars to life.

"Oh, thank God." He lets his head fall toward the steering wheel, his chin perched on top as he stares out onto the street.

"Were you worried it wouldn't start?"

"Mostly I was worried it'd blow up."

"Seriously?"

"Nah . . ." He pauses. "Well, maybe. I don't know if that was actually a risk. It did catch fire last summer."

"Why do you drive this thing again?" I ask him.

"What do you mean?" He runs his hand along the dashboard. "Listen to this baby purr!"

The engine is sputtering like an old man with a bad cough, almost like it might give out at any moment now.

"I wouldn't exactly call that 'purring.'"

"Want some tunes?" He turns the volume dial on the radio, a funky guitar playing over kicking drums before a female vocalist starts to sing. Huy bobs his head along to the rhythm of the song, doing his best to beat on the steering wheel in time with the music. I don't think he does a very good job.

"Not feeling Paramore?" he asks. "Scoot your arm over." He motions for me to stop leaning on the console that separates us, lifting the lid and showing off a collection of cassettes stored inside.

"Tapes?"

"Pick whatever you want."

"This is fine," I tell him, relaxing back in my seat.

"Fine," he scoffs, reaching into the console and pulling out another tape along with the empty case for the Paramore album. He switches the tapes out easily, and a second later another guitar fills the space, along with a tambourine. Then another sad voice replaces the last.

"Mitski." Huy answers my question without waiting for me to ask for it. "Good for a vibey night like this."

"A 'vibey night'—what does that mean?"

"You know, when it's nighttime, and the vibes are right," he says with a smile.

The "vibey night" is quiet around us, the music soft, the wind cold. But it feels nice, actually. It feels right to be here, even when I look down at my hand and then his. He adjusts in his seat, so he can face me better, leaning his head against the back glass of the cab.

"Why do you own so many tapes?" I ask him.

"Because it'd be too expensive to install a CD player in this thing."

"Yet another reason to upgrade to something else."

"Pfft, you don't know what you're talking about." He looks down at his hands. "I don't know, I probably could've afforded it if I didn't buy all of these. Noah told me to just buy a Bluetooth speaker and glue it to the dashboard."

"Also a nice alternative."

"I like the physicality of it, though. I like picking out a tape, reading my mood, knowing what I want to listen to. It's not the same as just picking a random song on Spotify."

I hope he knows just how pretentious he sounds right now.

"True, but Spotify playlists are easier to make," I argue.

"You'd think. But I've got my technique down."

"Really? You make mixtapes?"

"Here." He swings open the console again, and I hear the rattling around of the plastic cases before he exclaims "Aha!" and pulls out a tape, handing it to me.

The album cover is hand-drawn art, very messy, with the words *mixtape 13* written in lowercase letters on the spine.

"Give that a listen, tell me what you think."

"Okay, but . . . how am I supposed to listen to this? I don't own anything to play this on."

"Ugh, fine." Huy rolls his eyes, and for a moment I think he might just take the tape back, but instead he reaches over me, his arms stretching impossibly long to get into the glove compartment. From inside, he takes out a small black box.

"What is this?"

"A Walkman. Ever heard of them?"

"I know what a Walkman is," I tell him. "I've just never seen one in person."

"You could've just called me ancient to my face."

"You're not ancient," I say to him. "You just have very odd taste."

"I prefer 'specific.'"

"You want me to borrow this?" I ask.

"Yeah. The songs sound really good on tape. Adds to the depression element."

"Right." I take the player, eyeing it in my hand, glad that I have wired earbuds that I can plug right in. "I'll report back later."

"You'd better."

Something catches the corner of my eye, and I turn to look at an older Vietnamese man standing in front of the car, the headlights of the truck illuminating him in the dark. I nearly jump out of my seat, grabbing my chest as the man scares the living daylights out of me. He almost looks like a killer in a horror movie just standing there.

Okay, maybe that's a little dramatic. But I've always scared easily.

"Ba!" Huy rolls down the window, and watches as his father walks toward his side of the vehicle. "Gì vầy?" Huy asks him in Vietnamese.

"Ba nghe tiếng xe. Ba ra xem có chuyện gì."

"Hai đứa con thôi, Ba."

"Thôi, con nói bạn đi về đi. Khuya rồi."

"Mới seven p.m. mà!" I have no clue what Huy's saying to him, but the frustration is tight in his voice.

"Khuya rồi. Và tiếng xe ồn ào quá. Má không thích."

"Rồi, con hiểu. Để con chở Jude về trước đã. Không thì Jude phải đi bộ."

Huy's dad waves his son off. "Đi đi. Con lái xe cẩn thận nhé nhé. Ba mới sửa xong."

"Con biết, con biết."

I watch as Huy's father gives me a short wave that I return, and he walks out through the garage door and up toward the gate in front of their apartment door.

"Everything okay?" I ask him.

"Yeah, it's fine." Huy's voice is quiet, which feels so rare for him, so wrong. "Can I drive you home?"

"No way," I tell him. "I can take the bus, it's fine."

"Jude, please. If I drive you home, I don't have to go upstairs."

Oh. I didn't really expect that.

"Well, sure." I settle back in my seat, strapping the seat belt over my chest.

The music from Huy's tape fills the space between us as he drives me home. I want to say something, ask him if everything is okay. But I can't bring myself to do it, can't brave the wall that's gone up between the two of us.

His father sounded frustrated. Not quite angry, but definitely annoyed.

I wonder if that's a feeling that Huy is familiar with.

I close my eyes, listening to the music, the heat from the truck's vents warming me nicely. I could totally fall asleep right now. I almost do, actually, which is how I don't immediately notice we're driving past my apartment.

"I think you missed a turn," I tell him, looking at Google Maps on his phone, which no longer has a route on it.

"Oh, I didn't. Trust me." He smiles a sly grin.

"You're not going to murder me?"

"I swear." He holds his hand up as we reach a stoplight. "I'm just . . . correcting something."

"And you're trying to convince me you're not a serial killer? You're not very good at this."

"Just wait."

We're getting closer to the Presidio, and then we cut through MacArthur Tunnel. The dark turns orange as the music plays and I get my miniature *Perks of Being a Wallflower* moment. But the true treasure comes when we exit the tunnel, when Huy drives through the tollbooths and through the merging lanes.

Even through the night I can see those tall red arches, the wires connecting the bridge to the road. Huy rolls the windows down, letting the sharp wind blow through our hair as I stare at the night sky. There are no stars; this close to the city it's mostly a deep void, a helicopter flying around somewhere, but it's still very magical. Huy turns up the music to add to the moment, and I watch the bridge around us as it rises and falls all over again.

Before I'm ready for the moment to end, it does. And Huy's turn signal leads us off the main road and down a short driveway toward a parking lot that I'm sure makes for a great photo opportunity when the sun is out.

"There," he tells me, shifting into park. "Now you can't say you've never been across the Golden Gate Bridge."

"It lived up to all my wildest expectations," I tell him.

"I'm glad." He shifts into drive once more. "Ready to see it again?"

I smile at him, feeling a pull in my chest. "Of course."

"Is this it?" Huy asks as he pulls into a spot on the side of the street in front of our apartment.

"Yep, this is me."

"It's been an absolute treasure, Jude Ricci." He holds out his hand for me to take, and I do. His palms are warm.

"The feeling is mutual, Huy Trinh."

**115**

"Are you free this Saturday? I think I told you, we're playing again in Golden Gate Park, me and the guys. You should come this time."

"Oh, uh . . . sure," I tell him. "Thanks for the ride home. Text me when you get home, just so I know this death trap didn't break down on you."

"Aye aye, captain!"

He waits until I'm past the gate and through the front door before he drives off. I climb the stairs to an empty house, falling onto the couch and pulling out my backpack to do the homework that I couldn't do earlier because I was with Huy. But before I do that, I pull out my headphones and plug them into the Walkman, opening the compartment to put the tape in.

There's something so endearing about it, thinking of Huy picking the songs out just to record them onto something else when making a Spotify playlist would be about a billion times easier.

I'm in the middle of writing down themes in *The Crucible* when my phone vibrates. I rush to pick it up without even realizing just how eager I am to see who's messaged me.

No wonder humans get addicted to these things.

The first notification that comes in reads *Huy Trinh has accepted your follow request*.

And the second is a request from Huy to follow me.

The third notification comes from a DM.

> HUY: made it home safely.
> ME: good
> HUY: my mom is mad that I ate at naya before dinner
> ME: you chose it, not me

HUY: yeah, but blaming you is easier
ME: unfair

I back out of the messages, realizing that I now have a history of Huy at my fingertips. At least, the history he wants to show. There are pictures of him at games and him in his soccer jersey with much shorter hair. I have pictures of him with his teammates and friends from school.

I have pictures taken inside his parents' donut shop, pictures of his little sister playing her violin. The real surprise comes at the very bottom of his profile, a picture that maybe he forgot all about, or maybe he decided to leave it there just to have it.

It's Huy and Alice, posted a few years ago, when they were both much smaller. I'm surprised he's left it up because it's clearly from before he came out. The picture is simple, just the two of them sticking their tongues out at the camera.

Still, it's funny to see them like this, to realize how much they've changed in the time between then and now.

I wonder if they ever thought they wouldn't be a part of each other's lives. If that was a possibility that ever crossed their minds.

Not that they'll have to worry about that for much longer.

Because I'm going to make them friends again.

Just wait and see.

ME: still there?
HUY: yeah, trying to do homework
ME: same
ME: I won't distract you
HUY: probably for the best :)

HUY: see you tomorrow? I expect to hear your thoughts on the tape
ME: I promise
HUY: night jude ricci

I smile at the message.

ME: good night huy trinh.

# CHAPTER NINE

"Any fun plans for the day?" Huy asks as we walk out of school together, both of us freshly showered and aching from the exercises we did. It's like he always knows where to find me.

"Tutoring," I tell him, trying my best not to sound *too* excited. "By Alice. I bombed that last quiz." I'd practically gone to her on my hands and knees, both because I actually *do* need help if I'm going to survive the rest of my time at Hearst, and because more quality time with her certainly can't hurt.

We struck a deal after I promised to buy her dinner.

"Oh, that's cool . . ." Huy hesitates.

"Is it?" I ask.

"She's the reason I didn't flunk all through middle school."

"What about you?"

"Work," he says. "Got an early shift at the bakery after I get Hương to her violin lesson. They have to get some shopping done."

"Hương?"

"My sister. You're probably going to meet her at the showcase on Friday."

"Really?" That's when the final step clicks into place and I can start to picture the grand finale. At least to the first half of this plan. I might need Cal's help, though, to make it work. With two of them, there will be a lot of moving pieces.

"Yeah, my mom thinks that Hearst isn't a good enough

school for her, not enough focus on music. But my dad wants to make sure she knows all her options."

"Huh, well . . . not to brag, but I think our orchestra is pretty good!"

"Aren't you literally turning pages for Alice?"

"It's a very tough job," I promise him.

We round the corner of the block just in time to see Alice standing there at the bus stop, right where I told her to meet me, phone in hand, earbuds in her ears. She doesn't notice that we're there at first, and I do my absolute best to keep Huy's attention on me for long enough that the two of them don't notice each other until it's too late.

Alice freezes up as Huy and I both approach her. Huy doesn't notice until I call out "Hey, Alice!" because all his attention was on me.

It feels like a monumental moment, at least to me. Sure, the two of them have been in the same place at the same time. And at lunch, they sit maybe ten feet away from each other. But this is the first time that the two of them have been face-to-face in the days that I've known them.

I just need one of them to be brave, to take that first step, to turn this awkward moment into something more real.

Thankfully, Alice does exactly what I need her to.

"Hey, Huy," she says quietly, pausing before she says his name, almost like she's afraid. Her voice is barely audible above the passing cars and talking students who have joined us around the stop.

"Hey, Alice." Huy's a little louder, though no more confident.

"Are you ready to head out?" I ask her before I turn to Huy. "I'm going to need a lot of tutoring today."

"Yeah . . ." Alice stands there, still unmoving. Okay, so I'll have to push a little more.

"Huy, you were heading to the bakery to work, right?"

"Uh, yeah! Yep." It seems like my words have snapped him out of some trance.

I look back to Alice. "Maybe we could study there?"

This is perfect. They're both too distracted, too caught up in their own feelings to really realize what I'm saying. Their eyes are locked together, and they're falling. I know those looks. They're thinking about regrets, about lost time, about what they shared together and how they both miss it so badly.

Oh, I'm *good*.

"Come on," I tell Alice, the bus deciding to pull up before either of them can even think about what I've said. "Are you riding the bus today?" I ask Huy as I step on, keeping one foot on the platform. Since his truck worked last night, I have no idea what his call will be.

"Uh, no," he says. "I've got to get my sister first."

"Cool, then we'll see you later!" I wave, stepping on and scanning my phone at the card reader. Alice takes a spot near the middle of the bus, picking one of the seats that faces the back.

"Can we go somewhere else?" she asks.

"I feel like that went well!" I assure her. The uglier side of being a Cupid means pushing people to do things that they wouldn't normally be comfortable with. Putting yourself out there is one of the scariest things anyone can do.

"I don't know if I want to see him yet."

"You told me that you missed him," I remind her. "That you wished things could be different."

"Yeah, I do. But I just . . . you know . . ." For the first time in the weeks that I've known her, Alice seems at a loss for words.

"Well, maybe this will be a good thing? It might make things easier!"

"Jude . . ."

"Just give it a chance. If you're too uncomfortable, then we'll leave. Just say the word."

She looks at me for a moment before closing her eyes and letting out a long sigh. "I want the udon place at H Mart. I haven't been there in years because I didn't want to run into him. I always made my dad go there by himself."

"Deal. Udon sounds good."

"Besides, I miss his parents' donuts."

"You know, I still haven't tried them. Not since you stole mine."

"Oh." Alice turns back to me, looking excited. "You'll understand why I stole yours."

Trinh's Donuts is another bus ride away from where we get off, situated among a few restaurants and shops on a corner of the much more residential Sunset District. Traffic is already backed up running through Golden Gate Park, so by the time we make it on the 29 it takes us a bit longer than I'd like. But I keep telling myself it's fine. It'll be fine. We won't miss Huy.

The shop is situated on the corner, right across from the H Mart just like Huy promised. Trinh's Donuts is a small shop, sort of a hole-in-the-wall, the building painted a soft pink with a bright yellow awning that hangs over the large window, where a large—and deliciously painted—donut decorates the entrance.

I recognize Huy's dad behind the counter, next to a woman I'm guessing is Huy's mother.

"Thanh!" The woman I assume to be Huy's mother exclaims Alice's Vietnamese name, a smile wide on her face. She almost races from around the counter to come and wrap Alice in a tight hug.

"Lâu rồi con không đến thăm," Huy's mom says in Vietnamese, her words excitable. "Bác nhớ con nhiều lắm."

"Con cũng nhớ hai bác."

"Ba con khỏe không?"

"Vâng, khỏe." There's an unsureness to Alice's tone.

I'm totally forgotten about in the moment, which is fine by me. Reconnecting Alice to Huy's parents will take me a long way toward where I need to be.

Mrs. Trinh switches to English. "You're coming to hội chợ, right? I missed your cooking!"

"Oh, Dad wouldn't let me miss it this year."

"Good, good." Mrs. Trinh finally releases Alice from her hug, and notices I'm there. "Oh, hello!"

"It's nice to meet you, Mrs. Trinh. I'm Jude."

"Oh, it's Nguyen. I didn't take my husband's last name. That's a Western thing," she corrects me. I glance at Alice, watching her hide her face. "Jude? You're the boy with Huy in the garage the other night?"

"Oh, yeah. Sorry about that. I didn't mean to bother anyone," I apologize.

"Huy's been talking all about you," Mrs. Nguyen says. "I feel like we already know you." Now she wraps her arms around me and hugs me so tight I forget how to breathe for a moment.

"We were just going to order some coffee while we study," Alice says to Huy's mother.

"You don't want donuts?" Huy's mom asks.

"That'll be Jude's reward when we're done."

"Of course." Huy's mother finally lets go of me. "Take the booth in the back. No one will bother you there."

We order two Vietnamese iced coffees and set our stuff where we're told. Alice and Mrs. Nguyen make some small talk in Vietnamese as she brings us our drinks. Before too long, Alice is pulling out her textbook, and the moment I've been dreading arrives.

Is there anything more boring than math?

"Where's your test?" she asks.

"Uh . . . why?"

"So, I can see what you're missing," she says like it's obvious.

"Right, right." I'm more than a little embarrassed to show her the paper, marked all over in red, but it's gotten me here, right where I need to be. I just need Huy to show up.

We don't wait long, thankfully.

There's a door behind the counter that I'm guessing leads out to a storeroom or something, and just as Alice is walking me through the quadratic formula, the door swings open and Huy walks through.

"Mày trễ vậy!" Mr. Trinh says in Vietnamese.

"I know, Ba!" He moves behind the counter with speed, yanking his apron off a hook and tying it around his waist. "Hương took forever to get out of school. But I got her to her lesson."

"Đi làm đi."

"Vâng." Huy's voice goes low, and the frustration is obvious on his face the moment his father turns his back. He doesn't even see us right away, but when he does, our eyes meet, and I give him a sympathetic look.

"Jude." Alice actually snaps her fingers. "Pay attention."

"Right, sorry."

I try to focus on math as the shop gets more and more crowded. When I look over at the front counter, I notice that both Huy's parents are no longer hovering around, that it's just him having to bounce from the kitchen to the front counter to the dining area to collect trays and discarded paper bags when he gets the chance.

"Okay, so I want you to do your homework," Alice tells me, getting out her own notebook filled with her chemistry work. "And when you're done, I'll grade it."

"Yes, ma'am!" I say in a mocking tone.

"Don't make me smack you."

"Sorry." I pull out the homework, half done already thanks to some free time in bio. I *do* have some concept of what was going on, but having Alice explain things to me more slowly and in greater detail really helped. It's the style of schooling I'm more familiar with. When it was just Leah and me, there was plenty of time for her to sit with me, working me through steps until I confidently understood something.

"You two working hard?" Huy's voice surprises both of us, but when we look at the table next to us, we notice him picking up the plates and empty cups to take back to the kitchen.

"Jude got a twenty on their last quiz," Alice tells him.

Which might be the first full sentence I've heard her say to him.

"It was a twenty-six, thank you very much."

Huy lets out a low whistle. "You told me it was bad, but not *this* bad."

I want Huy and Alice to get a little more time together, but more customers come in, forcing Huy behind the counter for another hour. We don't see him again until we're delivered two cups of coffee in large white cups, complete with their own little saucers. Both of the cappuccinos have the art drawn in the foam, the same attempt at a leaf pattern. I say "attempt" because the shape has been totally lost, and looks more like a weird blob.

"What is this?" I ask him.

"I've been practicing my latte art."

Alice and I both stare at our cups.

"What's it supposed to be?"

"A leaf!" he says like it's obvious. "What else?"

"I shouldn't have any more caffeine," Alice tells him. "I'll be up all night."

"Oh, come on," Huy pleads. "One sip? I worked hard on these."

I take my cup, careful to avoid burning my tongue. The flavor isn't anything special, but then again, I know little to nothing about coffee so I'm not sure what I'm supposed to be tasting. "It is good!"

"I'll try it," she says, reaching for her purse.

"Oh no." Huy holds his hands out. "These are on the house."

"Are you sure?" Alice asks him.

"Of course."

Oh, I like where this is going. "Okay, well . . . thanks."

They both go quiet for a moment, but the scene doesn't turn awkward. Their gazes linger, but the silence is comfortable. Huy makes the first move, stepping away as an older lady approaches the counter to ask him something, and Alice's attention is turned back to the homework I've finished. I slide it over to her, letting her review it while her cappuccino sits there.

She hides a yawn with the back of her hand.

"This looks good. I think you actually learned something today."

"Gee, thanks. I love the confidence."

Alice goes for her bag, slipping her textbook back inside. "You still seem to struggle with the last few problems. We can meet tomorrow?"

"Yes, please. Too many letters were thrown around for me to keep track." I gesture to her still-untouched coffee. "You don't want this?"

"Nah, it's bad for me."

"Come on, Huy made it special for you." I know the gesture is symbolic, but if Huy comes back and sees that she didn't touch the drink he made just for her, it'll be a blow to his self-esteem.

"It's coffee, and I'm not even that tired—" She pauses when another yawn comes.

I just look at her.

"I'm not tired." She takes the coffee, downing almost all of it in a single swig now that it's cooled. "There. Pleased?"

"Very."

"When I'm up at three in the morning I'm going to call you."

"Headed home?" Huy asks, coming by to take my empty cup.

"Yeah, it's late," Alice says. "Dad's been texting me."

"Oh, well . . . tell him I said hello."

"Sure."

"Do you want any donuts? I'm about to toss out all the extras."

"Umm . . ." Alice seems to think for a moment. "I mean, I *did* promise Jude I'd buy them some." As if she wasn't the one desperate to have the donuts, like she's trying to play it cool in front of Huy.

"Come on." Huy nods to the counter. "Both of you. We've got too much left over."

Alice and I both stand at the front counter with our bags as we wait for Huy to split a dozen donuts between us.

"I tried to add a little variety," he says. Then he looks at Alice. "And extra blueberry for you, 'cause I know that's your favorite."

"Oh . . . thanks."

I swear I can see her blushing.

Yes! Yes! Yes!

"Am I going to see you at hội chợ?" Huy asks.

"Yeah, I think so."

"We've missed you," he says calmly. But I can read between the lines. He means *I* missed you. "I mean, my parents. They've missed your cooking."

This is the moment that you're looking for as a Cupid, when the emotions are running just a little too wild and the two people you're watching take the reins, leading themselves along.

"Are you coming to hội chợ, Jude?" Huy asks me.

Now why is the focus on me again?

"I don't know. Am I invited?"

"Yes, this is officially your invitation," Huy tells me.

"Good food, dancing, music, fireworks," Alice tells me. "It'll be fun. Neve's coming too."

"Okay." I nod. "When is it?"

"Few weeks," Huy says, folding the lids of the donut boxes down and sliding them over to us. "I can send you the details. We rent out the same strip as the farmers' market."

"I'll be there." Then I think for a moment. "Are you going to the Valentine's dance?"

"Probably not." Huy smiles. "I bet I'll be working. Unless someone invites me. Then maybe I could be persuaded."

There it is. I look at Alice, the idea now hopefully planted in her head.

"You never know," I say. "Someone could. It's not too late."

"We'll just have to see, won't we?" Huy hands me my box.

"Jude, are you coming to the bus stop with me?" Alice asks.

"Oh, uh . . ." I break eye contact with Huy. "Yeah. It's not that far from mine."

"Cool." Alice lets her purse hang off her shoulder. "Bye, Huy. Thanks for the donuts."

"No problem. I'll see you around?" It's almost like they've suddenly remembered that there's this wall between them. Or at least, they think it's still there. But I can see how it's broken around them. Alice and I walk out of the bakery with our donuts in hand, and I wait for Alice to get on the bus before I walk off toward mine on Geary.

I have a plan; pieces are set in motion. I can picture it so easily. At the recital, I know what I'm going to do.

I can almost see the finish line now. It's so close.

There's just a little further to go.

# CHAPTER TEN

Not to jinx myself, but I'm feeling *really* good about this. Even Leah loved my idea once I sat down and explained to her how I wanted to do things, what I'd need her to do. I give Cal the same spiel as I gave her earlier, the two of us spending another night together after Leah and Richard needed each other for a job, the leftovers of our takeout spread before us on the coffee table at Cal's house.

"You don't *have* to help me, you know," I tell him. "I know you've got your own assignments to worry about."

"Jude, please," he scoffs at me. "Besides, I've been *waiting* for the chance to see you perform in an orchestra ever since you showed me your schedule."

"It won't be much of a performance," I promise him. "Just me turning pages."

"Maybe Alice will be struck with some bug, and you'll really get the chance to shine?"

"Yeah, if that happens, I'll kindly ask you to run me down with Richard's car."

"I mean, it's a Tesla, so it's not like I even have to be behind the wheel." Cal laughs. "Do you really think that you're nearing the end with these two?"

"It feels that way," I tell him. Thankfully, I don't have to explain myself. Cal knows the sensation the same way that I do. That feeling that you're nearing something big, something that'll change the entire game.

Sometimes it's as simple as the lead in to a kiss, when you see the two people tilting their heads, their lips meeting, and that euphoric rush hits you. Other times it's slower than that, when a gaze lingers or fingertips touch by accident.

I can feel myself getting closer and closer. To that final moment, to passing the test.

To this all ending.

And that's all it takes to bring myself down. I don't know, it's dumb to think that I'm already so close with Neve and Alice, but I enjoy hanging out with them. I like being around them. They make me laugh. And it's nice to get to feel like a normal teenager. More than once, I've had to remind myself that I'm at Hearst to do a job, not to have fun.

"You okay?" Cal asks me. "You went all quiet on me."

"Yeah, I'm good."

But the way he looks at me tells me he knows something's up. Cal reaches for the remote, turning off whatever YouTube video essay he'd pulled up, because for some reason, he can avoid most overtly human things *except* long video essays about media he's never consumed.

"I want boba," he says, turning to me. "How does boba sound?"

"Really good, actually."

Cal takes my hand, leading me back out into the dining room. "We're going out to get boba," he tells me.

Cal and I grab our jackets, and we're out the door in record time, moving through the neighborhood until we find ourselves free of the winding streets.

"Is it weird that I don't want this job to end?" I ask him. Because I have to. I want to talk about this, and Cal obviously picked up on the signals. Why else would he have invited me out?

"Don't tell me you're enjoying it there?"

"I mean . . . it has been fun," I tell him. Because what's the point in lying? He'd be able to tell.

"But it's public school, with humans. *Humans*, Jude."

"I know they're humans."

"You're overthinking things. Just wait until you're finally done and you get to spend all your time with me again!" Cal takes my hand, pulling himself in close.

For the briefest of moments, I picture Huy's hand around mine instead. Strong, pulling me in close.

No. Nope. I can't think about that. That's what got me in trouble in the first place. I shouldn't even be having these thoughts. It's just because he's a cute boy, and it's normal to want cute boys. So long as I don't make the same mistake again.

I'm a Cupid.

That's what I'm meant to be.

"What's going through that frizzy head of yours?" Cal asks me.

"Do you ever wonder . . ." I hesitate. Once I verbalize this, there's absolutely no going back. But I don't like being alone in my thoughts. "You ever wonder what it'd be like to be human?"

Whatever emotion I expected from Cal, he doesn't deliver. There's no anger or confusion. He's not frustrated over me asking what should be a question that collapses the ground from underneath us. I'm supposed to be confident in my abilities; I'm not supposed to wonder about another life, what might be.

No, instead Cal just stands there, his face blank as we walk forward.

"Cal?"

"I'm just thinking," he says, his voice suddenly soft in an unfamiliar way. "I don't think so, no."

I don't know what sort of reply I expected. It's not normal to feel this way, I've been taught that my entire life.

And I'm not sure Cal would've told me the truth if he *had* ever felt this way.

He shakes his head. "Have you? *Are* you?" There's a soft panic to his words, barely audible, but I've known Cal long enough to hear it.

"I mean . . . kind of." I say the words, but suddenly, things with Cal don't feel as safe as they once did.

"Why? What do you think about?"

"About being normal, about . . . never mind."

"No." His grip on my hand tightens. "No never mind. Tell me. Please?"

"It's just . . . how do we know this is what we were meant to do? How do you know this is the life you were supposed to lead?"

"Existential," Cal remarks. "Heavy stuff."

"You don't have to answer that."

"But I will," he says. "It's a hard thing to pin down. You know? But I've just always felt confident in what I do, what I can do, the potential. I like helping people fall in love. Don't you?"

"Yeah, I do," I tell him. "But sometimes I look at humans and I wonder if they have something figured out that we don't."

"Well, if that were true, we wouldn't be needed, would we?"

"Yeah." I force a laugh. "Right."

"I think that you're just scared," Cal says. "And I don't mean

**133**

that in a bad way. I think anyone in your position might be scared. It's a heavy thing to have to carry."

"You're telling me."

"And I know that . . ." He pauses, and I can almost hear what's coming next like a prophet. "I know that what happened last summer might still have you worried. But Richard wasn't just hyping you up for no reason, Jude. You're an *amazing* Cupid, and you're good at what you do."

"Do you really believe that?"

He nods. "Your confidence being shaken is normal. You only truly fail if you stay down when you fall."

"God," I groan. "That was the corniest thing you've ever said to me."

"I think I got that from a movie you made me watch. Did it help?"

"Kind of." I hate to admit it, but I do feel better now, in a way. Cal's right—it's just my anxiety getting to me.

To become human would mean leaving this all behind, sacrificing everything I've built to leave Leah and Richard behind.

And Cal . . . a life without Cal would be a quiet one, maybe. But it'd also be so lonely.

I'm a Cupid. I belong in this world. I belong with Leah and Richard, and I belong with Cal. This is my home; these are my people.

# CHAPTER ELEVEN

"Oh wow, you clean up nicely," Alice says as she unlocks the front doors of the school for me. It's weird being at the school after-hours, all the lights off, no students milling about.

It's eerie.

"Thanks," I tell her. "I'm the most uncomfortable I've ever been."

Sure, I've done my makeup and my hair: I've tried to go for something natural looking, no patterns or anything ornate like that. Some foundation, eye shadow, light blush, my brows. The most outlandish thing I did was draw on some fake freckles. But the outfit itself is too formal—for some reason, I decided I should wear a tie. *A tie*.

"If it helps, you don't look it. It's just a couple of hours. Think you can make it?"

"I'll survive."

"Come on, we're just setting up in the auditorium."

I follow Alice through the empty hallways that seem so eerie without any students walking through them.

"Are your parents coming?"

"My dad is."

"Just him?" I ask.

"Well, considering my mom divorced him and moved back to Vietnam, I doubt she'll show."

Oh. "Ouch."

"Eh. It was a few years ago. I'm fine with it." Her voice is so nonchalant.

"I mean . . . should you be, though?"

She actually laughs at that. "Not like I have much of a choice, do I?"

"I guess not." I go quiet.

"My dad and I are fine as we are. I've already been through all those emotions. I accepted a while ago that she's not coming back. And I don't blame her. She never wanted to marry my dad. She felt like she had to. She never wanted kids—she didn't keep that a secret. It's just how life went."

"That's still not fair to you," I say.

She snorts. "You my therapist now?"

"I feel like that's a normal thing to say."

"Yeah." She kicks her feet as we continue along our path. "I don't know, I'm angry at her, but I'm not angry with her, if that makes any sense. I *was* angry at her, but I was also happy. That she got away from this life she clearly didn't want to live. It just sucks knowing that I'm one of the reasons she didn't want to live it."

"Alice . . ." I pause.

"Please don't say something corny like 'It's okay to not be okay.' I don't think I can handle it." She lets out an odd sound, one that's clearly trying to be a laugh but doesn't quite sound right.

"No," I tell her. "It's not okay that it's not okay. And it doesn't have to be."

She stares at me, water behind her eyes.

"I can't imagine what that feeling is, what you've been

through." Yeah, maybe we're both missing parents in some way or another, but I never knew mine. "And it's not okay that your mom did that to you. You don't have to pretend that it is." Okay, I guess I'm in full-blown therapist mode. The last thing I expected when I walked through these doors was to have this heart-to-heart with Alice.

But . . . I like her. She's a nice person, despite the rocky exterior that she's built around herself. Maybe I don't know her as well as Neve, or Huy, but I do feel like I know her in a way.

I feel like she's my friend.

And it's clear that this has been weighing on her.

She wipes at her eyes without thinking, and of course they come back streaked with black. "Ah, fuck!"

"Come on." I close the gap between us. "I keep a bag in my locker."

On the other side of the school, we're in complete privacy. I offer Alice a wipe to clean both her eyes, giving me a mostly fresh canvas to start from.

"Thanks," Alice whispers.

"Of course." I ready my primer. "It's my fault anyway."

"Right." She laughs, rubbing the primer into her skin. I don't own any foundation that matches her more golden skin tone, but with some careful blending, I can make things work. "Thanks," she says softly. "For what you said back there."

"No thanks needed." I use a deeper shade of eye shadow to blend out the foundation and concealer she has on. I know I told her that I don't know what she's feeling, but at least Alice got to know her mother before she left.

I stare at her carefully, drawing her eyeliner in an extremely careful single stroke. Replacing her eye shadow and mascara, I look at my work.

It feels good to know what I'm doing.

Once we get to the auditorium, we find Mr. Lawson racing around. I've never seen an actual chicken without its head, but if I had to guess what it looked like, I'd say Mr. Lawson is doing a pretty good impression.

"I thought this was just a showcase for some kids," I whisper to Alice.

"It is, but I'll remind you that the number of kids who sign up for orchestra helps determine the budget every year. The more kids he has, the more funding. Not enough kids and . . ." She makes a cutting motion at her throat, sticking her tongue out for a little dramatic effect.

"That's harsh."

"The public school system, baby!" Alice sings. "Mind you, the county didn't bat an eye at the cost of the football field renovations last year. But Mrs. Jackson, the art teacher, has to buy canvases and paint out of her own pocket."

I step backstage with Alice, where she switches into flat shoes and grabs her drumsticks. Mr. Lawson manages to squeeze in two full rounds of rehearsals before the time for the doors to open comes, at which point the curtains draw to a close and we're allowed to step backstage to get water and snacks.

Soon enough, though, we're being called back out. Alice and I nod at each other as we take our seats, and I close my eyes, breathing. It feels weird to say that I'm nervous when my only responsibility is to flip pieces of paper. But it's nerve-racking to be faced with this many people.

Imagine my surprise when the curtain is pulled back after Principal Kurt gives a rousing speech on the importance of arts and music (which earns a silent scoff and head shake from Mr. Lawson) and I see all the seats are filled, with some kids and parents left standing since they came in late.

Immediately, I can pick Leah and Cal out of the crowd, and they both smile at me, Cal taking a picture.

I smile back, but my eyes wander, looking for someone else.

I find him toward the middle of the audience. Dressed in a dark red button-down and khaki pants, his hair trimmed just an inch and brushed away from his face. I recognize Mr. Trinh and Mrs. Nguyen next to him on one side, and a little girl who looks almost identical to her older brother sitting beside her. Huy gives me a short wave, close to his chest. And I give him one right back.

I knew that he'd be here. He told me that.

But knowing he'd be here and seeing him here are two totally different things.

There's this beat of silence that feels like it carries the whole world. Mr. Lawson stands in front of us, tapping his baton on the music stand.

I ready myself, hunching toward the stand with our music. And with a wave of Mr. Lawson's hand, we begin. I find my groove with Alice effortlessly, the practice really paying off.

When I dare to look up at the crowd, I can see smiles on their faces, videos being recorded. And then my eyes meet Huy's again, and his meet mine.

He smiles so bright it's distracting, and I feel that jump in my chest that breaks through even the nerves of keeping Alice in time.

"Jude!" I hear her whisper.

When I look, she's nodding at the sheet music, signaling for me to turn the page.

"Sorry!"

My eyes meet Huy's again, and I feel that familiar panic. The one that settled in when I was at camp, doing my best to get these two teenagers together, when I just so happened to spy Leo as he was helping a kid with a skinned knee, spraying an antiseptic spray and letting the kid hold his hand while he put a Band-Aid on one-handed.

He looked up at me, and he smiled.

I felt like the ocean pulled me under like a stone. It was immediate, turbulent, entirely out of my control.

I'd fallen in love.

And when I look at Huy, when he smiles at me . . .

I feel that all over again.

The room goes silent, and when I break eye contact and see the way Mr. Lawson is looking at me, I realize that I've missed my cue. I flip to the final page of the sheet music, the music echoing through the hall. Mr. Lawson turns back around and gives everyone a bow, the crowd erupting in applause. Everyone sets their instruments down, and while everyone else is standing for their applause—Mr. Lawson reminding everyone that we'll be taking a short break before the theater department puts on their medley of songs from *Wicked*—I step off the stage.

I can't breathe.

It's like the collar of my shirt is wrapping itself around my neck, slowly, agonizingly ripping the breath out of my lungs. I know that I am breathing because I can feel the air entering my body, but it burns, like I've been running in subzero temperatures. It's painful. I step past the poor girl being painted green into the single-person bathroom, locking the door before I fall against the wall, sinking slowly. The more rational part of my brain tells me that this floor is filthy, that I shouldn't be sitting here. But with each passing second that voice is getting quieter, being snuffed out until there is nothing left except Huy.

The way that he looked at me tonight, the way his lips stretched into those dimples and he showed off his two front teeth, which are just a little crooked. I don't know why these feelings have pulled me completely under, leaving me to drown in them.

But I know what they are.

Because I've felt them once before.

And I can't let myself slip into them.

I'm not in love with Huy. That'd be so stupid. To fall in love with a human again, and after I just met him? That's not how it works.

He's a *human*.

And he's meant to be with Alice.

To even admit these feelings exist out loud would be enough to set Leah off, to pull me from this job, possibly move me out of the Bay Area just to get away from these two boys who took my heart without my permission. To erase Huy's memories of me.

Have we never considered how unfair a thing that is to do with humans, to mess with their memories without their consent? How fucked up is it that I'm only considering this now?

I never even asked for this life, for these powers.

Would life be less complicated as a human?

No, right? As a human, there's no Leah, no Richard, no Cal. There's no comfort in helping people find the person they love, working to get them together. I like doing that. And what does a human life even look like for me? Would the Cupids simply kick me out, leave me to roam the streets all on my own, figure out things for myself? Would Leah help to take care of me? Or could she not be bothered? I can't imagine her being that cruel, but would she even have a choice? I'd no longer be their responsibility, after all.

So, I guess my question has two answers.

(a) Fall in love with a human I've known for two weeks, become human, allow my entire life to be upended to the point that I have zero idea what'll even happen to me.

Or (b) live a life of comfort, doing something that I'm good at while never ever getting to love this boy back, never getting to determine my own fate, never getting to live the life that I might want to live and being forced to serve some "greater purpose" in the universe all because my life was decided for me before I was even born.

God, I hate my stupid fucking brain.

There's a soft knock on the door.

"Hello?" It's a voice I don't recognize. "Sorry, we need to get in there."

I stand up, double-checking myself in the mirror and grateful that I've avoided any tears. I flush the toilet, run the sink for a bit, and try to focus, regain what little composure I was managing before.

I have a job to do. It's time to grow up and accept my responsibilities as a Cupid. Enough messing around and dreaming of something I can't be.

I step out of the bathroom, whispering a sorry to the girl whose entire face and hands are now a sickly green color to perform as the Wicked Witch of the West. I don't remember what her actual name is.

My phone dings in my pocket, and I chastise myself for hoping that it might be Huy.

CAL: Where'd you go? Are we still doing this?

Right. I am here to help Alice and Huy get together. That's my role in their life. Not to be their friend, not to fall in love, not to go to school or perform in the orchestra or anything like that. I'm a Cupid.

A Cupid.

This is my role in their lives, and to want anything else is wrong of me.

I have a duty.

ME: yeah, coming out now
CAL: okay, I see Alice, she's talking to Neve
ME: i'll find huy

I swallow a hard lump that almost refuses to go down as I climb back onstage and slip down the steps hidden on the side. It's easy to find Huy. He's alone, near the corner of the room with a piece of cake in hand, his family nowhere to be found. I grab my own precut slice of cake before I walk over toward him. It's dark chocolate with a thick layer of frosting, the perfect ammunition for what I have to do here.

In all honesty, I'd prefer it if I could talk to Alice and Neve instead. But Cal's been nice enough to help me out here, which means I need to take the lead.

I can't give up now, not when I've gotten so close.

Huy finally sees me, and his eyes light up.

"There you are!"

It's unfair how he literally has a piece of cake stuck to his teeth and he's still so perfect looking.

"Here I am."

"I must say, your page turning was superb. I think you saved the whole show?"

"Oh, hardy har har, you're *so* funny!"

"I'm serious!"

"I messed up a few times. I was late."

"If it makes you feel any better," he says, "I don't think that anyone noticed."

"You think?"

"Oh yeah." He takes another bite of the cake, leaving a trail of frosting on the corner of his mouth. "I mean, I didn't realize until you said something. So, I think you're safe."

"You've got a—" I rub at the corner of my own mouth. "Frosting."

"Oh!" And instead of using the napkin in his hand, he just licks, and on the wrong side of his mouth too.

"No, here." I take my napkin, dabbing it softly with my tongue and hoping that he doesn't think it's gross before I wipe the stain away.

He leans down to be more level with me, and I realize that we're inches away. I've seen his face before, I've seen it nearly every day for two whole weeks now, and it still feels like I notice something new every time I look at him. Like now: there's a tiny scar, right below his eye. It points like an arrow to the dark brown of his iris, which pops with these hints of something light, something softer.

I hate how things have already changed, how a crush makes you look at someone in a way that you've never seen them before. He looks so different. Except it's not him who's changed. It's me.

"Thanks." He stares at me, and only me.

"Yeah, no problem." I have to stop my heart from exploding out of my chest. "Where'd that scar come from?"

The question slips out so naturally I'm not sure I'm even the one who asked it. But it floats there, in the ether, my words spoken.

"Oh, this one?" He points, pulling his skin a bit. "Soccer game. My teammate wasn't paying attention, shot the ball too hard. It whipped me really good."

"Ouch."

"Well, you know what they say about men with scars—they're super sexy," he says with a purr that makes me cringe.

"God, please never talk like that ever again."

"What? You don't like my sexy voice?" He then shifts to something deeper, leaning in even closer. "This doesn't do anything for you, Jude?"

"Please!" I push him away. "Ugh, you're violating my ears."

"Oh, I can violate more than that!" he says. "Wow, that sounded so wrong. I'm so sorry."

"Whatever will you do to make it up to me?" I ask him.

He wiggles his eyebrows. "I can think of a few things."

"You just keep digging that hole deeper," I tell him.

"Oh, speaking of holes—" He stops himself, unable to even

think about finishing that sentence. "I'm sorry, I'm done, I'm done."

"Promise me?" I'm sure my cheeks are a shining red. I'm grateful that I'm already wearing blush to help hide it.

"I do, Scout's honor."

My phone *dings!* again.

> CAL: still doing this, right???
> ME: yes
> CAL: okay, I'm going for it.
> ME: 👍

"Pressing matters?" Huy asks, pretending to sneak a peek at my screen.

"Nope," I tell him, turning the screen off and sliding it into my pocket. I turn to find Cal heading toward Alice and Neve.

"Looking for Cal?" Huy asks me, and suddenly his voice goes very . . . neutral. Not like he's annoyed or anything. It's just very un-Huy-like.

"Oh, uh. No? I mean, maybe?"

"Maybe?" He chuckles. "He stopped by before the show started, said hello."

"Really?"

"Mhmm." Huy takes another bite of his cake.

I don't know how to feel about Huy and Cal having a conversation without me being there. But Cal knows what he's doing; it's not like he'd say something that he's not supposed to.

"The two of you are cute together." Huy's words linger in the air before I truly hear them.

I turn to him slowly, wondering if I've actually heard him right.

"Wait, what?"

But before he can answer, I hear a crash and the sound of Alice saying "*Really?*" while another person tells her "I'm so sorry, oh my God!" My eyes meet Cal's, who is smart enough to not be *directly* involved in the accident. Some older-looking guy starts to apologize profusely while he offers her napkins, and Neve goes to Alice's side, leading her through the crowd. Earlier, I planted an OUT OF ORDER sign on the women's bath-room door and jammed it shut. Now, with any luck, Alice will want to clean her dress badly enough that she'll go for the men's room instead of searching around.

Which means it's my turn.

"Oh, yikes," Huy says, his eyes following Alice as she brushes past the crowd of people. "You think she's okay?" For a moment, it looks like he's going to go after her without me needing to ruin his clothes.

I don't want to risk it, though.

"Yeah." I take a step back, carefully watching the people around me. I'm still thinking about whether Huy thinks Cal and I are together.

Isn't it so funny how our brains control everything we do, that we're only alive because of what they do; they tell us to breathe, tell our hearts to pump blood, control the trillions of nerves in our bodies that make us feel the fucked-up rainbow of emotions that we're forced to experience on a daily basis?

And yet the brain does so much without our permission, thinking thoughts that we don't want to think, as if we aren't really ourselves. Just puppets for this weird little organ that would have no reason to exist without us.

I hate my brain for making me feel things for Huy that I shouldn't.

"You okay?" he asks me, his brows furrowing close together.

"Yeah, yeah . . . I'm fine."

My phone *dings!* again.

CAL: We don't have much time.

I don't reply to the message.

Cal's right, I don't have much time.

I'm still hanging on to Huy's words. I don't know if I'm a believer in alternate universes. I believe in them the same way I believe in aliens. I mean, how could I not? I'm literally a magical being meant to help humans fall in love. Aliens existing out there somewhere isn't *that* far-fetched. And the universe is a big place.

But if there *are* an endless number of universes out there, that means Huy and I had to have found each other in at least one of them. There exists this perfect universe out there where we're both human, where Cupids don't exist—or maybe they do and I'm just not one of them—and we still found each other.

If the theory is true, there exists one perfect universe out there where this life that I want for myself isn't impossible. Where I'm the happiest that I could be because I'm allowed to be with Huy Trinh, and I'm allowed to love him.

I hate them. Almost as much as I hate this version of myself. The one who can't love him.

I don't have time to react to the push. Suddenly, I feel a hand on my back, firm and unmoving as this lady passes behind me at the same time. And I swear, at least for a moment, that I see Cal.

I'm forced forward, my momentum only stopped when Huy reaches to grab me by both arms. But it's too late to stop the plate from falling out of my hands, from careening the few inches cake-first onto Huy's shirt. We collide, my face hitting his chest. The panic sets in as I realize what's happened.

"Oh my goodness, are you two okay?" The lady who allegedly caused all this grabs me by the shoulder.

I step back, conscious of just how close Huy and I are to each other. That's when I look down, averting my gaze, and see the giant stain on his shirt. My plate falls to the floor as we both stare at the huge mess.

"Shit, Huy," I say slowly. "I am so sorry."

"Oh no!" The woman who caused this whole thing covers her hand with her mouth.

"It's fine," Huy says calmly, and I believe him. "I hate this shirt anyway."

"Come on, bathroom." I take him by the shoulders and we break through the doors to the gym. We cross the hallway just in time to see Neve exiting the men's room.

Perfect.

"You too?" she asks.

"Cake," I say.

"You?" Huy asks.

"Alice, and salsa!" Neve exits back into the gym. "We need seltzer."

Huy and I pause at the bathroom door.

"I'm going with Neve," I tell him.

"Oh, okay. I'll be in here, I guess."

"Hot water," I warn him. "And don't scrub, dab."

"Got it." He opens the door, and I listen before it shuts, the sound of his shoes squeaking against the tile. Then, once the door is closed, I can't hear anything else.

Before I forget, I grab the OUT OF ORDER sign from the women's room and place it on the men's room door. This way, no one will bother them. I also shoot a text to Cal, so he can distract Neve. Hopefully he'll think of something other than spilling food—I think we've lost enough clothing for one night.

It'll all be worth it, though. Two garments sacrificed for these two people to get together, to be happy forever, to finally reunite and realize their feelings for each other never really went away, they just needed more time.

I sink against the wall, staring at the floor, at the patterns in the linoleum.

It's for the best.

I don't know how long I stand there, or how long I'm supposed to stand there for. I can't just wait for them to come out, and I guess, at some point, Huy is waiting for me to show up with something to help him clean his shirt. But I can't run the risk of interrupting what could be a pivotal moment.

Just *talk* to each other.

You'd be surprised how many issues between people would be solved if they just had a conversation. And yet humans act like it's the hardest thing in the world.

The door to the gym opens again, and I dare to look up just to make sure Neve hasn't broken through, but it's Cal.

"How'd it go?" he asks, keeping his voice low. I'm not sure if we need to be whispering right now.

"They're in there," I say. "Now it's in their hands."

I can't influence what they'll say to each other, the words that they'll choose. All I can do is hope that they'll say the right ones, that I've influenced the two of them enough to say what they need to.

"Then you did what you could," Call tells me.

"Right." Then I remember. "Did you push me?"

"What?" He looks at me with obvious confusion.

"In the gym? Did you push me into Huy?"

"I didn't. I pushed the lady who pushed you."

"Why would you do that? I had everything under control."

"You're seriously angry?" He crosses his arms. "You were the one taking forever just to spill cake on a shirt."

I'm not angry; I'm more annoyed. I had a plan, and it was my decision to pick the moment to strike. I didn't need Cal to make that call for me.

"I was going to do it. I was totally in control," I tell him. "This is *my* assignment, remember?"

"I do," Cal tells me. "Do *you*?"

"Whatever." I lean against the wall. He's right. It's dumb to be mad right now. There are more pressing matters at hand. It doesn't matter how it happened. What matters is that it did.

"Well . . ." Cal looks toward the door. "Should we listen in on them? Neve is heading out to the closest corner store for some fizz. I'd guess that'll give us about five more minutes."

I hesitate, wondering if that's the right move before I nod at Cal. We squat low to the floor, daring to open the door just an inch.

"You think it'll come out?" I hear Huy ask.

"Dude." Alice sighs. "I have no idea. I think you're only making it worse."

"Jude and Neve are supposed to come back with something. Maybe it'll help."

There's a beat of silence, the sound of scrubbing. I can only guess that Huy didn't listen to what I told him.

Then Alice says, "You and Jude seem like good friends."

Huy doesn't answer, not right away at least. There seems to be an eternity that stretches on and on between her question and when Huy finally gives her an answer.

"Yeah, I guess so." Then another pause before Huy asks, "What?"

"Nothing."

"Alice . . ."

"I was just making an observation."

"But I know what you were thinking," he says. I wish *I* knew what she was thinking.

"No, you don't."

"I know you better than you think."

That's when the bubble bursts. "You haven't known me for years, Huy. So don't start now."

It feels so wrong to be here, to listen to this conversation.

"Alice, I . . ."

She doesn't say anything.

Huy pauses, and for a moment, I think he's going to let this slip away, to let this conversation pass by, set me back weeks.

But he doesn't.

"I'm sorry."

More silence, barely filled in by the sound of running water.

"I didn't know how to talk to you," he says. "I guess . . . I don't know. There wasn't a reason to be afraid, but I was worried. I thought that you might hate me, that you wouldn't understand me."

Seconds tick by like hours.

When Alice doesn't say anything, he continues, "I was really confused and scared, to be totally honest. And I know that doesn't excuse ghosting you like I did. But I hope it explains how I felt."

"Huy, I get it. I mean, I don't because I don't know what you were going through. But I do understand to a point. I'm not mad at you for coming out or being trans. Please never think that. I'm just . . . you were my *best* friend. I loved you. And then you stopped talking to me."

The faucet is turned off, the sound of still-dripping water echoing off the tiled walls.

Alice continues, "I just wish that you would've told me half of what was going on with you. I wish you would've had a conversation with me instead of just deciding for me."

"I know," Huy says.

"You didn't owe me a coming out. You didn't owe that to anyone; it's your choice if and when. But I just wish you'd told me something. Anything at all. Instead of ignoring me." Alice lets out a shaky breath. "I know that you were scared, and I was too. I lost my best friend. And that really fucking sucked."

Huy doesn't say a word, which is probably the safest choice.

Alice needs to get this out; she deserves that chance. She's been hurting for so long, and the person who caused that hurt is right in front of her.

There's never been a better time.

"I was angry with you because I was scared, and without you, I was all alone," Alice continues. "I didn't have anyone, not until Neve."

"I know."

"Tell me why."

"What?"

"Tell me why what happened *happened*."

"I . . ." Huy pauses. "I was scared too."

More silence, more quiet. The dripping finally stops.

"I was scared of how you'd react when I told you who I am. I don't know why, because I knew that you would've accepted me. But I didn't know that for sure, and I was worried that you'd hate me. And then, at camp, all the boys welcomed me. None of them cared. None of them judged me. And I felt like a real boy for the first time. It felt so effortless, so natural. It was the first time that I ever felt like I belonged somewhere, and I guess I fell so hard into it because I was desperate. I wanted to feel as boy as I could, and they helped me do that." He breathes.

"Huy . . ."

"And it wasn't fair, to put that on you." I can hear the tears, his voice going hoarse. "I know, and I'm sorry. You're right, I made that decision for you. I didn't want to hurt you. So I thought ignoring you was the easier option."

"You did hurt me, Huy. But I've never hated you."

He laughs. "Your stares from across the cafeteria make me skeptical of that."

"I've been angry at you. Annoyed, frustrated, but above all of that, deep down I was happy to see you become who you really are, to be comfortable in your own skin."

"God." He sniffles. "That was *so* cheesy."

"Stop ruining my moment!"

"I'm sorry, Alice. I'm so sorry." Huy lets a sob slip, and my heart breaks for him. I hear something, a strange sound that I can't make out.

The words come quietly. "I love you, Huy."

Four words that end my world.

And four more are yet to come.

"I love you too."

I close the door, forcing Cal to step away.

"We should give them privacy," I tell him, and he nods just as Neve rounds the corner, a bottle of seltzer in her hand.

I block her at the door. "They're having a moment."

"Seriously? Alice hasn't mauled him?"

"It's complicated," Cal says. "I'm Cal, by the way." He holds out his hand, and Neve returns the gesture with a confused look on her face.

"Just give them some time," I say.

"Okay, but I've got to get this to her."

We stand out there, counting the minutes to ourselves before Neve has finally had enough waiting around. She knocks on the door. "Everyone's decent?"

"Huy's got his nipples out," Alice says.

"I don't mind if you don't!" Huy laughs, but I can hear something in both of their voices. It's clear that the tears, silent as they were, were heavy. Huy is indeed standing there with his nipples out, his binder folded on the sink because even it couldn't escape the cake stains. The skin around both their eyes is red, rubbed raw, and there's a pile of used paper towels in the sink.

"The store had these too," Neve says, pulling two Tide pens seemingly out of nowhere and handing one to Huy. "Everything okay in here?"

"Yeah, yeah." Alice turns back toward the mirror, brushing her hair away from her face. "I messed up my makeup again, Jude."

"How do the clothes look?" Neve asks.

"Umm . . . well . . ." Huy looks at his shirt in the sink, soaked through now thanks to how he was washing it. "At least Alice's dress looks okay."

Alice steals a look at him in the mirror before she turns toward Neve and me. "Can you see it?"

There's a dark stain on the front that you can catch in the right light, but I think that's just because it's still wet from where she's cleaned it.

"It looks better," Neve tells her, leaning against the sink. "So . . . we missed something, didn't we?"

Huy looks at Alice.

And Alice looks at Huy.

I want to disappear, to vanish completely. I don't want to be here anymore. I want to run out of the school and never come back here, never ever see the two of them happy ever again. And that is so selfish of me, I know that. I know what it'd mean to abandon this entire story after working with them for so long. But I hate how much love they have for each other in their eyes, and I hate how Huy is looking at her.

"No," Alice says. "Nothing happened."

"Riiiiiight," Neve replies. "You two just look like you've been crying your eyes out for no reason?"

"We're fine," Huy says, turning away. "Aren't we?"

"Yeah." Alice stares down at her dress. "We're fine."

Huy's eyes find my petrified form in the mirror. He smiles at me, and I crumble to pieces. "Just fine."

# CHAPTER TWELVE

"Impromptu sleepover tonight?" Cal asks as we step out onto the front steps of the school, leaving the event. It's gotten so cold out, and I was stupid enough to leave my coat at home.

"Is it still impromptu if we plan it?" I ask.

Cal sticks his tongue out at me. "Semantics."

"I can't," I tell him. "I, uh . . . homework."

"You don't have to do your homework," he says. "It'll be fun! We'll watch *Nobbing Hill*."

"I'm serious, Cal. And it's *Notting Hill*."

"*Maybe Be My Always?* You love that one."

I don't even bother to correct him on the title this time. I just say, "Not tonight."

"Okay, okay. Text me when you're home?"

"Yeah." I nod. It's late enough that Cal doesn't want to take the buses, so he orders a Lyft instead, and I wait the five minutes outside with him until it arrives.

"Love you," he says as he gets in the car, then blows me a kiss through the air.

"Love you too." The words feel so shallow to say out loud.

Cal might not want to ride the bus this late at night, but I don't mind, especially with how quiet it tends to get. But before I do that, I just want a moment to myself. I walk back toward the school, taking my seat again on the front steps. It's cold, but after sitting in the chill for a few minutes, it's starting to feel nice. Sure, maybe I can't feel my fingers, but who needs fingers?

I should feel good about tonight. I should feel proud of myself.

It's not an easy feat to get two people to repair a relationship the way that Huy and Alice did. And sure, they probably still have a ways to go in terms of figuring out what this friendship looks like now, but that's why I'm here, to help clean up the messy ends that are left over.

Half my job is done.

The next half is for them to admit their feelings for each other, to reignite that spark that they once had. And sure, a middle school romance can't compare to a high school one. Hormones are running higher, and they're old enough to know that a relationship is more than just holding hands and passing notes in class. Not that those aren't instrumental parts, don't get me wrong, but this time we'll be going for something more real.

And then I'm done.

Just like that.

There will be some sort of grand gesture at the dance. I can probably pay the DJ to play a special song . . . the lights will come down . . . maybe I can arrange it so that they're the only ones on the dance floor . . .

A love story for the ages.

Wouldn't that be perfect?

I can feel the tears welling up before I have a chance to stop them. I put my fist to my mouth, biting softly to distract myself, to give myself anything to do other than sit here and wallow in my own misery. I don't want to cry; I shouldn't be crying over a boy. A *human* boy. But my brain feels so overwhelmed, and it's the easiest thing I can think of to do.

I should tell Leah the truth; she'll get me out of this. No matter how Richard feels, she'd pull me out without any hesitation at all. She could help me, send me off somewhere far where I won't confuse my feelings and royally fuck up my life.

My heart was left too open. And Huy Trinh walked right in, left his shoes by the door, and made himself comfortable.

"Pathetic," I whisper to myself, wiping my eyes and watching the sleeve come away stained black and brown and beige. "Fucking pathetic." I sniffle.

"Well, I for one thought your page turning wasn't *that* bad."

His voice makes me jump.

Because life can't be any crueler than to deliver Huy Trinh to me again. Right when I'm feeling at my worst.

"Right, ha." I try to laugh off the scene, wiping my face even more.

"What are you doing out here?" he asks, stepping slowly down until he's right next to me.

"Just waiting for the bus," I tell him. "It won't be here for another twenty minutes."

"I could give you a ride."

"You drove here?"

"Yeah. Don't you have a jacket?" he asks me.

"I . . . no . . . it was warmer when I got here."

"Jesus, Jude. It's freezing out."

"I know." I turn my gaze to my knees, tucking closer into myself. I don't know what it is, but something about his tone makes me feel ashamed. I don't even realize that he's placing something over me until he already has, when a shadow falls over me and I feel something heavier on my shoulders, the soft texture of the corduroy under my fingers.

"You're going to catch a cold," he says as he slips his jacket over me.

"But you—you're not cold?"

"I'll be fine." He smiles at me, those dimples making another appearance. "Besides, I'm parked a block away, I'll survive. Let's go."

"You don't have to take me home," I tell him. I don't want to pull his jacket in closer, but it smells like him, and it's so warm.

"I know I don't have to." His voice is calm. "I want to."

Huy offers me his hand.

"Now, don't make this more difficult than it has to be. My mom raised me to be stubborn, and I *will* get my way."

I can tell there's no winning tonight. So, I take his hand, and let him hoist me into the air with him. For the second time in one night, our chests almost collide as he picks me up. He lets out this low laugh as he saves me again, staring down at me. It'd be so easy to steal a kiss right now, to ruin my entire life in just a single move. What is wrong with me? To know that I'm so willing to do that for a boy who can't love me back, who isn't allowed to love me back.

Huy doesn't say another word until we're in his truck. He cranks the heat to high, which doesn't do a lot, and he apologizes for it before he asks me how I liked the mixtape that he gave me.

"It was good," I tell him. "It was hard to keep track without the artists on the paper. I liked that one where the girl screams at the end."

"Phoebe?" he asks.

"I think so?"

"Let's see." Huy reaches down between my legs once again, digging for his backpack. "If you like Pheebs, then you'll like . . ." He seems to shuffle around for a moment before he finally plucks out another tape and hands it to me.

"'The Depression Mix,'" I read out.

"Phoebe, Car Seat Headrest, Sufjan Stevens, Japanese Breakfast, Clairo."

"Your basic white cis depressive starter pack."

"You know, Noah made the exact same joke." Huy finally shifts the truck into drive. "Just goes to show you lack originality. And Michelle Zauner is Korean."

"Well, we both already knew that I'm not original." I pull the jacket closer around me. It smells of ginger, orange.

It's like a punishment.

With how little traffic there is, it only takes him ten minutes to get back to my apartment. Far too quickly for me, and yet every second passes by in a terribly sweet agony, the radio mimicking my feelings as a girl sings about love.

"So." Huy stops at a rare red light. "Do we need to chat about why you were crying?"

"Huh?" I ask like I didn't hear him.

"You were crying when I came outside. But we don't have to talk about it if you don't want to."

I don't say anything, because I'm not even sure what I could possibly say to excuse what he saw.

"It was nothing," I tell him.

"Okay."

And he leaves it at that. No prodding or pushing; he just lets it go.

Maybe talking about it would help, but I can't talk about what's going on with him.

"Relationships are weird," I tell him.

"You're telling me."

The light turns from red to green.

"Have you ever had feelings for someone you shouldn't have?" I ask him. It's a bold question, one that I absolutely should not ask him. But everything I've done lately feels like it's been done against my better judgment.

Huy lets out an awkward laugh, and despite the light change, he doesn't press the gas. There's no one behind us anyway.

"Well . . . I don't know, that all depends."

"On?"

"On whether the person I like thinks that we shouldn't be together."

So, he does still have feelings for her. I mean, I knew that he did. I wouldn't have been assigned to him if he didn't, but this is confirmation right from the source.

"What do you think?" I watch as the light turns red.

Huy smiles awkwardly, and there's more than a hint of sadness to the look that he gives me.

"I think that I'm grateful to have this person in my life, and I don't want to mess it up by getting feelings involved."

"You're scared that'll happen?" The light goes green again.

"Happened once before, and I lost my best friend because of it."

"But you and Alice talked it out?" I don't want to switch the subject so quickly, but it happens.

"Yeah, I mean . . . we talked it out, but it'll be a while before we're back to where we were. We might never really be. She lost a lot of trust in me. I can try to earn it back, but I have to respect her feelings if I can't."

"That's admirable." The light turns yellow. We haven't moved.

"I wish it felt that way."

"I think you should give it a chance."

"What?" Red.

"The crush." My stomach twists around and around, my ribs ready to split. "I think it's worth the risk."

"Seriously?"

I nod. "You never know how someone really feels. If the feelings are strong enough, then it might be worth the risk."

"And if they reject me?"

I shrug. "Then you have a final answer. Isn't that better than just stewing in mystery?"

"Not from my perspective." Green.

That makes me laugh. "Trust me." I tell him because this is what he needs to hear in the moment. I don't want to say these words; I want to tell him that she isn't worth it, that Alice isn't the person for him. But that's not what I'm here for. That's not my lot in life. "It's better to know for sure than to dream of what could have been. You owe that to yourself."

Yellow.

He hesitates, staring ahead for a few seconds before he lets out a breath through his nose. "I'll think about it."

"You should."

We sit there. The light turns red.

Then green again. Huy finally presses on the gas, inching us forward.

"Where'd you learn so much about love?" he asks.

"I know a thing or two about crushes," I say to him. "I'm in the business of love."

"Right, right . . ." He laughs, and I turn, staring out the window as we drive off.

# CHAPTER THIRTEEN

More people are around for Huy's game the next day than I expected there to be.

The Polo Field is a large, expansive area in Golden Gate Park, meant to accommodate multiple kinds of sports so leagues can rent it out during their seasons. It seems far too large for what ends up just being a friendly soccer game with Huy, some of the guys from the Hearst team, and other boys from a different school.

But whatever works.

I wave at Huy as I spot him beyond the gated area, helping another boy set up a goalpost at the far end of the field. He hasn't said anything about his jacket yet, and I walked out of the house without it this morning.

I'm still not sure if I did that on purpose or by accident.

And to be quite frank, I don't think I want to know the answer to that question.

I climb toward the bleachers, mostly made of stone on top of these wooden platforms that add a charm that the aluminum ones at Hearst lack. That's when I see Alice and Neve seated near the middle, a blanket laid out underneath them, lunch boxes and mini-coolers ready to go.

"We were wondering when you'd show up," Neve says.

"I'm early," I tell her, climbing the steps carefully. "They haven't even finished setting up the field yet."

"Yeah, but we expected you to be here first," Alice chimes in, snapping open a Tupperware container of grapes.

"Why would I have been here first?" I ask them.

Alice and Neve both eye each other, giggling, which honestly hurts worse than if they'd just straight-up insulted me.

"What?"

"It's nothing," Neve tells me.

"It seems like something." I almost want to run back home, to abandon this game and this day.

"Jude, it's nothing," Alice promises. "I swear."

I climb up to the row behind them so I can sit between them, grabbing a tangerine and peeling it carefully.

"How's your dress?" I ask Alice.

"Dad took it to the cleaners this morning, just to be safe. Apparently, they think they can make it 'brand-new again,' so we'll have to see."

"Mhmm!" Neve swallows the grapes she's been chewing on. "How did things go last night?"

"Good, yeah . . . we talked. I didn't want to wake up Dad, so we ended up walking down to Baker Beach. It was freezing."

My ears perk up. "Wait . . . the beach?"

"Yeah, Huy wanted to talk some more, this time without everyone around. No offense."

"None taken," I say plainly.

"We walked around for all of ten minutes before the wind picked up and he drove us to NaYa. And we just caught up. It was nice."

They must've talked after he dropped me off. Which is totally normal, it's a totally normal thing to have done. It's great, in fact. He's making moves without me having to intervene.

This is good.

"You think the two of you are good now?" Neve asks.

Alice smiles in that slow way, like she's remembering something that he might've said. Like she's a girl in love with a boy.

"I don't know. I mean, no. Not straight away. But it's better."

"Good." Neve leans in, resting her head on Alice's shoulder. "I'm glad."

"Yeah . . . me too."

I hate how her kind words make me feel so nasty on the inside. I should be happy, ecstatic. Completely independent of me, the two of them spent time together, started to get to know each other all over again. All while I lay in bed covering myself in a jacket and crying myself to sleep like the pathetic mess I am.

I should be so happy for them.

But I can't force the feelings that aren't there.

As the hour stretches on, more people show up to play. The bleachers remain mostly barren, a few bystanders showing up to support their friends, and a couple who spend the entire first game making out on the top row because this is the prime space to do that. Huy shuffles the ball toward his teammate Ricky, who kicks it high into the air, speeding toward the goal for the final point they need to play to their game of twenty. Huy and his boys throw their arms into the air and cheer around one another, racing toward the sidelines with smiles on their faces, bodies covered in sweat and dirt and grass stains.

Neve and Alice both stand to walk toward the fence that separates us, so I follow them.

"You made it!" Huy says, chest heaving as he struggles to catch his breath.

"Of course," I say.

"You guys played good," Alice adds.

"Yeah, but their defender is a beast." Huy lifts up his shirt, doing the thing that boys do the best. And I'm too gay to not stare at the V shape that disappears below the waistline of his shorts, eyes following that trail of sparse hair. I catch Alice staring too.

Or maybe she catches me.

"Alice, can you refill my water bottle?" Huy asks, and she nods, so he tosses it over the fence and Alice and Neve race off to find the nearest water fountain. I almost join them. I'm not in the mood to be trapped with Huy again. Even with a barrier between us, things feel too close.

Maybe once all of this is done, I can ask Leah or Richard to erase my memories of him.

"Cutie." Huy's voice jars me.

"I . . . what?" Cutie? Why would he say something like that?

"Cutie?" Huy points through the fence, over my shoulder, toward Neve's lunch box. "Can you hand me that cutie? Or is Neve gonna eat it?"

The oranges are settled on the blanket. The blue label reads CUTIES clear and bright on the side.

Jesus, I need an ice bath. Or maybe a lobotomy.

"You good?" he asks me.

"Yeah, I'm fine," I lie to him. "Just tired."

"Late night?" he sings.

"Guess we both had one."

He looks confused. "What does that mean?"

"Nothing." I sound so bitter. "Alice just told us you went to the beach?"

Alice didn't do anything wrong. In fact, she did exactly what I need her to do. She took charge of the situation and sought out time with Huy without me needing to push her.

"Yeah, I just wanted to talk to her. Is that okay?" he asks.

"Why wouldn't it be?"

Fuck me. Shut the fuck up, Jude. *Shut up!*

I climb the steps to grab the orange, tossing it over the fence just as I hear my name being called. But not by Huy, and not by Neve or Alice. No, I look up and spy Cal walking along the side of the field toward us. He's dressed warmly, for the cold weather, and has two cups of coffee in his hands. We play a game as I look at Huy as he looks at Cal looking at me.

Then Huy turns back to me, making that expression where his lips disappear. Is he disappointed that Cal is here? Relieved? Annoyed?

"Hey," I say to Cal. "What are you doing here?"

"Thought you could use some help," he says in a quieter voice. "Hey, Huy!" Cal waves as best he can with coffee cups in hand. Then he passes one over to me. "Here, I got you your usual."

"Thanks."

"So . . . soccer! Huh?"

"What about it?" I ask him.

Cal's brows furrow. "Are you mad that I'm here?"

"No, no," I promise. "I'm just tired. And I didn't expect you."

"You seemed stressed last night," he says.

I don't want to have this conversation in front of Huy . . . but when I turn back to him, he's moved away to talk to Noah and another guy from Hearst whose name I don't know.

"What's wrong?" Cal asks me.

"It's nothing," I tell him as I lead him to our spot on the bleachers. "Nothing."

I catch Alice and Neve as they pass Huy his water bottle, to a grateful response. Alice and Huy exchange a glance that lingers, before the girls return to the bleachers.

"Hey—Cal, right?" Alice asks when she gets to us.

"Right!" he chirps. "Sorry about your dress last night."

"Why? Not like it was your fault."

Cal and I share a look, and as Alice and Neve sit back down, Neve looks around, picking up her bag and rummaging through it for a moment before she turns to me.

"Did someone take my orange?"

The other team takes game two, which means we're going into game three, and it's another forty-five minutes of sitting in the cloudy cold as we watch sweaty boys run around chasing a ball. I'll totally admit, Huy's a powerhouse at this game. Not that I understand all the intricacies, or even what his role as the captain means he does, but he's impossibly fast, his footwork a blur as he steals the ball from the opposing team. He almost makes it look easy. In fact, I might believe that it was if after every point he manages he wasn't doubled over, trying to recover his breath.

Huy leads the team to an early advantage.

They're ten points ahead when it happens. I barely even have the time to realize that something has gone wrong before Huy's on the ground, crying out in pain. Another player tried to kick the ball out from underneath him and missed. He tripped over something, and he was *just* close enough to Huy that when he fell forward, he fell right onto Huy, both of them taken to the ground.

The other boy gets up.

Huy doesn't.

He screams.

Someone blows a whistle, and the entire game comes to a halt. I'm on my feet first, Alice and Neve not far behind me. Already, both teams are gathered around him, Noah kneeling down to keep his head elevated. Noah asks Huy if he feels like he can move.

Huy can't get an answer out, though; it's like the air has been punched out of him, his face twisted in a permanent grimace. He's not bleeding, which seems like a good sign, but I'm not a doctor.

"Shit, dude," I hear another player whisper. I think it's the guy who tripped him.

"Huy?" I fall to the grass next to him.

"Fuck, my arm." He winces, pulling it close to him. I think he's finally catching up with himself.

"Everyone back up." Noah commands the situation effortlessly. "Jude, keep his head up."

I do exactly what I'm told, putting my hands to the back of Huy's neck and keeping it softly elevated as Noah takes Huy's wounded arm, holding it gently.

"I think it's my wrist." Huy winces again.

"I'm going to apply a little pressure, okay?" Noah says.

Huy nods hastily. All it takes is Noah grazing his wrist for Huy to grunt in pain.

"Fuck me!" He grits his teeth.

"Okay, yeah. It's likely broken. We need to get you to a hospital."

"Should we call an ambulance?" I ask.

"It'd be faster to drive him to the Kaiser ER on Geary." Noah turns to Huy. "Okay. Do you think you can stand up?"

"Yeah, yeah." He hesitates, and another boy from the team grabs his hand to help him up, careful of where he touches Huy's body, as if he's afraid that Huy will fall apart. Once he's on his feet, though, Huy's steady. Neve races back with the ice pack she had with her in her cooler.

"Here, use this."

"I'll pull my car around," Noah tells him, handing Huy off to another teammate, rushing off toward the exit.

"Can someone call my parents?" Huy asks.

"I'll do it," Alice tells him, phone already in hand. "I'll ride with you."

"Okay." Huy sighs. "Thanks."

She puts a hand on the small of his back and begins speaking in Vietnamese once one of Huy's parents answers the phone. It feels like I'm caught in the eye of a tornado, standing around in the calm as everything around me spins completely out of control. The entire accident seems to have sped right past me, and I'm struggling to catch up as most of us follow Huy and the teammates who are helping him toward Noah's car just as he pulls around, letting Alice into the back seat first before he carefully helps Huy buckle his seat belt.

Alice rolls down her window, calling over to me and Neve. "I'll text you guys with updates."

"Please," Neve pleads.

"Jude." Huy calls me over. "Can you get my stuff?"

"Yeah, of course."

"Thanks."

"Okay, Huy's parents are already on their way to the emergency room," Alice tells everyone, and Neve and I take a step back as we let Noah drive off, already so careful with his turns as he exits the parking lot.

"What about his truck?" Neve asks.

"Do you have a license?" I say.

"Uh-uh, you?"

I shake my head.

"His parents will just have to come back and get it," Neve says, letting out a deep sigh.

"Okay, guys!" Someone from the opposing team settles in. "Let's get back to the game, you boys pull in two subs."

Without Huy here to play, Neve and I don't see much reason to stick around. "I wish we could've gone with them," I tell her as I help her pack Alice's things away.

"At least Noah knew what he was doing," Neve says.

I silently agree with her.

"Is he okay?" Cal asks me.

I didn't even realize that Cal hadn't moved from his spot. I guess he saw the chaos and didn't want to add to it.

"Not really, they're taking him to the emergency room."

"Ouch." Cal winces. "Are we leaving?"

"Yeah. Just let me get Huy's stuff." I turn to Neve. "Are you going to head home?"

"Yeah, my mom was dying for some mother-daughter time

today anyway. She wants to go through her prop collection and start donating things." Neve zips up her bag. "Just what I wanted to do, sift through severed heads and alien masks."

"Severed heads?" Cal asks with a generous amount of hesitation.

"Neve's parents design props and effects for horror movies," I clarify.

"Ever see *The Hendersons*? Or *Dear Killer*?" Neve asks.

"Can't say that I have," Cal tells her. "Jude mostly makes me watch rom-coms."

"Ah, well. You're not missing out on much." Neve throws her bag over her shoulders. "I'll text you tonight, okay?"

"Yeah, sure. I'll keep an eye out."

"Bye, Jude. It was good to see you, Cal!"

"Good to see you too!" Cal waves as Neve exits the field. "She seems nice."

"Yeah, she's really great." I feel that bitterness along my tongue again. Because Neve is a good friend. But she won't be for much longer.

"Well . . . now you get to spend the day with me!"

"Yeah . . ." I try to sound as thrilled as Cal does.

"Do you want to grab some lunch or something? I know it's still early."

Actually, despite my hunger levels rising, I don't really have much of an appetite after seeing Huy writhe around in pain with a broken arm. "Are you hungry?"

Cal shrugs. "I could eat. It's a good day for Volcano Curry."

The moment he says that, it triggers something in me, and my stomach growls. At the very least, it'll be warming.

Filling too, so I won't have to worry about food for the rest of the day.

"Volcano Curry sounds good."

"Great!"

I gather Huy's stuff and let Cal lead me out of the park, Huy's backpack slung over my shoulders.

# CHAPTER FOURTEEN

Alice texts Neve and me five hours later in our group chat.

> ALICE: confirmed broken wrist, he's getting it wrapped up
> now.
> NEVE: Wrapped up??
> ALICE: cast will come later, he'll be back to get that done in
> a few days
> ALICE: his parents are PISSED
> ME: yikes . . .
> NEVE: tell him we love him
> ALICE: 👍

I don't really know what I feel like doing. The curry katsu isn't sitting well in my stomach as I go about the rest of my day with Cal, which he's labeled a "self-care day" in the hope of cheering me after noticing my mood was down. He brings out the face masks and my nail kit from the bathroom, pulling a few different nail polish colors out for me.

"You want me to paint your nails?" I ask him. "You hate when I paint your nails."

"I know, but you're in a funk. And it cheers you up."

"That obvious, huh?" At least he's right. I pull out my cuticle pusher. I can't explain why it's super relaxing to sit here and work on his nails. I guess maybe because there's a definitive answer as to whether or not I've done a good job. Like, when I'm done, I can sit here and look at what I've done and know if I'm proud of it or not. I can tell if his nails (or my nails, or Leah's nails) look good. Same with when they let me practice my makeup on them. And if they don't, I can start over without too much fuss.

Or just wipe the slate clean and try again another day.

After all, my nail skills are good, but they don't compare to my makeup ones.

"Do you want to talk about it?" Cal prompts.

I guess if there's another soul in the world who might understand—or at least sympathize—with what I've been feeling, it'll be Cal.

But now? I feel so hesitant, wondering if it's the right move. I don't like the idea that I can't trust Cal, because I know that I can.

"Do you ever . . . start to miss the people that you've worked with?"

His shoulders visibly slump. Like he's thinking, *Not this again.*

"Like the couples that we help?"

I nod. "Or the people you meet when you're with them."

"I take it this is about your human friends?"

Well, I can't exactly deny it. "Yeah."

"You've gotten really close to them; I can tell just from the few times we've hung out together."

"I know that there's a timeline here. A ticking clock or whatever. And I don't think that I'm ready to say goodbye to them."

"Well, Jude, we know going into this that these relationships aren't permanent. We're in and we're out."

"I know." I drop his hand, letting my face fall to the coffee table harder than I mean it to. "Ow."

"Come on, don't pout," he tells me, scooting closer and letting me lean against his shoulder. "It's understandable, I think."

"Really?" My voice is muffled.

"I mean . . . yeah. It's your second long-term assignment? You've never really gotten to hang out with humans our age before. Besides last year." His tone makes him sound like he doesn't want to bring it up. "I think it's normal."

"It doesn't feel that way." And for the first time it occurs to me that Cal might just be telling me what I want to hear, and not what I *need* to hear.

"You just need to finish the job, and then you'll be done. It won't matter after that because they'll forget all about you!" He has too much levity in his voice, almost like he's thrilled by the idea of the gang forgetting who I am.

I want to vomit.

I finally pick my head up. "You never answered my question."

"Which one?"

"Have you ever regretted having to leave someone behind?"

"Well, no, I haven't," he tells me. "I don't think I've ever had any humans that I'd call 'friends.'"

"So, you don't know what I'm going through." Maybe it's cruel of me to phrase it that way. I just want him to be honest with me.

"I guess not."

"I'm sorry, Cal. I didn't mean it. I'm just . . ." I let my head fall again, softly this time. "I've been so confused lately, and worried."

"It's a part of the job. This is exactly why we're not supposed to let the humans get to us. We're better than them."

Are we, though?

"What if I don't want to leave them behind? What do I do then?" My voice is barely louder than a murmur, and at first, I have to assume he hasn't heard me.

"I wish I knew what to tell you," Cal says after a moment of silence. "It's just the life that we live."

"Do you ever get tired of it, though?"

"What do you mean?"

"I mean . . . when we're older, on our own, we'll be sent to live somewhere else, to be a Cupid wherever we're needed." We're both lucky that we've been able to stay in the Bay for our entire lives, to be granted stability by Richard. Not every Cupid our age is so lucky, and once we're eighteen, tested, and let out of the house, labeled fully independent Cupids capable of taking care of ourselves and others, we'll be told where to go, unable to settle. There's not even a guarantee that Cal and I will get to be near each other. I can only hope that we'll stay in each other's orbit.

It's a lonely life, that of a Cupid.

I go on. "It doesn't fill you with dread? Knowing that this is our life, that there's nothing more out there?"

"Would you rather be human?"

I don't say anything at first, which I know is bad because silence is just as much of an answer as me saying yes. But I honestly don't know what I think.

"Sometimes I think I'm jealous of them," I tell him honestly. "They get to do whatever they want, live their lives however they want."

Love whoever they want.

Which isn't even true; it isn't a universal human experience. It's a privileged one. If I were human here, in San Francisco, I'd certainly have more freedom than most of the planet. In other places, I might not be allowed to be myself; I might've been given parents who hated me for being trans or queer. Add to that me being white in a society where that makes everything easier. I'm afforded benefits that not every human has access to, be it because of their skin color or where they were born or how they identify.

"You don't . . . want to be human, do you, Jude?"

"No!" I shoot up from Cal's lap, my words coming out too quickly. "I mean, no . . . I don't. I just wish that I could have what they have, even for a little bit."

"Well . . . you have me, don't you?" Cal looks at me, sadness in his eyes.

And I feel that sting of guilt in my heart.

"I do." I feel like an asshole. All this time I've been worried about leaving behind these people who I just met, when my best friend has been sitting right next to me the entire time.

"I'm sorry, Cal."

"I know," he says softly. "But remember how complicated they are? How messy they get? I mean, if they need an entirely different set of people just to help them fall in love, imagine how much more help they need. I'm surprised there aren't Cupids out there for their anxieties."

"I think they call them therapists."

Cal laughs, and I try to laugh along with him, but my chest is so heavy.

I wish this felt natural.

What if I don't want to forget them? What if I don't want to move on? Why is that the worst thing in the world?

"Thanks, Cal," I say, because I think it's what he wants to hear.

"You're welcome."

We continue the night with *The Wedding Planner* and order pizza from this Italian place in our neighborhood. Cal falls asleep during the last act, and I'm too lazy to turn on anything new, so I just let *The Devil Wears Prada* auto-play. Cal leaves his head in my lap, and I carefully let my hand trace the back of his neck, the skin behind his ears.

He looks so peaceful like this.

Just as Andy is undergoing her big transformation and figuring out how to be an assistant, my phone lights up. A photo from Huy comes in. He's in a dark room, giving the camera a thumbs-up with his hand wrapped in a white bandage.

> HUY: I livd.
> ME: how badly does it hurt?
> HUY: pleae, the doczs loaded me on pin kilrs
> ME: that explains the typos then
> ME: should you be texting?
> HUY: nt the meds, hand makes txting hard
> HUY: cn I cll???

I look at Cal in my lap, wondering if it's the right move. But before I can even make a decision, my phone screen flashes with Huy's name. I stare at it, wondering if this is the right thing to do.

It's not.

But I accept anyway.

"Hey," he says quickly. "Sorry, I cast dialed you, and I couldn't end it in time."

"It's okay," I promise him. "Cast dial?"

"It's way harder to text than you think it'd be."

"So it's not the painkillers?"

"No, but those are hitting pretty hard." Then he pauses. "Wait, why are you so quiet?"

"Cal. He's sleeping."

"Oh, sorry. We can talk later—"

"No!" Again, too loud. But it's too late. "I mean, I don't mind. He's a heavy sleeper anyway."

I look down at Cal, relaxing back into the couch, careful not to disturb him.

"How do you feel?"

"Like shit," Huy groans, his voice going soft as well. "I tried to sleep for a bit, but I kept rolling onto my arm and waking myself up."

"Alice said that your parents were angry."

"Yeah. My mom went on a whole rant about how she said playing soccer would kill me one day and how she was right."

"It *was* really scary," I tell him. "I didn't even realize what was happening until you were on the ground."

He laughs at that. "If it makes you feel any better, I don't remember much."

"Really?"

"Mhmm. One second, I was running around. Then I felt the air leave my lungs, like someone punched me straight in the chest. Next minute I was on the ground, and it felt like there was no air left in my body."

"Jesus."

"It's Huy, actually. You should know that by now."

"God, you are not funny." I shake my head. "Not even a little bit."

"Your laughter says otherwise."

"I'm hanging up now."

I don't think he believes me for a second.

"What are you doing?" he asks. "I'm bored."

"Watching a movie."

"Which one?"

"*The Devil Wears Prada*," I tell him.

"Where's that streaming?"

"Netflix."

"Is there any chance you'd be down to start it over?" he asks.

I'm literally *always* down to rewatch *The Devil Wears Prada*. "You want to watch a movie over the phone?"

"Anything to keep me from going downstairs just to hear my mom tell me how dangerous soccer is and how she and my dad will have to cover my shifts at the bakery for the next few days."

"Did she really say all that?"

"You'd think I'd get a little bit of sympathy. But I guess not. She means well, though." He tries to laugh it off, but it doesn't sound real. "So . . . would you restart the movie? For me?"

"For you? Of course."

"Let me get my laptop."

I move out from under Cal, careful not to wake him as I slip a pillow under his head and pull the blanket around him, then move to the chair next to the couch, remote in hand. It's easy to just hit "Start From Beginning" and pause while I wait for

Huy, listening to the sounds of him wrestling with himself on the other end of the line.

"Are you okay over there?" I ask him.

"It's harder than you might think to do things one-handed, okay?"

"Sounds to me like you need to try harder."

"And it sounds to me like you should bite me."

"Ouch, hit a nerve, did I?"

I can practically hear his smile through the phone.

"Are you ready now?" I ask him.

"Yes, I'm ready."

"Okay . . . hitting play in three . . ." I start.

He continues, "Two."

And at the same time, we say, "One."

"Do you see Miranda as the villain?" Huy asks as the ending of the movie approaches.

"I think Andy's a villain for littering in that fountain," I tell him. "Honestly, I've watched this movie enough times to wonder if there really is a villain."

"No villain? I thought stories had to have those."

"I mean . . . sure, Miranda is tough. But it's proven that she's only that way because she cares about what she does, and she wants the same from the people around her *because* it's so important. She keeps people at a distance to protect herself. Andy, she just wants to follow her dreams. And sure, the dude is hard to get along with, and he could be less whiny, but I don't know. I don't think he was really wrong either. I'd be mad if someone forgot my birthday."

"I think I can see that," he says. "When *is* your birthday?"

"Why?"

"I'm curious."

"Only if you tell me yours."

"Deal."

"March fifteenth. Your turn."

"August eighth."

Huy being a Leo makes *so* much sense, and I don't even subscribe to the zodiac thing.

"So, wait, you think a story doesn't need a villain?"

"No. Not a real one at least. Sometimes the circumstances are the real bad guy."

"Then what is there if there's not a villain?"

"The self-discovery, going for what you want. It's why I still think this movie counts in the canon, even if there isn't a lot of romance." What's worse, there's technically cheating.

"The romance canon?"

"You know, the pantheon of rom-coms. The stories that date back to Jane Austen and before. What we consider the core stories."

"Okay, I think you're getting in a little too deep for me."

"It's not that complicated," I tell him.

"I trust you."

"*Prada* has all the things you'd expect. The discovery of oneself and going for what you want. At the end of the movie, despite the future that awaits her, she makes the decision to head into the unknown, to leave behind the comfort of a promised life so that she doesn't lose a piece of herself. It's a journey that many a rom-com protagonist goes on."

"I can see that," Huy says to me. "Do you think she makes the right choice?"

"Well, based on the ending, we know she does."

"Right, but if you were in her shoes, if there was no script to go off, if you had to make the choice to leave behind a guarantee for something else, would you?"

It doesn't hit me until he's said the words.

"I don't know," I tell him. "It's hard when you don't know."

"Well, yeah. But you have to make those decisions all the time, right? Unless you're secretly a psychic." He laughs, and then pauses. "You're not, right?"

"If I were a psychic, I would've told you not to play that third game today."

"Fair enough." He sighs. "But you didn't answer the question."

"Go for what you know, right? Isn't that the safest option?" I tell him. Because it's true. Why wouldn't you go for what's promised?

"The unknown doesn't intrigue you?"

"Would you do what Andy did?"

"Maybe. You never know what's out there, right? You never know if there's something better waiting for you unless you go for it."

"But the safety?"

"Isn't that a bit boring, though? I mean, what's life without a little risk?"

"Risky."

He pretends to snore, grunting out an ugly sound. "Ugh, snooze fest."

"There's nothing wrong with wanting to keep things the way they are."

"But if you do that, you never know what else might come your way. Who was that guy, that poet . . . ?"

"I have bad news: There are a lot of poets."

"We talked about him in English. The road-less-traveled guy."

"Frost." I'm all too familiar with him after the poetry unit I had to do.

"Yeah! That guy. He took the road less traveled and look at where it got him."

"That was a metaphor," I tell Huy. "The poem is about irony, about people who always wonder what the other path looked like. The regret that they carry with them. About second-guessing yourself even when it's too late to do anything about it."

"Maybe, but isn't poetry up for interpretation?"

"I'd agree with you if we didn't spend two entire days dissecting that thing. The poem has a meaning."

"Not if I decide it doesn't."

"You can't just—"

"Too late!" He stops me dead in my tracks. "I've made an executive decision. Frost was a hack; the poem has no meaning."

"You can't do that."

"I can." Huy pauses. "I was elected . . . the . . . mayor of poetry."

"The *mayor* of poetry?"

"Mhmm."

"Elected by the people?"

"For the people," he says. "So, I've signed that into law."

"You're impossible."

"And you're no fun."

There's that smile again, so obvious on his lips.

"Besides," he continues, "you don't know if the promised path is the best option either. Andy could've been fired; she could've lost who she truly is, her relationships. She could've ended up just like Miranda."

"Right, but that's a movie," I tell him. "This is real life."

"Maybe. But that doesn't mean the risk isn't worth taking sometimes."

"You'd give up your whole life for some unknown future? Really?"

He hesitates, as if to prove my point. But then he finally answers me. "If I thought that version of myself might be happier, then why not?"

"It's not always about happiness," I tell him.

"I know, which is why I think you should chase it when you can."

His words sting, like salt in a wound, and I have to remember that I can't just decide to go against the grain, to decide against everything that I've ever known for some potential nothing. Besides, there's no guarantee that I'd ever get the chance to find Alice again, or Neve.

Or Huy.

This is my life.

And it's my duty to live it in service to humans, to be a Cupid. That's it.

"Oh jeez. It's soooooo late." Huy stifles a yawn, which then makes me yawn. "I should go to bed."

"This was fun," I tell him. "And I got to show you my favorite movie."

"Is it your favorite?" he asks.

"Yeah."

"Huh."

"What?"

"Nothing," he chuckles. "This just means I have to show you my favorite."

"And what movie is that?"

"Ah-ah, no spoilers."

"And I'm not the fun one?"

"You're not," he says to me. "I'll show you, one day. Don't make plans for Monday."

"I already don't have any."

"Good. Can you bring me my homework?" he asks.

"Yeah, I can do that."

That smile. "Good, I'll see you then."

"Okay."

"Good night, Jude Ricci."

"Good night, Huy Trinh."

# CHAPTER FIFTEEN

Against my better judgment, I keep my promise to Huy, gathering all his homework that following Monday so that I can deliver it to him. I shouldn't, I know that. Not with everything going on, not with Huy and Alice being on the cusp of something special, not with the Valentine's Day dance being just over a week away.

But he asked me to, and I can't think of a good enough excuse to get Alice to do it.

I come close, during lunch. Saying that I have an appointment that I forgot all about, or that I really need to do my reading for English.

But I also know that I don't have much time left.

Counting today, there are ten days until the dance, until this plan comes to fruition and the pieces of the puzzle connect. That's ten days with all of them. Ten days of being their friend, of laughing with them at lunch, of stealing Alice's hot fries and Neve begging us for a horror movie marathon. Ten days until I don't get to do this anymore.

It doesn't matter. That's what I have to tell myself. Everything they know about me is under false pretenses. My entire life is a lie to them. Which makes me wonder if any of it was ever real.

Or was this all just one big act? Has my entire life been a performance?

Who am I really? I know that I like romantic comedies, and

iced chai lattes from Starbucks. I love the mango bingsu from NaYa, and I like walking down to Baker Beach when it's sunny out. I know that I love Cal and Leah and Richard, and that they're the only family I've ever had. I know that I love doing my own makeup, and that it helps me see who I really believe that I am, at least on the outside.

I know all of this about myself, and more.

But is that really who I am?

Huy texted me his address last night so I know the way back, and I head there after school, the Walkman affixed to the outside of my pants pocket. Huy was right—this is very much a depression tape. So many people singing about their fathers, their boyfriends, their girlfriends, their dogs.

Still, I like most of the songs, even if they make my heart feel heavy.

The bus pulls into the stop on Balboa, and I backtrack toward Seventeenth Avenue to walk down to Cabrillo.

The Trinh house is *actually* a house, not an apartment. In the evening sun, I can see the three stories, by the looks of it, if you count the garage. And just like every other home around it, there's no denying that it belongs in San Francisco, with the soft, almost mint-green siding, and the burnt-orange trim of the windows and doors.

The staircase to the front door spirals a bit, giving the Trinhs a rare front porch where a bench sits surrounded by lush winter plants that are able to survive the chilly air. I hit the doorbell, making sure to wipe my feet on the doormat that reads WELCOME!

The front door has this frosted glass inlaid in the middle, so as Huy approaches, I can make out this blurry vision of him, his olive-green hoodie giving him away. The door swings open, and there he is. His arm is wrapped carefully in bright white bandages and a black sling.

"Jude!" Huy smiles at me, bringing himself in for an awkward hug. "God, it's been two whole days with just my family. I'm ready to jump off the roof."

"That bad, huh?" I step inside, slipping my shoes off to join the pile by the door.

"I'm literally desperate for anyone."

"Am I your first visitor?" I ask him.

"Alice came by yesterday—she brought me sundubu."

I change the subject. "When do you get your cast?"

"Tomorrow. Then I can actually go back to school."

"Well, I call first dibs on signing it."

"You think I was going to let anyone else have the privilege?" Huy swings toward the stairs so quickly that I'm afraid for his arm. "Movie time?"

I follow Huy up the stairs to his room.

"Is this where the magic happens?" I ask him.

"What? No, that happens onstage." Huy falls onto his bed recklessly, not seeming to mind his arm at all. "This is where I sleep."

"Of course," I joke. "How could I not realize?"

The room is small, about the size of mine, with one large window that looks out onto the street below us. Huy's unmade bed is tucked right against it in the corner, and I'm sure on cooler nights, the setting is perfect for a little reading or watching a movie. I'm jealous. My only view is of our backyard, and the Orthodox church we live near.

The rest of the room is so quintessentially Huy. Posters of every singer I can think of him mentioning hang on his walls. There are black-and-white photos of an older woman and a young girl, as well as pictures of Huy when he was much younger. A Vietnamese flag, yellow with three stripes running horizontally through the middle, hangs next to a trans pride flag.

And on the wall opposite me, starting on the floor, running at least ten rows thick and as high as his desk nestled into the other corner, is his tape collection. Some I'm familiar with, but others I've never seen nor heard of before.

"Jesus."

"My dad thinks I should donate some." He rubs at the back of his neck.

"How many do you have?" I squat in front of the collection. I'd say it's half official releases, half mixtapes, which still seems ludicrous. Some of them bear titles as simple as *study vibes* or *for jogs around ggp*. But others get more specific, like *crying on a friday afternoon* or *julien baker: life ruiner*.

"Last I counted, it's at four hundred, but that was a while ago."

"I still maintain my stance that Spotify is easier to manage."

"Maybe for you," he says with a grin on his face. "But sitting down, picking a tape out, or a record, or a CD . . . I like that physical part of the experience. Actually finding something instead of scrolling, scrolling, scrolling." He lets his head fall back on a pillow. "God, I sound like such a hipster, holy shit."

"Yeah." I laugh with him. "You do."

I spot a framed movie poster on his wall. It almost looks hand-painted, the title *The Dark Crystal* written out in elaborate font.

"Now what is this?"

There are no humans on the poster, only weird-looking elf guys, and some scary bird thing.

"You're telling me you've never heard of the 1982 dark

**194**

fantasy epic sleeper hit *The Dark Crystal*? It's my favorite movie. Jim Henson, the guy who did the Muppets? He made it. My parents couldn't afford that many English lessons for me growing up, but they wanted me to learn, so when my grandmother would babysit, she'd play me all her old VHS tapes and DVDs so I could learn that way."

"That's sweet."

"*Dark Crystal* was my favorite, even though my grandma was sure it'd scare me."

"Was she right?"

"At first. But I got brave enough one day."

"Is that what we're watching today?"

Huy likes this question, I can tell. "If you want to."

He reaches for the space between his bed and his nightstand, pulling a laptop free of its hiding place. Then he looks back at me. "What are you doing over there?"

He pats the space on the bed next to him, maneuvering so he sits against the wall.

Because of course we can't just go downstairs and watch this movie. I do as I'm told, and crawl onto the bed with him. This feels weird, and not the good kind of weird either. Our shoulders nearly touch as he takes the laptop and shifts it so I can still get a good view.

He finds the movie and hits play. The screen turns black, and the narration begins.

"'Another world, another time. In the age of wonder . . .'"


"Jude?" Huy's voice is in my ear, distant but warm.

Then I feel a tapping.

"Hmm?"

"Jude."

"What?" I mumble, keeping my eyes shut. Why is Huy in my bed with me? That's weird, right? That's a weird thing that's happening. And I feel like I should be more concerned, but I'm comfortable. I open my eyes slowly, adjusting to the orange light that's filling my room. I turn to see Huy there, looking right at me with his warm brown eyes. Then everything washes over me like a bucket of ice water.

"Oh my God!" I jump away from him, still on the bed as the adrenaline in my heart begins to pump irresponsibly fast. "Oh God."

"You okay?" He puts a hand to my back.

I hate how nice it feels. "Yeah, yeah. Just surprised me is all."

"Sorry."

I cover my face with my hands to hide my embarrassment.

"I fell asleep?" I don't know if I mean for it to be a question.

"Yeah, you did."

During the movie he really wanted to show me.

On his shoulder. I feel asleep on his shoulder.

"I'm sorry," I tell him. "I didn't mean to . . . you know."

"It's okay. It's not everyone's cup of tea." There's something in his tone that I don't like. Distant. Cold.

"You can start it again, if you want." I dare to look at him, and my God, is that a spot of my drool on his shirt? Kill me now, please.

"I would, but my dad wants us downstairs for dinner."

"What? How long was I sleeping?"

"The entire movie, plus I watched some YouTube videos, so about two hours."

"I can't believe that."

"It's okay, I promise. It's just a movie." He turns away from me.

Right, except it's not just that. I should go home; I should leave now before I dig my hole even deeper.

But then I hear the footsteps, and Huy's little sister, Hương, comes to the top of the stairs.

"Huy, Dad said come down for dinner."

"Okay, we'll be right there." Huy closes the laptop and sets it on his nightstand. But she doesn't leave the doorway.

"Why is a boy in your bed?"

"Hương, Jude isn't a boy, they're nonbinary. I told you."

"Okay, so why is another person in your bed? Are you two dating?"

"Just go back downstairs—we'll be there in a second!" Huy reaches for one of his pillows, chucking it at the doorway, but Hương is gone before it even hits the floor. "I'm sorry about her."

"It's okay." I think he's talking about the misgendering, but it's her dating comment that leaves its mark. "I, um . . . I actually don't think that I can stay for dinner."

"Oh." He looks even more hurt. "Are you sure? My dad made extra for you."

"Yeah." I stand up from the bed. "I forgot, I'm supposed to be home."

"You could take it to go, we'll get you Tupperware."

"I'm sorry. I should go."

I don't wait for him; I just step out of the bedroom and start racing down the stairs. Unfortunately, Huy is right behind me.

"Jude, slow down. What's wrong?"

"It's nothing," I promise him, except it is. It's everything.

I can't deal with this anymore.

"I'll see you soon, okay?" I stop at the door, barely taking the time to slip my shoes back on. I don't even bother to tie the shoelaces.

"Jude, it's nice to see you again." Mr. Trinh comes into the foyer, an apron tied around his waist. "I hope you're hungry."

"It's nice to see you too, Mr. Trinh," I say to him, and I do mean it. "But I actually have to leave, I'm so sorry."

"Oh, that's disappointing. We'll have to have you over some other time."

"Yeah," I tell him. "I'd love that."

A lie. A flat-out lie.

"At least let me drive you home?" Huy offers.

But I stop him. "You can't drive with one hand," I tell him. "I'm fine, I swear."

"Okay . . ." I can tell he doesn't believe me, not for a second.

"Bye!" I shout as I rush out the door, nearly tripping over myself as I go down the stairs.

"Yeah, bye."

I'm such an embarrassment.

Stupid.

Stupid.

Stupid.

I walk until my chest is heaving, until my thighs are starting to hurt a little. I reach the Great Highway and the seawall, where the parking lot sits empty because it's too cold and too dark to be out here. The tide fades out as I stumble through the sand. I should go home, but I can't. I need to be alone. I need to be somewhere that has never been home to me because I can't deal with this anymore. I can't deal with these feelings that I want to pull out of my body. I can't deal with a future where Huy

Trinh won't know who I am; I can't deal with a future where he isn't a part of my life. Whatever this job was, this assignment, this curse, it's ruined my life harder than Leo ever could've.

There's a log, situated in the sand, for anyone who wants to use the firepit that sits there open, ashen, charred wood left behind.

I wish that I'd never met him.

I was always taught that love was a blessing, that love was what kept us all going. Love for one another, platonic and romantic, one-sided or mutual. I was taught that love is the universal language, that it'll be what saves us all, that it's the very reason that I exist, that I have a future, a responsibility.

I was taught that love is the most important thing in the world.

So why, sitting here, can I only think of love as a cruel curse, as the thing that is keeping me trapped here, with a future that seems to hold no hope for me at all?

This is what I deserve, for letting this happen again. At the first hints, I should've told Leah and Richard, gotten them to take me off this assignment.

Because Leah was right.

I'm not ready; I never was. I might not ever be again. Because what are the fucking chances? That I'd make the mistake of falling for a boy, only to let it happen all over again.

I just have to get them together. I have to put an end to this.

I have to.

It's for the best.

That's what I have to tell myself.

It's for the best.

It is.

# CHAPTER SIXTEEN

The easy thing about not technically having parents is that it's so much easier to skip school.

Sure, Hearst calls me, thinking that I'm Leah, leaving a message to warn me that unless I submit a doctor's note by the end of the month, my absences will be listed as unexcused. Apparently, I only get five of them a year.

On Tuesday, I go to Japantown. There's an AMC there where Cal and I have watched movies. There isn't much playing, just leftover movies from last year and a few early-in-the-year stinkers. But I manage to spend the entire day there, only making my way home once I've seen the moon almost crash into Earth, a family drama about a Chinese American family, and a rom-com about two exes reuniting for their daughter's wedding.

There are a handful of differences in that last one that keep me from relating too hard to it.

On Wednesday, I know that I can't sit through six hours of movies again, so I ride the train over to Oakland. At least this way I can guarantee that I won't see anyone that I know over on this side of the Bay.

Distance won't help, though, that much I know. I could travel anywhere in the world, and yet I'd still be drawn here, to this city, to this boy.

•   •   •

I go back to school when I desperately don't want to.

I have a duty that I've been neglecting. Huy and Alice aren't together yet, despite getting them along this path. There is still work that needs to be done.

And it's my job to see it through.

I manage to dodge Huy in English, but when I walk into algebra, Huy is seated on top of my desk. Alice is twisting around to talk to him. I can't hear them. For a beat, I just stand there, looking at them, picturing this as their life together. Huy laughs at something that she says, and he feeds her a slice of an orange he's struggled to peel, if the shredded remains of the peel on his desk are any indication.

I don't belong here with them. This isn't my world, my life.

And I need to accept that.

I don't have a love story.

"There you are!" Huy booms when he sees me.

Alice's eyes shoot toward me, and she smiles too.

"Hey, Jude. Where you been?" she asks.

"I, uh . . . was sick."

"Oh!" Alice reaches to grab the neckline of her sweater, stretching it over her nose and mouth. "Are you still sick? I can't get sick right now. I'm not missing hội chợ."

"No, I'm fine. It was just a stomach bug," I tell them both. Huy makes no motion to move as I sit at my desk, which makes for an awkward position. That's when Alice fully swings around to face the both of us. Huy fishes around in his pocket for a moment before he produces a black Sharpie, handing it to me.

"What's this?" I ask.

"A Sharpie," he says. "You can write with it, draw with it, even dye your skin. Though I'd advise against that."

"Do I even want to know?" I ask.

"No," Alice answers for him. "You do not."

"I got my cast." Huy lifts his arm, pulling back his hoodie sleeve and giving me a full view of the green cast that wraps itself all the way up to just below his elbow. "And you told me you'd sign it."

"He wouldn't let another soul touch it," Alice says.

"Noah tried, but I stopped him."

"Me?" I stare at the Sharpie again. "Why?"

"I promised you'd be first, Jude." He seems so genuinely sincere it's almost heartbreaking.

"Ugh, I'm going to vomit." Alice digs in her backpack to get her notebook, giving Huy the space to give me his arm. "Won't you two just get a room already?"

I want to vanish, to disappear.

"Jealousy isn't cute, Alice," I reply, not as quickly as I'd like.

"Please just sign the thing," Alice says. "I've been dying to cover his arm in dicks."

"You know, that's very immature of you," Huy says in a voice so oddly straight that I can tell in an instant that he's messing with her.

"Jude, *please* hurry." She clasps her hands together. "I have so many good ideas."

For some reason, I start thinking too much when I'm putting the pen to his cast. *It's stupid, just sign your name, you don't have to write anything extra.* I write out my name quickly, four simple letters, and hand the Sharpie to Alice.

"Finally!" She puts the ink to his cast, writing out her name in bubbly letters, even adding a heart over the *i.*

The bell rings and Mrs. Henry calls for everyone to take their seats, but Huy still lingers above me, unmoving.

"Hey," he whispers at me, "you okay? After . . . you know, the other day? You left in a hurry."

"Right. I'm sorry."

"It's okay." He pauses, biting at the bottom of his lip. "Are you still interested in going to hội chợ tomorrow? I can give you a ride."

"Oh, I . . . uh . . ."

Want to say no. I should say no. For my own safety.

Tết could be an amazing opportunity to push Huy and Alice together, though. Dancing, food, music, the energy of something monumental.

The Valentine's Day dance is still the goal. But this could set the stage wonderfully.

"Yeah," I tell him. "I'm still going."

"Nice. It's in the Sunset, so I can pick you up around five?"

"Sounds good," I say, as he heads back to his seat.

By the time we make it to lunch, Huy's cast is more black than green, with the boys from the soccer team finally getting their chance to make their mark. Neve even rushes over to snatch the Sharpie from Ricky, leaving me and Alice alone at the table.

"Excited for tomorrow?" she asks me.

"Yeah, it's going to be . . . fun."

"You don't sound so enthused," she says slyly, tapping her nails on the cafeteria table. "Could something be the matter?"

"What? No. Why would it be?" I sputter. "I'm just . . . still under the weather, that's all."

"Do you know what caused it?"

"No."

"Mhmm . . ."

"Speaking of." I switch the topic just so effortlessly. "What about the Valentine's Day dance?"

"What about it?"

"Have you got your tickets?"

"No," Alice scoffs. "I'm not going to that thing. Neve already has me helping make decorations with the art club after school today. There's no way I'm wasting my Wednesday on that."

"Really?" I glance over my shoulder at the soccer table. "There's no one you want to ask?"

"Not really." But when she looks up, I catch her staring at the soccer table. Just for a second.

I don't know whether to press it or not. I should, but I can't bring myself to.

Neve comes back, takes her seat next to Alice, and proclaims, "I got it!"

"What?" Alice asks.

"My name, on the cast. Had to avoid three different penises, but I managed to get it on there."

"I hope you mean *drawn* penises . . ." I can't help the look of disgust on my face.

"Please, unless a penis is attached to a beautifully bodacious babe, there's no way I'm going near one of those. Too . . . weird looking."

"I'm begging us to change the subject," Alice pleads, covering her face.

"Aw, babe," Neve coos, bringing Alice in. "Your fear of the penis is natural."

"Please!"

"Neve, are you going to the Valentine's Day dance?" I ask, giving Alice the change of topic that she's been searching for.

"I've worked on that stupid heart-shaped disco ball in art for a month now, I'm not missing the dance."

"I thought we were gonna watch movies?" Alice asks, her voice lower, almost as if I wasn't supposed to be privy to this conversation.

"I told you I wanted to go. Jude, are you going?"

"I think so." I kind of have to, don't I?

"You gonna ask anyone?"

I freeze. "Why would I?"

"Because it's a *Valentine's* dance." Neve says this like it's the most obvious thing in the world. "You should ask someone."

"Who are you going with?" I ask.

Neve turns to Alice, and from under the table, she takes Alice's hand, showing it to me. "Alice, of course."

"Do I really have to?" Alice whines.

"Come on, you know how hard I've been working on these decorations. I want to enjoy the actual dance."

"But no one goes to these things," Alice tells her. "Dances are overrated."

"They're fun," Neve tells her. "And we already have a bunch of tickets sold. So, we're going. And you're going to look cute and you're going to have a good time."

It doesn't sound like a request.

"Fiiiiiiine. You owe me."

"Good girl." Neve pats Alice's hand. "And now we just need to find Jude someone."

"You really don't have to do that," I tell her.

"Come on, you've been at school for a few weeks now. No one's caught your fancy?"

"Ew." Alice sticks her tongue out. "Don't call it 'fancy.' You're not a grandmother."

Neve rolls her eyes, but Alice doesn't notice. "So, no one? Not a soul?"

"No," I tell her. Certainly not anyone at this school, and definitely not this boy at the neighboring table with nice hair and sweet brown eyes. Not a boy with an oddly compulsive need to collect a dead medium of music, who loves a weird movie about Muppets.

Not the boy who loves to bake and play soccer with his friends on the weekends. Not the boy who is meant for someone else, who I've been tasked to help find his actual one true love.

I look at Neve, and I swallow hard.

"There's no one."

When I get home later, the house is totally empty. The only evidence that Leah's been home is a note on the refrigerator door.

*Gone for the night on a job—don't wait up!*

So, I'm alone. Again.

You know, usually I might appreciate that. I used to love these nights alone, having the house to myself, watching whatever I wanted, listening to music without my headphones on, practicing makeup or going through my closet. On bolder nights, I'd venture out into the city, go to Japantown or the Castro and just walk around, people watch. Or text Cal, see if he wanted to hang out, get dinner, go somewhere, or watch a movie or something.

Tonight, though, I slump on the couch, pull out my homework. The last acts of *Death of a Salesman* need to be reviewed for a test next Friday. And then it hits me that by the time the test arrives, I won't be a student at Hearst anymore. I'll no longer be in their system, and Mr. Benson will have entirely forgotten about me, one extra desk situated right behind Huy.

I flip through our streaming services, looking for anything that might help me pick myself up, but every movie seems like the wrong choice. I don't want to watch the girl get the boy, or the girl get the girl, or the boy get the boy. I don't want to watch two people fall in love, resisting each other the entire time only for the last fifteen minutes of the movie to come, for them to accept their feelings despite all the odds stacked against them.

Which just means that I should watch *My Best Friend's Wedding*, but my attention span doesn't last past the opening musical number before I'm on my phone, staring at Huy's Instagram. I wander around the apartment like a ghost, going to my room to listen to music before immediately turning it off. Huy's Instagram still lingers there on my phone, his story refreshing. So I click on it, embarrassed when I see the *Uploaded 1 Min. Ago.*

And it's literally just a shot of his shoes on the black-and-white tiled floor of the bakery, pleading for someone to come and hang out with him because he's bored.

As the sun begins to set, I make my way into the kitchen and open the cabinets and the fridge. There's not much to eat—some leftovers, bags of chips, frozen stuff. None of it calls to me, though.

But you know what does?

Curry. For the second time in how many days now?

Is there ever such a thing as too much curry, though?

It's the first bit of excitement that I feel all evening. I grab my keys and phone, putting on the headphones plugged into Huy's Walkman while I ride the 29 down to the Sunset to my favorite Japanese curry place.

I confirm that I want the curry katsu, spicy, and wait, taking my bag when it's brought to the counter, turning up the music when I start my walk back to the apartment. It's only when I realize that I'm accidentally passing by the back side of Trinh's Donuts that I dare to look up. God, my timing is awful.

Huy's coming out the back door, a trash bag at his side. He lifts the black plastic lid of the dumpster without much effort and slings the bag in with ease despite his sling weighing him down.

And before I can decide whether or not I want to see him, he spies me first.

His expression is different now. Where I might expect that grin that's become all too familiar to me over these last weeks, there's a . . . something. He almost looks distant before he waves at me, his arm stiff, and I wave back, correcting my course and turning right to head for the shop despite every single voice in my head telling me that it's the wrong move.

"What are you doing out?" he asks as I approach.

I show him the bag. "Volcano Curry."

"Ugh, I'm jealous."

"Are you closing?" Is it already eight?

"Yeah, just wrapping up," Huy calls out, averting his gaze for a few precious seconds. "No chance you want to keep me company?" He almost sings the question. I can't say no to him, despite every bone in my body urging me to reject this offer, to leave Huy standing out here in the cold, confused as to why I don't want to be around him. I just can't let him go.

"Sure."

That's how I end up helping him clean the tables and counters. Which isn't even my responsibility, but after watching him struggle with the broom for five minutes, I hop in.

"Are your parents still mad at you?" I ask him. "Over the arm?"

"I get nightly lectures, and my mother prattles on about how right she was." He sounds so annoyed. "But that happened before the wrist too, so . . ."

"She really hates you playing soccer that much?"

"They think that it's irresponsible, that I'm putting myself in danger." He looks at his arm. "Can't argue with them now. Five years of playing and the worst injury before this was some friction burn and a bout of athlete's foot. And the ball to the face, I guess." He begins to wipe down the front counter. "It's whatever. It's not like it'll matter once I graduate anyway."

"What does that mean?"

He steals a look at me. "Nothing. Don't worry about it."

"No. Do you want to talk about it?"

"You don't have to listen to me, Jude."

"I don't *have to*," I tell him. "But I want to."

The look on his face tells me he doesn't appreciate having his words turned against him. "My parents and I had this big argument last year when I started talking to Coach Thompson about school picks, scholarships, maybe playing pro one day. He thinks that I'm good enough, and I've had scouts from colleges come to some of my games."

"Seriously? That's amazing, Huy!"

"Yeah, if only my parents shared the sentiment," he tells me. "They think I'm being *unrealistic*."

"Ouch."

"Yeah . . . at the end of it all, I just told them what they wanted to hear. There was no getting past them."

"So just like that, you're giving up on your dreams?"

"I mean, I don't even know if that's my dream. I don't know if I want to play professionally. It's not exactly a popular sport in America. I just . . . I wish that they would've listened to me." He lets out a sigh. "When Hương wanted to play violin they tossed her into lessons. They joked the other night about the second mortgage they'd take just to get her into a nice arts school." He leaves the rag on the counter, his face sinking. "I'm sorry, you don't want to hear about this."

"You don't have to apologize for your feelings. They're not a bad thing," I tell him matter-of-factly.

"Yeah, but you're not my therapist," he says, with a quiet frustration to his voice. "It's just hard. Sometimes . . ." He pauses, looking around like he's suddenly conscious of the idea that people might still be around, but the door is locked, the lights off, and there's not a soul to be seen anywhere outside. "I don't know, sometimes it feels like they don't like me."

"I'm sure they love you, Huy."

"No, not love. *Like*, as a person. I wish that they liked me."

The tears are welling up behind his eyes, and I can't stop myself from wrapping my arms around his body. I don't know why I'm doing this, it just feels natural. He needs a hug. I know that feeling all too well. It's such a simple concept, the touch of another person, their warmth next to you, that pressure that you feel, that comfort.

A simple concept, sure. But a life-changing one too.

"I'm sorry," he tells me. "I didn't mean to get so intense."

"It's okay."

"I guess I've never talked to anyone about how I felt before."

"I've got ears. I can listen."

"Thanks, Jude." He finally returns the hug, pulling me close to him. I can smell the vanilla and taro smells that stick to his clothing. The sugar on his skin.

Finally, he pulls away and says, "We have some curry to address."

With the two of us eating, it's easier to sink to the floor, sitting next to each other with the container between us.

"God, I could marry this curry," Huy says with his mouth half open.

"I don't know if that's allowed just yet."

"Just wait, one day, we'll approve human/curry unions. Mark my words."

I can't help but notice how close our knees are right now, pressed together ever so slightly. He's wearing his pair of jeans with the holes in the knees, the sparse black hairs poking out.

"I'm sure the streets will be filled with people celebrating."

"All the smart people will." Huy points his fork at me. "So . . ."

"So . . . ?"

"You're really okay, after the other day?"

"The other day?" I know what he means, but in my delusion, I hope that pretending I don't will free me of having to have this conversation. "How was I acting?"

"I don't know, kinda weird. You rushed out of the house so

quickly my dad asked me if I'd said something to hurt your feelings."

"Oh, no . . . I mean, I'm fine. I promise."

"You sure?"

I nod.

"Okay, just . . . you know. You're my friend, Jude. If you want to talk about something, I'm willing to listen."

I wish I could tell him the truth; I wish the words *I'm a Cupid* could come out of my mouth so easily. It would explain so much, and then maybe—maybe—I could try to save myself. But why would he believe me? Or any of it?

Besides, I'm already in enough trouble.

Who knows what would happen if it was found out that I told him the truth.

"Thanks," I say. "But really, I'm good."

Huy moves back toward the refrigerator, coming back with two bright Thai iced teas with the plastic lids tight across the top. When he hands me one, he casually asks, "So, are you going to the dance next week?"

"Yeah, I think so," I tell him. "You?"

"Maybe. No one's asked me."

"*You* could ask someone."

"Indeed, I could." He props his good arm behind his head and leans against the counter before he realizes how uncomfortable the cast makes that angle. "Who are you going with?"

"No one," I say, sipping the sugary-sweet tea.

"Really? That's surprising."

"Why?"

"Because . . ." He trails off. "I don't really know why I said that."

I look at him, confused. "Who would I go with?"

**212**

"I don't know. You could go with Cal, right?"

"Oh, Jesus, no!" Okay, it comes out with a little too much force behind it. "Cal's just . . . he's my best friend."

"Ohhh." Huy draws the word out. "Okay then."

"Did you really think that we were dating this whole time?"

"I mean this in the best way possible, Jude. Are you sure that you're not dating him?"

"Uh . . . yeah. I think I'd know if I were dating Cal. Besides, I've never been in a relationship before."

"Really?" Huy asks as I start to play with the cuffed leg of my jeans.

"Yeah. Is that surprising?"

"I don't know. I mean, I'm still getting over the Cal thing." Huy takes a soft breath, letting it out through his nose. "So, you've never been in love before?"

"I never said that." I don't know why I can answer that question honestly. I don't think about it, it just slips free. "I've been in love before. Definitely. Have you?"

Huy hesitates, and for a moment, I'm worried I've offended him. But I can't give up this chance to learn something. His honest answer could be everything for me.

"I guess what I had with Alice—you know, before everything— at least, maybe that was love? It's been such a long time, and we were literally like thirteen. And I don't think any thirteen-year-old actually knows what romantic love feels like."

"Probably a safe thing to assume," I say, forcing the words out. I need to probe a little harder. "Even now, though? You don't think you might have feelings for someone?"

"Why?" Huy flashes that familiar lopsided grin. "You have news for me?"

My face lights up. "No!" I say a little too quickly. "I was just . . . I don't know, curious. We were having a conversation!" I try to twist the words to make it seem like *he's* the weird one.

"Yeah, I don't know." Huy pauses. "It's always hard to tell. You know what they say about high school relationships not lasting, so you have to wonder if it's worth it to get all tied up in another person."

"I think that's a little pessimistic."

"Maybe. Plus, TMI, but my shots tend to ramp up the hormones. Sometimes I'm never certain if a feeling is mine, or just the way my body is reacting. Besides, I'm young; I have my whole life ahead of me to fall in love with the right person."

It's not what I want to hear him say. Then again, I doubt even under the most familiar circumstances that Huy would boldly admit "Yes, I'm in love with Alice" here in the middle of a closing donut shop.

"Sometimes, though . . . I miss that familiarity," he admits.

Oh?

"Yeah?"

"Yeah." Huy pauses. "I guess I have you to thank for that."

"What do you mean?"

"Without you talking to her, I doubt that Alice and I would've been able to patch what we once had." He turns his head, like he's having a normal conversation. "I've known for years that I've missed her, that I missed being her friend, whispering private inside jokes in class, staying up all night FaceTiming, walking down to the beach or Golden Gate Park. And now we have that again."

I want to disappear, to vanish. This is what I'd hoped for, right? This is exactly what I planned. I can't even ask myself why it feels so wrong, because I know the answer. I know why it hurts, and I can't stand that I feel this way.

But this is all a good thing.

Huy smiles warmly at me, and I try my best to smile back at him. Because that's what he needs me to do for him, because that's what I'm supposed to do. I've set the scene for Huy and Alice's epic love story.

This is all my fault.

"You should give love a chance," I tell him. "You might be surprised."

"Maybe." Huy's expression sinks, if even for just a brief moment. I notice at least that much. "Where'd you learn so much about love anyway?"

"I watch a lot of rom-coms, remember?"

"Right, right." Huy brushes his hands on his apron.

"I think I'm going to give you your own advice," I say to him. "That you should chase whatever makes you happy."

"After you told me all about how the safe path is the better one?"

"Hey, we're talking about you here, not me." I sip my tea again. "It's easier to give you advice."

"Very *do as I say*," he tells me.

"Exactly."

He nods, palming his tea in his large hands, playing with the plastic lid. "Okay . . ." he says. "I'll think about it."

"Really?"

"Yeah . . ." He looks at me, and he winks. "What's the worst that could happen?"

# CHAPTER SEVENTEEN

It's a weird feeling.

Knowing that tonight will be it. I mean, not *it*, but close to it. In the movie starring Huy and Alice, tonight will be the night that they remember falling back in love with each other. There will be food, shared laughter. Huy will pull Alice to the floor to dance, and the two of them will get all hot and sweaty, escaping outside to the cool night air to steal a moment alone.

They won't say a word, not at first. But the feelings will be there. Something will finally click, and the two of them will be pulled right to the edge of the cliff.

And I'll be there to push them over.

"Jude?" Leah calls from her spot on the couch. Today's a rare day off for her, so she's been enjoying herself by catching up on *Drag Race*. "You're pacing around the house, honey. You're starting to make me nervous."

"I'm sorry," I tell her, waving my hands back and forth in front of my body. There's something simple about the action that's keeping me cool and calm. "I'm just worried."

"Tonight's it? The big finale?" Leah asks me with so much pride in her voice.

"Not quite—it's the setup for the big night. I want the feelings to be *cemented* tonight. Then boom! They kiss at the Valentine's Dance on Wednesday."

"Shame you couldn't strike this on a year where Valentine's Day is on a Friday."

"You're telling me."

"But I mean, this is it? It sounds like you've reached the end!" Leah eyes me. "I feel like you should be happier. You look depressed."

"That's one way of putting it."

"You're nervous," she tells me.

"Is it that obvious?" I don't mean to snap; it just comes out that way.

"Whoa! Okay, let's turn the attitude down a notch."

"I'm sorry, I'm just . . . What if I fuck it up now? What if I've made it *this* close to the finish line, and I stumble?"

"Do you really think that'll happen?" Leah gives me a reassuring look, and I know she's saying this to try to make me feel better.

"I don't know!" I tell her, falling to the couch dramatically.

"Okay." Leah reaches for the remote, realizing just how serious the situation is. "Let's talk this out. I want you to tell me what could possibly go wrong tonight."

"I don't get Huy and Alice together."

"You're not trying to get them together tonight—you said it yourself. This is the last night of prep."

"I could fail. They could say something they don't mean, they could hate each other again, and this entire month will just go *poof!* up in smoke. And I'll have failed Richard, and the Cupids, and you'll be disappointed in me, and—"

"You think that you'll disappoint me?" Leah asks, her voice quiet. "Look, I get scared all the time, Jude. It's just that as an adult, I'm expected to hide it better."

**217**

"You're great at hiding it." I can't remember a time when I've ever seen Leah scared.

"I was scared when I was your age, the first time I was sent out to get my first couple together on my own. You wanna know what happened?"

She takes my silence as a reply.

"I used the same plan you did the other night. I thought that tripping the guy and getting him to spill wine on this girl's dress would lead to a funny moment. They'd go to the bathroom, try to clean things up, laugh about it. You want to know what really happened? She slapped him."

"Really?"

"Yeah, in retrospect it's pretty funny. But there was no laughing then, just angry shouting as she chewed him out in front of a dozen people at a college party. It was ugly."

In the years that I've known her, I've never really heard Leah talk about her failures. Her success stories, sure, but never her failures. I guess it was kind of this unspoken rule?

"And after that, I caused a car crash. Just a fender bender on the street, nothing serious. But fender benders don't really bring people together. Another time I accidentally caused a flock of seagulls to attack this couple. I tried to *When Harry Met Sally* these two kids in college and they made it just into Oakland before she made him get out of the car and hitchhike back to campus because there was no way she was driving all the way to Texas with him."

"How come you've never mentioned these stories before?"

"Because they're embarrassing," she says bluntly. "But they happened. Because . . . well . . . that's what happens. You fail at shit, you fail at life. It's one of the things we have in common

**218**

with humans." Leah puts her hand on my knee. "I know that things feel really big right now, and that you have this need to prove yourself. But if something goes wrong, if tonight is a bust or even if it goes well and you fumble at the dance, you know what'll happen?"

"I . . . no, I don't."

"You'll come home, go to sleep, wake up the next morning, and you'll try again. And yeah, you won't feel great; you might even cry like I did the first few times. But it's just what happens. You fail, and you try again."

"That feels easier said than done."

"Oh, make no mistake, it is, but that's why I'm here. And Cal too. And Richard isn't going to care if you mess up."

"He won't?"

"No, because he's failed too. And so has Cal, and literally every other Cupid who's ever been in your position."

"Then why did you think I wasn't ready?" I ask her.

"Because when you came home that afternoon, when you told me what happened, I suddenly pictured this entire future where I didn't get to be your big sister anymore. And it terrified me."

"Leah . . ."

"I love you, kiddo, a lot. And the thought of losing you . . . it's scary."

I can't keep myself from leaping at her, wrapping my arms around her shoulders and pulling myself close to her.

"I'm sorry that I caused that."

It takes her a moment to register what's happening, but she wraps her arms around me, her face in my neck. "It's okay, Jude. It's okay."

To think I was willing to let a boy ruin this for me, to take this life away from me, to take Leah and Cal and Richard and everyone else away.

When I pull away from Leah, I realize that my eyes have watered enough to ruin my mascara.

"Ah, shit." I wipe my eyes, my finger coming back black and brown from my eye shadow.

"Go," Leah urges me. "Go fix it before that boy gets here."

I'm on the floor in front of my mirror bed when Huy arrives, trying my best to patchwork together my previous look while music plays from the Walkman. I hold my breath as I redo my eyeliner, trying to re-create it as perfectly as it was before.

I hear the doorbell, Leah rushing to get it, footsteps coming back up the stairs, and then a knock on my open door.

"I didn't want to ruin whatever moment you're having here," Leah says, hovering in my doorway. "But Huy's here."

"Oh, okay." I stop the music, grabbing my jacket off the end of my bed. I'm prepared to go out into the hallway, grab my shoes, and go out to Huy's truck. But when I step out of my room, I nearly collide with Huy.

"Oh." I hear his all-too-familiar laugh. "Sorry, I didn't mean to—"

"Huy." I whisper his name softly. "Why did you come inside?"

"It was freezing out there!" Leah says before heading back downstairs.

Huy quickly adds, "Don't worry, the tent is heated. You'll be safe."

"Cool, so, uh . . ." I readjust my jacket. "Ready to go?"

"Well, hold on," he tells me. "I'm still getting the feeling back in my fingers. Plus, you've seen *my* room . . ."

"You don't want to see mine." I step in front of him. "It's a mess."

"Oh, come on. Just a peek? It's only fair."

I let him step past me. It feels like Huy's the kind of person you could never win an argument against, even when he's in the wrong. Which is probably the most dangerous superpower of all. He walks through the door, peeking around the weird hallway that leads into my actual bedroom. He stares at the bed, at the dresser, the photos that sit on top of it, the rows and rows of makeup and nail supplies, my tall mirror, and the postcards and prints that decorate my wall.

"Everything you expected?" I ask him.

"And more."

"So, you've been dreaming of my bedroom?"

I'll admit, it's nice to see him flustered for a moment. "No! That's not what I—" He turns, finally seeing the smile on my face, and he realizes that I'm messing with him. "You're not funny."

"Not liking how the tables have turned?"

"How are you liking it?" he asks, ignoring me and picking up the Walkman from the floor.

"It's depressing," I tell him. "And it's hard to remember which songs I like."

"I'm gonna guess . . ." He hesitates. "MUNA is a favorite?"

"Which one is that?"

"'Runner's High' on this tape. And 'What I Want.'"

"Yeah." I recognize the titles. "I like those."

"I'll let you borrow the full album."

"Only if it's on tape."

He smiles. "Deal."

Huy sets the Walkman down, going back to the dresser, his eyes gliding over the brands that I've collected. I'm grateful that my nerves forced me to clean my room just to give myself something to do.

"You have a lot here." He hovers over all the bottles and palettes and brushes. "Do you really use all of this stuff?"

"Not all the time," I say. "My skin would be terrible if I did that. And some days I just can't handle a lot on my face."

"I guess it's like a comfort for you, though?"

"Kind of." I pause. "I don't know, I guess it makes me feel more like myself. It feels natural. And it's a skill that I've spent years working on, so I feel really proud of myself when I can make something out of an idea in my head. And I like feeling pretty, like I look good." I stop myself. "That probably sounds stupid."

"No," he says almost immediately. "It doesn't."

I don't say anything.

He keeps talking. "Before I came out, my mom tried to teach me how to put everything on. But I hated it, and I fought her like every step of the way, wiping off anything she put on me. Eventually she got frustrated, called me wasteful, and stopped trying."

"Really?"

"Oh, I was a *dramatic* child," he tells me. "Like I'd pull off my church dresses the second my parents turned their backs because I hated wearing them. But the makeup . . . sometimes I miss it, actually."

"You do?"

He nods. "I tried it again at some point. I watched these videos from trans guys and drag kings. I thought I could figure out how to shape my face better."

"I'm going to guess it didn't go well?"

"My mom laughed when I showed her. She said I looked like a clown—she wasn't too off base on that one. She helped me clean my face off and look a little more presentable."

"Oh my God . . ." I can't help laughing.

"It's not funny!" he says with just as much levity in his voice.

"I know, I know. I'm sorry." I try to straighten my face, but when I look at him again, I crack up all over.

"I'm glad that my pain is humorous to you. It didn't help that all my gender envy came from K-pop idols, with their perfect skin and nice hair, the androgyny that seemed so effortless. God, Jungkook had me spiraling for weeks one time."

"Would it hurt your feelings if I said I don't know who that is?"

"No. In fact, it's probably better that you don't. I don't want to cause you any accidental dysphoria."

"I appreciate it," I say, hesitating, wondering if I should say the next words that come out of my mouth. "Do you want me to do your makeup?"

"Would you really?"

I nod. "I don't have your tone for concealer." Much like Alice, Huy has these golden shades to his light brown skin, and he's darker than her, so there's 100 percent no covering up or blending in. But makeup doesn't begin and end at concealer and foundation. And I can still do plenty with the tools I have on hand.

"That's okay," he tells me.

"Then sit." I grab my primer, and my go-to bag, the place I keep all my usual choices when I don't want to think too hard about what I'm putting on my face. I signal a space on the floor in front of me.

"Do we have time?" he asks.

"I can do this in five minutes, trust me." I open the bag.

Huy finally sits down, and once I sit down too, I'm face-to-face with him again. It feels oddly intimate, to be on the floor together. He's looked at me before, but now, it's like he's looking into my soul. He bats his eyelashes like it's on purpose, and I have to look away.

"I promise it'll be light," I tell him. "Nothing heavy."

"Okay."

"And if you want it taken off, please just let me know. I've got wipes here. It can be washed away in seconds." I hand him a hair band, showing him how to loop it around his neck first and then pull up to get his hair out of his face.

"Thank you."

I carefully rub his skin with the primer, and he finally closes his eyes when I ask him to so I can actually focus on something besides the way he's looking at me. I can imagine bolder greens and yellows making his eyes pop, or maybe even a soft purple on his cheeks. But we're not going for anything out of the box, not right now. With no concealer or foundation to use, it means that I get to focus on his eyes, and since this is a test for him, I decide to go a little more natural. Deep browns with golden undertones that match his skin almost perfectly.

He smiles as I bat his face with the brush.

"What?" I ask him.

"Feels weird."

"You get used to it."

With the first layer looking good, I grab a softer pink shade for his lips, applying a thin layer. "Look at me," I tell him, and his eyes open. "Do your lips like this." I press mine closer together, making them an awkward line and rubbing them together like I do to get my gloss to spread evenly.

Huy laughs again and does exactly what I say.

"Don't laugh. You have to do it."

"I'm doing it!" he argues, closing his eyes again when I grab the eye shadow palette, settling on my natural nude colors, going for a soft brown and a harsher brown to really bring out the shape of his eyes and the warmth of his gaze.

"Open again."

When he does this, his eyes pop with the softer color that now surrounds them. He doesn't look like a new person—I'm good, but not *that* good. But the softer touch brings out his eyes so well.

"I'm going to do eyeliner." I show him the pen. "Then mascara, and you'll be done."

"Okay." He closes his eyes again.

"I need them open," I tell him.

"Right." He almost sounds nervous.

I get it. I have to lean forward, directing him to look up so I can ever so gently run the pen along the fine line of his eye to get that stark black contrast that highlights the colors I've added. "Stay very still," I remind him.

"I know."

"And don't talk."

He zips his lips, and I get too close for comfort. Close enough to count the long eyelashes that flutter with every careful breath he takes, close enough to see the thin hairs that connect his two brows, close enough that I can see the soft hazel in his brown eyes that almost casts them in a golden shade.

Close enough to know how beautiful he is.

Who am I kidding? I could know that from a mile away. He could be a dot on the horizon, inching farther and farther away from me, and I would forever know how beautiful Huy Trinh is, and how unfair it is that I won't know him a week from now.

The mascara comes next, my touch soft and careful, and then the rose blush that dusts his cheeks like a soft cloud, covering the bridge of his nose from one side to the other. It's a subtle note, but it adds necessary color.

Huy has to pull away, wiggling his nose, his eyes going crossed for a moment.

"What? Too much?"

"No, it just tickled." He grins. "Thought I had to sneeze."

"Well, get back here. I want to add a bit of highlighter." I dust my brush onto the highlighter palette, sprinkling a touch on his nose and cheeks.

Huy wiggles his nose a bit. "That felt weird."

And I'm done.

I stare at him. The way the black line traces his eyes, and the soft glitter in the eye shadow makes his eyes glow in the light. The blush warming his cheeks and the pink of his lips that I can't take my eyes off.

I know what that gloss tastes like, and I crave the sugary flavor.

"How do I look?" Huy asks me, blinking softly.

I have to look away, even though I desperately don't want to. Like he might vanish if I turn my head. I search for my mirror and hand it to him, letting him take in my work.

"Do you like it?" I ask.

"Yeah." He keeps staring at his own face. "I love it."

"Here." I reach back into the bag, handing him the pack of

makeup wipes. "Use these tonight. Don't just use them, though. Actually wash your face."

"Got it." Huy takes the pack. "I'll give them back to you at school."

"Don't worry about it."

"Are you okay?" Huy asks me, his head cocked to the side.

"Yeah," I whisper slowly. "Come on." My voice is drier than I realize, like I've been choking on something. "We should get going."

# CHAPTER EIGHTEEN

The street has completely transformed since the last time I was here. And now, instead of the rows of tents and trailers, there's one single white tent that covers an entire block and some of the sidewalk. Leading up to it, there are tables for those brave enough to sit outside in the cold, though I guess the large grills filled absolutely full of food are enough to keep them warm, along with some additional food trucks that seem to prepare all kinds of Vietnamese dishes from savory to sweet.

Despite the size of the tent, there are so many people crammed inside that it's hard to maneuver at first, and it only seems to get worse the closer you get to the middle, where all the tables are set up for people to eat. Along the perimeter sit the people preparing food, the warm smells wafting their way into my nose and making my stomach gurgle. And on the far side of the tent, surrounded by speakers and screens, stands an older man saying something excitedly in Vietnamese as most of the crowd laughs along with him.

"Come on, I think Neve and Alice are here already." Huy nudges me forward, taking my hand so we won't lose each other in the crowd, but the joke's on him, because the feeling of his skin against mine only makes me want to totally vanish.

We have to move toward the back of the tent—or is it the

front? Alice and Neve are there, sitting next to each other while Alice feeds Neve pieces of fried squid.

"Mhmm!" Neve's eyes go wide when she sees us, trying her best to communicate with a mouth full of food.

"You guys made it!" Alice finally notices us. "We saved these seats."

They each move their bags from neighboring chairs.

"Thanks." Huy pulls mine out for me.

I don't say anything.

"How bad was parking?" Neve asks, finally swallowing her squid.

"Just two blocks away, not that bad," Huy answers.

"Your parents were already asking about you," Alice tells him. "Wondering where you were."

"We didn't mean to be late," Huy says over the music. "We lost track of time."

"Doing what?" Alice asks.

Huy gives her the full view of his face, waiting for her to finally notice.

"Wait!" She reaches, grabbing his cheeks and pulling him in close. "You're wearing makeup."

"Jude did it," Huy says.

"He looks so good, Jude!" Neve says.

"Better than normal."

"Thanks." My voice still doesn't carry any farther than my own ears.

"Ladies, please." Huy relaxes back into his chair. "There's enough of me to go around."

"*Anddd* you killed it," Alice says to him. "Congrats, Jude. You made him even more insufferable."

"I didn't think that was possible." Neve steals another piece of squid.

"Jude!" Alice calls me out, suddenly switching the topic of discussion. I think she sensed my discomfort. "Is this your first Tết?"

"Yeah," I tell her, not appreciating the spotlight being on me. "I mean, I know what the Lunar New Year is, but I've never been to the actual festival before."

"We call it hội chợ," Huy tells me. "Tết is the day, the new year, and hội chợ is . . ." He looks around at the ensuing chaos. "All of this!"

"Aren't you two hungry?" Alice asks. "We grabbed extra chả giò." She pushes a plate of egg rolls toward us, which Huy is all too happy to pluck from.

"I think we'll probably do a lap," he says, chewing softly. "I need to find my parents."

"They're over there, in the corner near the stage." Neve points before she gives Alice a sharp look. "*Someone* might've gotten dessert before she ate dinner."

"Okay, but they were going to run out of blueberry. I didn't want to run that risk," Alice argues.

"That part I get, but you wolfed it down before we even found a place to sit."

Alice looks all too proud of herself. "It was good."

Huy laughs—and I can't help but notice how much more comfortable they are with each other. How I caused this, how I helped these two friends find each other again.

How this is all my fault.

Alice's gaze lingers before she says, "Go eat."

Huy says "Come on!" really loudly and jumps up. As I follow him, I wish I could command my heart; I wish that it would listen to me. I wish whatever chemicals in my brain that controlled my attractions would just give me a break.

We start at one end of the endless line of food, weighing all our options, my stomach only growing more and more hollow with every passing vendor. There's bánh mì, of course, and smaller plastic tubs of all kinds of soups and pickled onions with scallions. Fried chicken that makes my mouth water. Like the chả giò Alice grabbed, and thịt kho—which Huy picks up two orders of for us—nem chua, and chả lụa. There's also mountains of desserts, the sugary-sweet air filling my nose, and stalls dedicated to boba and Thai tea.

It's a literal food heaven with how many options there are and how everything smells and looks more delicious than the last options.

Huy spies his parents right where Neve said they'd be, closer to the end of the line, tucked near the stage with their full donut selection on display, with a mobile frier going just outside the tent. They've also brought other desserts too, like these white jellies, and much smaller but longer strips of fried dough covered in powdered sugar.

"Ah, there's Jude!" Mr. Trinh smiles at me when he spots us. "Thịt kho, you got that from Lam's? Good stuff!" Mr. Trinh clacks at me excitedly with his tongs.

"Yes, Ba," Huy answers for me because I have no idea when or where we got this food; all I know is that the longer I stand here with it, the more my stomach grumbles. "How's everything here?"

"Good, no one but Alice wants sweets yet, so we're prepping."

"Do you guys need any help?" Huy asks.

Mr. Trinh waves off his son. "No, no. Enjoy your night, Huy.

Please." Then he turns to me. "Jude, are you free next week? We need a make-up dinner."

"Oh, uh . . ." Again, the focus is on me, and again, I hate it. "Yeah, I should be."

Except I won't.

"How's next Friday sound?"

I nod, forcing out my best fake smile for Mr. Trinh.

"Good!" he says. "Huy can give you a ride from school."

Except if everything goes right, Huy won't even know who I am come Friday. He'll never remember making these plans with his father, he'll never remember stealing a donut for me, he'll never remember leading me back to the tent and feeding me a piece of squid because he wants to see how I'll react. As if I've never had squid before.

Alice won't remember me either. And neither will Neve. No one in this tent will. Whatever impression they once had of me will be replaced by a shadow. If they ever try to recall the memory, my face will be blank; they'll be so unsure of who they were with that night, the name *just* on the tip of their tongue before they lose it, before they decide it's not worth remembering.

I wish I were them.

I wish I didn't have to remember this night. I wish I didn't have to recall the pop music in my ears, the smell of the food, the braised pork touching my tongue. I wish I didn't have the sound of Huy's laugh committed to my memory, where I guarantee it'll live for such a long time.

I don't want the image of his smile, his giddiness as he takes Alice's hand and they lead each other to the makeshift dance floor, spinning with each other, her hand looped together with Huy's non-sling hand as they've never looked happier.

There's a moment when Alice stumbles, someone knocking into her by accident as she collides with Huy's chest, staring up at him. I can almost imagine the moment playing in slow motion for her, because I've been in her shoes.

I've never hated her more.

Which is awful to think, and only makes me feel worse about myself. In this moment, in this life, I'd give anything to be able to swap places with her. Huy smiles, and they both laugh almost like they're drunk or something before they're forced to clear the floor. The tent flaps at the back open and these two large, ornate dragon puppets dance their way in, the crowd going absolutely wild at their incredible feats of acrobatics. Seriously, they're leaping onto each other's legs, jumping high in the air, moving in careful synchronization all while controlling the face of the dragon they're dancing with.

And after that, the San Francisco and Oakland dance teams all file out, dressed in gorgeous áo dài with these large fans as they twirl around onstage. It really is a magical festival.

"God, I wanna marry this pig." Huy's eyes flutter closed as he finally finishes seconds of his food.

"Get a room, why don't you," Alice tells him, biting into another donut.

"I would!" Huy tells her. "I absolutely would get a room with this pork and make sweet love to it all night."

"Stop!" Alice shoves him. "You're going to make me vomit."

"I'm so sorry our love is forbidden to you." Huy slumps toward her, laying his head on top of hers. "I thought you'd be more progressive than that, Alice."

"Sorry, I'm porkphobic. I just can't support human/pork unions."

"The two of you are going to make me sick," Neve says as she nabs a spring roll.

To think, a week ago, the two of them had no idea what to say to each other. Two weeks ago, they didn't know what their feelings were. And three weeks ago, they hated each other.

That was me.

I helped them find this again.

It's all my fault.

I just need them to say something, to say anything at all. But that can't really happen here, can it? As much fun as I'm having, as easy as it's been to forget myself, a tent packed to the brim with people all fighting to have conversations of their own doesn't exactly lend itself well to the heart-to-heart conversations.

I need to get them outside. Out in the night air where they can be alone.

I watch as Huy takes another piece of pork, flying it toward Alice's open mouth like she's a toddler, deviating at the last second to eat the meat instead. I should be proud of what I've accomplished. Even if they weren't in love with each other, I helped two people who'd lost their way find each other again, recover this friendship that clearly meant so much to the both of them. I should be proud of what I've done here.

I need to get this over with. I *want* to get this over with.

So I can finally catch a break.

"I think I'm going to grab one of those fruit bowls," I tell Huy because he's the only one who can hear me right now.

"Sounds good!" He nods, turning back to Alice and Neve.

With the two of them distracted, I can go for the tall heat lamp that we've been seated next to this entire time. It's been doing its job, keeping us and the neighboring tables warm, but

I need a little more from it right now. I carefully turn the knob as far as it'll go, cranking up the temperature.

I don't hang around, waiting for it to climb. I just go and grab my fruit bowl. By the time I make it back to the table, everyone's foreheads are visibly shinier. Huy's even moved spots, picking seats closer to Alice and Neve, bent down like they're having a serious conversation—a conversation that ends when I'm back at the table.

That can't be good.

"Whew." I pull on the neck of my sweater. "Is it boiling in here? Or is it just me?"

"Not you," Alice whines, falling forward onto the table and catching herself with her hand. "I think I'm going to do a lap outside, get some air."

"That's probably a good idea." Neve grabs her purse.

"Come on." I nudge Huy. "We can get some fireworks."

"You seriously think they'd let us do fireworks in the city?" he asks, standing tall. "We'll get you some sparklers, though."

"Hmm . . . I'm not sure if that's good enough."

Huy just laughs, putting his hand on my shoulder and leading me out.

"What were you guys talking about?" I dare to ask as we finally step outside, where Huy can actually hear me now.

"Oh, it's nothing." He puts his hand back down. "Don't worry about it."

But how can I not? How can my brain not run wild with the idea of what they were saying behind my back? Do I smell? I steal a whiff of my armpits, and it's not that; thankfully my deodorant is doing its job. Do they all secretly hate me? Has this entire month just been one long prank on me? Or maybe they're all secretly Cupids? Maybe Huy, Neve, and Alice were planted by Richard; maybe this has all been a test, different from the test that I thought it was supposed to be, and they wanted to see if I'd crack. Like Richard *specifically* chose Huy, knowing he was super charming and the kind of boy I'd fall for.

No, that doesn't make any sense.

So then . . . what were they discussing?

Alice and Neve go right for another dessert truck while Huy leads me to the booth where they're handing out sparklers. We stand feet away from each other, drawing shapes that hold in the air for a split second before they're gone.

Alice and Neve loop back to us. "Here, do something cute," Alice says as she whips out her phone.

"Make a heart or something!" Neve calls from behind her.

It feels so wrong, but my brain doesn't fight against making half the shape in the air. When Alice shows me the pictures she took, there isn't a single one that matches up properly. Mostly thanks to the height difference.

But I don't mind.

They're all perfect.

"Come on." Huy nods as the sparklers go out. We've kept walking away from the tent, and I don't even notice at first that Alice and Neve aren't following us anymore.

When did that happen?

I look around for Alice, but Huy is insistent about pulling me toward something, down the street, toward the beach.

"You had fun?" he asks.

"Yeah, definitely! The food is fantastic."

"Good." He grins, showing off his dimples. "I'm glad you had a good Tết."

"Did *you*?"

"I think my stomach hates me," he says, patting his belly. "But I'm not complaining."

"When did you start having regrets?"

"Around the third order of xôi gấc. But it's *so* good, Jude."

"I know, I know. I had it too."

The breeze picks up as we near the beach, but oddly enough it's calmed down a lot from earlier. I can actually hear when Huy talks to me, and it doesn't feel like my ears are going to snap off at any moment.

"Want to see the water?" Huy climbs the sloping sidewalk that wraps around a dune.

"Sure."

I follow his lead, down through the sand. There's a huge drop-off from where the tide essentially formed its own short cliffside in the sand. Huy leaps down before he offers me his hand, which I gladly take.

"I like the ocean," I tell him out of nowhere.

"Yeah?" Huy doesn't look at me, he just looks at the water.

"I come to the beach a lot, when I can't think. Or when I'm thinking too much."

"Does that happen often?" he asks.

"You've known me for a month, you tell me."

"I don't know if I'd call you an overthinker, Jude."

"You can't read my mind. Trust me, it's a mess up here."

"I'll just have to take your word for it, huh?"

I look at him. "I guess so."

He lets out a long sigh. "I like the water too, the beaches. It reminds me of home."

"Back in Vietnam?" I ask.

He nods. "I don't have many memories of it; I was too young when we left. But my parents have shown me pictures and home videos of our village, and a lot of my family that's over there will FaceTime. But I have these specific memories of the beach. Listening to the crash of the ocean waves, the sand in my toes, the fishing boats coming in from a long day at sea, the smell of the salt air."

"Do you want to go back?"

"Yeah, eventually. My parents want to take my sister—she's never met most of my family. They just need to take the time off from the bakery. Which . . . Lord knows when that'll happen." He shakes his head, letting his gaze drift down toward the white sand. "Maybe when they're retired and I take over for them."

I sigh, breathing out through my nose.

"I wish you'd follow your dreams," I tell him again.

He waits a beat. It's nice to not have to wonder if I've offended him. If I have, then I can erase his memory, and I've freed myself of this entire situation.

"I wish I could too," he says. "But it's complicated."

"I seem to recall someone telling me about the road less traveled," I remind him. "About following your dreams."

"Ah, see, that's so much easier said than done, though." Huy huffs. "And even easier when they're not your dreams."

"Can you do something for me, then?" I turn to him.

"Uh . . . sure."

"At least *try*?"

His brows furrow. "You make it sound like you're going somewhere. Are you leaving?"

No, I'm not.

And that's the problem. I'm not going anywhere. I'll be stuck in this city, living every single day knowing that Huy is somewhere out there, holding hands with the girl that I wish were me. It'd be so much easier if I *were* leaving, if I convinced Leah to move us somewhere far, far away.

"No," I finally say. "I just . . . you know. I want to see you fulfill your dreams."

He lets out a breath. "Maybe one day I can make it happen. Who knows."

"You don't until you try?"

"Yeah, I guess."

I tease him further. "Be bolder, Huy Trinh. Go for the things that you want."

He looks at me. "Yeah?"

"Yeah."

"I feel lucky to have you in my life, Jude Ricci."

That's surprising to hear come from his mouth, his lips forming the words slowly. He turns fully toward me, standing just barely two feet away as he smiles.

"I feel the same way about you," I get brave enough to tell him.

Because why not? Why keep this from him? Everything else about what we've had has been a lie, a fabrication.

I want to tell him the truth. Just for once. I want something to be from *me*.

"You're a good person," I say to him. "I know that sometimes you might not think so, that you doubt yourself, your abilities, and your relationship with your parents. But I want you to know that you're a good person."

"Jude." He moves closer as the words spill out. "Where is all of this coming from?"

"I just want you to know that," I tell him. "Please?"

"Okay." He smiles down at me, but there's something new here. Something different.

He's different. At least in this moment, he's different.

"What is it?" I ask him.

"Nothing." I can see him chew on his bottom lip. "It's nothing."

There's a glow behind his eyes when he blinks and turns away, walking toward the water.

I follow him. "No, don't say that. What's wrong?"

"Nothing's wrong." He stops walking, and faces me again. "And that's the problem."

"What does that mean?"

He looks down at the sand, like he can't meet my eyes right now. The moment is long, the space between us growing distant.

"Do you remember what you said to me?" he asks, finally breaking the silence. "The night that we watched the movie on the phone?"

"Ummm . . ." I rack my brain for a bit. It seems like so much of my life has been dedicated to conversations with Huy, it's hard to remember exactly what I've said. But I remember most of that night. "About risk, about taking chances?"

"Yeah." He sighs, and a cloudy breath escapes his lips. "I'm going to take a risk here."

"With what?"

"Telling you the truth."

"Huy."

"It doesn't matter what your reaction is. If you hate me, you can tell me to fuck off. I just need to get this out and if I don't do it now, I don't think that I'll ever find the courage again."

"Huy—"

"I like you, Jude. More than like you."

This can't be happening. This can't. It's like the sand begins to swallow me whole, wrapping around my feet like cement blocks that will drag me farther and farther into the earth. It'd be preferable to die, slowly suffocating in the ground where I once stood.

None of that happens, though. I'm not stuck here; I can move if I want to.

I just don't want to.

Huy goes on. "I was confused at first. Because I saw you with Cal, and I didn't want to interfere or mess with a relationship. And I was happy for you both. But then you told me that you weren't dating, that you're just friends, and I . . . well, it didn't help my feelings. I might not be able to make decisions about my own future, but I can make a decision about you, to tell you how I feel. Because I don't know if I can sit with the feelings anymore. I need you to know." He lets out this sad, forced laugh. "And I really need you to say something so I don't keep making an asshole out of myself."

The wind cuts like a knife, chilling my skin. This is what I wanted, right? To hear how he felt, for him to admit his feelings for *me* and not for Alice. As if my life couldn't possibly get any worse.

I got exactly what I wanted and I've never felt lower.

"Don't say that, Huy," I tell him. "You don't mean any of that." I wish I could conjure up something bolder, something above a whimper, but I can't.

Huy freezes, his gaze shifting toward me. "I do, Jude. I mean every single word."

"No." I shake my head. "You don't. You're not in love with me."

"You can't tell me how I feel. Only I can do that."

"Well, you're mistaken. You're confused."

"I'm not confused." He steps closer, and I can't stop myself from recoiling, from nearly falling over myself into the sand as I try to get away from him. I can see the fear on his face, the realization that he's made a mistake. "Jude, please. Let's just talk about this?"

"I can't," I tell him. "I can't talk to you about this."

"Why not?"

"Because . . ."

*Because I want you.*

*I want to kiss you.*

Because I want to ruin my entire life for some boy who I've known for *days*.

Because I want more than anything to say the words back to you, to take your cheeks in my hand, to taste the gloss on your lips and feel your hands on my body.

I want that so bad it scares me.

"I can't let you love me," I tell him.

"What does that mean?"

"It means what it means. You can't fall in love with me. That's not how this was supposed to go. I'm not the one that you fall in love with."

He only looks more confused. "How was it supposed to go?" There's a clear frustration in his voice.

"Alice. You're supposed to be with Alice!"

"Jude, you're not making any sense."

"You're not in love with me, Huy." As if I can salvage this moment, convince him that his feelings for me are simply

**242**

misguided, that if he just directed them toward Alice he'd be so much happier.

If Huy is in love with me, and not Alice, that means this was a waste of time.

It was for nothing.

The pain, the anxiety, the panic, the thrill, the excitement, the joy.

Everything.

All for nothing.

"Please don't tell me how I feel," he pleads. "It's one thing for you to not return these feelings, but I know what they are, Jude. It's fine if you don't like me back, but you're being mean."

Good. Maybe I can convince you that I'm not worth it. That I'm not worth anything at all.

"You don't love me, Huy. You can't love me, and I can't love you."

"Can you at least look at me?"

I realize that I haven't been looking at him. For good reason. Because when my eyes meet his, I see the tears welling up.

I did this. I hurt him. And I wish it felt good, because that would bring an end to all of this. But it just makes me want to die, to know that I caused this, to know that his heart aches because I can't be someone who we both want me to be.

I want to kiss him; I want to be with him, to hold his hand. I want a future with him, to go to the same college, to find our lives together, to get married, adopt, grow old, and die with him. I want Huy Trinh more than anything I've ever wanted in my entire life.

Which is exactly why I can't have him.

"No." I pause. "I can't. I'm sorry."

"Okay." He slumps onto the log, and then he starts to laugh. And all I can do is stare at him, wondering just what comes next. "I'm sorry."

I don't want him to be. Because nothing about this situation is his fault. The only thing he did was love, and that's never a crime.

"I don't want you to be anything," he says.

"If things were different . . ." I start to say.

But he stops me.

"Please, Jude," he interrupts. "Just leave me here for a bit."

I nod, but he doesn't see me. I start walking back toward the road, almost stumbling as I climb the hill, the sand burning my eyes. I cry on my walk to the bus line, avoiding the festival and any lingering faces, avoiding Neve's and Alice's texts wondering where I've gone.

I want to go home. I want my bed. I want my blanket, my pillows.

But instead of getting on the California, I walk down to the 7, and ride for a while until I reach the 37 and take that to Twin Peaks Boulevard.

I climb the hill, to that familiar brown house where the lights shine from the inside.

I ring the doorbell at the gate, and a voice chimes in.

"Hello?"

"Cal? It's Jude." I can't say anything at all without crying.

"Jude? What's going on?"

"I need you," I tell him. "Please."

# CHAPTER NINETEEN

There's the quiet sound as the gate at the front of Cal and Richard's yard opens, and by the time I climb the steps, Cal is standing there waiting for me, dressed in a worn T-shirt and pajama pants.

"Jude? Baby, what happened?"

When I see the look on Cal's face, I can't keep it back any longer. The sobs begin, and I manage to say, "He's in love with me." I fall forward, Cal catching me on his shoulder. I feel the weight of his hands, one on my back, the other in my hair.

"Come on," he whispers, pulling me away so he can look me in the eye. "Let's go inside, yeah?"

I nod pathetically and follow him into the house.

I don't explain what happened, not at first.

And he's kind enough to give me the space that I need.

He leads me up to his bedroom and lets me lie there on his comforter, conscious of the sand I'm probably leaving behind before Cal comes back from downstairs a minute later with hot chocolate that I don't want to drink.

God, I feel so pathetic.

Every time I close my eyes, I can see Huy, sitting there in the dark.

Cal climbs into bed next to me, setting our beverages on the nightstand before he curls up next to me, letting me put my head in his lap.

He doesn't say a word; his hand just finds my hair and begins to play with the curls.

I want to lie here and not have to think about the world outside this bedroom. The world where Huy likes me.

He found the courage to admit his feelings to me and, like the coward I am, I told him that it's impossible. Because it is. Because the responsible thing would've been to tell Leah and Richard a long time ago, to have gotten out early, before all this had a chance to get out of my hands.

Now it's too late.

Because what do I do now? What do I do with myself?

Why am I like this?

Why did I let this happen?

Why?

"Cal?" I whisper his name because it's the only word I can think of right now.

"Hmm?" I can barely see him look down at me, his usually comforting smile making me feel so much worse for no reason at all.

"He said that he loves me."

Cal's hand stops playing in my hair, and his brows furrow, nearly meeting in the middle. "Who?"

I hesitate. "Huy."

What good will more lying do for me?

"He said that he's in love with you?"

I nod, feeling so numb to everything around me.

"Huh." Cal's left just as speechless as I was. But the words are out there now. Cal knows, and I know, and Huy knows. And that fills me with a sense of dread that I cannot explain. Like something is going to go wrong any minute now, even though it already has. "How did you respond?"

"I told him that it can't happen." I sit up, wiping my nose with the sleeve of my jacket. "That whatever he wants . . . it can't be."

"That's good." Cal hesitates. I can tell there's something else on his mind, something that he isn't asking me.

"I failed," I tell him. "Again."

"You didn't fail, Jude. This happens."

"No, it doesn't." I slip off the side of the bed, letting myself fall to the floor so I can pull my knees up to my chest. Might as well try to make myself as small as I feel. "It's never happened to you, to Leah, to Richard."

"Well, you don't know that," Cal says to me. "I mean, it's never happened to me. But you know how secretive Richard is." Cal climbs off the bed just to sit down next to me. And I let my head fall to his shoulder.

"What's wrong with me, Cal?"

"Nothing, Jude. Nothing is wrong with you." He puts a hand on my thigh, rubbing small circles there in the denim.

"Then why did this happen? Again! What's wrong with me? Why can't I control my feelings, why can't I just be a normal fucking Cupid? What the fuck is going on in my brain that makes me fall in love with these human boys?"

"Wait . . . Jude?" Cal sits up straight, leaving me behind. "You're in love with him too?"

Cal turns to look at me over his shoulder, and all I can do is stare at him.

"Jude . . ."

I tell Cal, "I didn't even realize it was happening again. Not until it was too late."

"Huy falling for you is one thing, Jude. But you falling for him. You know the consequences of that."

"I wouldn't have let anything happen."

"Do you know that for a fact?"

I don't, actually. Because I certainly dreamed of kissing Huy, of wondering what his lips taste like, what his hands would feel like on my waist. I've pictured a life with Huy, holding his hand as we walk down the street. If we were allowed to be ourselves, to follow our dreams, he could play soccer, and I could . . .

That's where the dreams have to stop, a blank space left for whatever I might do. Because I don't know what I'd do if I wasn't a Cupid.

I don't know who I am past that.

That scares me. More than Huy falling for me, more than me being in love with another human.

I don't know who I am.

And I don't know how to find them.

"Nothing would've happened," I repeat, my voice lower, shamed.

"You have to be careful, Jude. I almost lost you once before. And I don't like the idea of losing you again."

I don't say anything.

"If you'd kissed him—"

"But I didn't."

"Or if he'd kissed you! Humans are spontaneous. What if he'd done it without warning? He could've ruined everything."

"Huy wouldn't have done that," I tell Cal.

"You don't know that."

"I know him better than you do." I don't mean the words to come out so sharp, but the hurt on Cal's face is immediately clear. As if I could feel any worse than I already do.

"I'm sorry," I tell Cal. "I didn't mean to—"

"It's okay," he says. But it feels like it's anything but. "I'm just . . . I can't lose you, Jude. You're my best friend. You're . . ." His voice trails off.

"I know, Cal. It was a slipup." So why is there a part of me that feels so much relief knowing that Huy returned my feelings? Because in a different world, we could've been together. Could've been happy. That other Jude out there, the human Jude in another universe, somewhere out there they had this same night. And they were able to take Huy's hand, to tell him that they love him back.

I hate that version of myself.

Why do they get everything that I want? Why is their life so easy?

Why can't that be me?

Why can't I be happy?

"Jude?"

I peer up at Cal.

"What are you thinking?"

I pause, unsure. "I don't really know, to be honest with you."

"Have you told Leah? Richard?"

I shake my head.

"You probably should, so they can help clean this up."

"I know."

"They won't blame you, you know. You don't have to tell them that you reciprocate these feelings." It sounds so clinical, the word *reciprocate*.

"It's not his fault," I say to Cal, hiding my face in my crossed arms. "It's mine."

"But they don't have to know that."

"It's not right. To lie about that. I don't want to."

"Jude, he's a human. He doesn't have to matter to you anymore. He's probably already forgotten all about you."

I hesitate, unmoving.

"You did the spell, right? You erased his memories?"

"Not yet." I can't hide my shame any deeper. "I didn't have enough time."

"It only takes a few seconds, Jude."

"I know, Cal!" I can't sit here anymore. I stand up, unable to stop myself from pacing around Cal's room carefully. It's like my body has too much energy in it. "I couldn't do it. I wasn't thinking, and I just wanted to get out of there, and—"

Cal steps in front of me, stopping me by grabbing my hands. I know that he means all the best in the world in this attempt to calm me down, but I have to pull away. Stopping me isn't doing anything except building up the fire in my stomach again. Growing, roaring to life until it all spills out of me.

"It's okay, Jude."

"No," I tell him. "It's not. Stop telling me that it's okay."

"It will be, though. When we tell Leah the truth, she'll help you out."

I adore Cal with every fiber of my being. I love my best friend. But there is no *we* here. At the end of the day, he's not the one who fell in love with a human, he's not the one who let their walls slip, who let another person in when that was the last thing they should've done. He didn't let a boy ruin his life.

"I'm sorry," I say to Cal. "I don't know if I should've come here."

"What do you mean?"

"I think I should've just figured things out on my own."

"Jude, it's okay. I'm your friend." He closes what little gap there is between us. "I don't like seeing you hurt." Cal takes my hands. "I care a lot about you, Jude. And seeing you do this to yourself twice now, it's hard to sit here and bite my tongue."

"Cal, what are you doing?"

"I'm right here, Jude. I always have been." He leans in a little closer. "And I'm tired of hiding my feelings for you." His voice remains soft as the last words in the world that I want to hear right now reach my ears. "I've just been waiting for you to see it."

"Please, Cal . . . I can't do this right now."

"Jude, I—"

That's when he goes for broke, when he leans in and plants a kiss on my lips that I didn't ask for, that I have no reaction to. It lasts barely two seconds. I count them down in my head, waiting for the moment that this will end. And thankfully, it does.

"Why would you do that to me?" I ask him, my breath shaky. "Why now?"

"I . . . I don't know," he says. "I'm just tired of pretending that I don't have feelings for you."

I take my hands back, stepping away. "I think I'm going to go home."

"Jude, please." He reaches for me, but I pull away.

"I just want to be left alone. Okay?"

He lets his arms fall to his sides, then slowly nods. I can notice the telltale signs of tears, the way his mouth twists and he closes his eyes, unable to look at me from his shame. It's a stance that I know well, despite Cal never having been that much of a crier. I can still feel his lips on mine as I walk out of the house, down to the bus stop. I can feel his skin pressed against mine. Have I always been like this?

If being a Cupid has taught me anything, it's that we're incredibly lucky to get one person who wants to be with us, who wants to spend the rest of the night with us, let alone the rest of our lives. My future is right in front of me. Cal is a Cupid, so we could be together. It wouldn't disrupt anything.

My Cupid future is within my grasp, and I still can't hold on to it.

Because I love Cal; he's my best friend, almost my brother. I cannot and do not want to imagine leading a life where he isn't beside me, making me laugh, comforting me, helping to pull me back from the edge when I'm climbing atop it. But I don't love him romantically. I can't give him that, and I don't want to pretend.

I can't do that to Cal.

I can't do that to Huy.

And, most of all, I can't do that to myself.

# CHAPTER TWENTY

As pathetic as it is, I don't leave my bed the whole weekend.

Leah dotes on me, taking my temperature and making me soup. I know that I need to get out from under the sheets, I know that I need to sit Leah down, to have a conversation with her, tell her the truth. There's a chance she already knows. If Cal told Richard, he would've told her.

I don't know if Cal would betray my trust like that. Or if the more cruel choice is to make me do it myself.

I feel so unfair for forcing those feelings onto him. Cal has never been anything except kind to me, beside me for every mistake that I've ever made, encouraging me when I needed it the most.

He's always been there. And I never noticed how he felt.

The hand-holding, the kisses, the moments of affection . . . they always just felt so natural with him. I never questioned how I showed my love for him despite me knowing it could be read as romantic, even if I never saw it that way.

This is my fault.

Every time I close my eyes, I see the pain on Huy's face as he told me to leave.

He'll forget me. He'll forget the way he looked at me, why he was on that beach for so long. He'll never remember the glances that we stole from each other across the classrooms. He'll forget that day in culinary arts when I mixed up the salt and sugar and made the most repulsive yellow cake ever. He'll forget the repeat trips to NaYa after school, and the shared dessert. He'll forget my love of chocolate donuts. He'll forget taking my hand. He'll forget showing me his favorite movie. He'll forget our night shared on the phone. He'll forget me watching him play soccer.

He'll forget me.

Every inch of me.

But how can I ever forget him?

"How are you feeling?" Leah asks when I brave the living room, with my Crocs on for comfort.

"Not great," I tell her, slumping onto the couch.

She reaches over, putting the back of her hand on my forehead. "You don't have a fever, so that's good."

"I'm not sick," I admit to her. "I just didn't want to leave my bed."

"I could tell," she says. "I wanted you to take your own time."

"You could tell?"

"You're a lot whinier when you're sick."

"Am not."

"You so are, Jude-bug. But that's not what's important right now." She readjusts on the couch so that she's facing me, her legs tucked underneath her. "What's going on in that little head of yours? How did the festival go?"

"Terribly."

She frowns. "I'm sorry to hear that. Do you still think you can meet the deadline? We could talk to Richard. What can I do to help out?"

"It's not that," I start to say. "I mean, it's impossible. We can't fix what happened."

"Jude, you're worrying me." She puts a hand on my knee. "Tell me what happened."

I take a deep breath. There's no reason to hide the truth from her, not anymore. Not when there's nothing to protect, nothing to hide from or behind. I have to learn how to face the consequences of my actions.

Again.

"Last night, Huy admitted that he has feelings for me," I say. "And I have feelings for him too."

Leah closes her eyes, breathing deeply. I can't blame her. I can guarantee that I'm more trouble than any other Cupid my age. I wonder if she's ever wished that she'd gotten Cal instead. A kid who knows what he's doing, who knows the rules, who knows how to set up firm walls to keep humans from getting in.

"I didn't mean for it to happen," I say before I remember those are the exact words that I said to her when I explained what happened to Leo. "I promise you."

"Jude . . ." She opens her eyes and sighs again.

She doesn't know where to begin.

We just had this conversation six months ago, where she explained to me over and over again the dangers of what I'd done, the risk I'd put myself in, the harm I'd done to my future by allowing a human to infect my brain the way that Leo had. I wanted to argue that it didn't feel like a risk, or an infection. That it felt good to be wanted by someone, to share the moments that Leo and I had together before they were taken away from me.

I don't know how long we both sit there in complete silence. Somewhere, the house settles, the floorboards creaking, the pipes making a noise as the heating kicks on. I just want this to be over, for her to yell at me and to tell me how much of a disappointment I've been. I want her to say that she's sending me somewhere else, that she doesn't have the capacity to deal with me anymore.

"I'm sorry," I say, because I need the silence to be filled, I can't take it anymore. "I swear I didn't mean for it to happen."

"I know." She still won't look at me, her voice curt. "But it did happen, and that's all that matters."

"I told him that I couldn't love him back. That it wouldn't work out."

"You didn't give him a reason?" She finally looks at me. And I shake my head. "That's something, at least."

"What do I do?"

"Have you erased his memory?"

I shake my head again.

"Do that, before the day is over. As for what happens next . . ." She stands. "I'm going to call Richard, ask him his opinion. But if it's left up to me, we're leaving this city."

*"Leaving?"*

"It's clear that you can't be trusted." There it is. A shock registers on her face for a tiniest possible fraction of a second that tells me even she's surprised by what she's said. But it's out there now. "I'm sorry, Jude. But it's the truth. It's clear that there's something that boy . . . that Leo did to you, and it's hindering your ability to do your job."

"But I told Huy that we couldn't be together, and I didn't kiss him or anything. It's done."

"No, it's not." Leah steps closer to me, reaches out to put a hand on my shoulder. "Jude, I love you, and you have such a big heart. But in this line of work that can be such a dangerous thing. This is twice now, in just six months. It's clear to me that you aren't ready to be out there, in the field. Not anymore."

"So what do I do?"

"We'll go together," she promises. "And maybe we can explore other options. You could research couples for other Cupids. You could be more administrative, like Richard. There are a lot of roles for Cupids that you could take on."

"Because I'm a failure."

"You're not a failure, Jude, you're—"

"But I am," I tell her, feeling the bile rising in the back of my throat. "I failed at this, and I've been a failure for a long time. Whatever edge I used to have, I lost it. And I don't like what that means for me."

"Jude, you're not making any sense."

I stand up, tucking my hands under my armpits because that's where they belong. I can't tolerate the idea of them just hanging there awkwardly anymore.

"What if I don't want this life?" I tell her.

I'm not really prepared to say it, and she's clearly not prepared to hear it.

"What does that mean?" she asks.

"What if I'm tired of the rules of being a Cupid? What if I've liked pretending to be a normal teenager for the last month? What if I've liked having friends? Hanging out with them, going to school, doing homework! And having these feelings for Huy. It feels natural. It feels good." I finally take a breath. "The only reason it felt wrong to love him was because I'm living a life that I never agreed to live. Because I'm not human."

"Jude, you don't know what you're saying. You're a Cupid. You're meant to be a Cupid."

"How do I know that? How do I know that there's not some better life out there for me? If I were human, I'd get to be happy. I'd get to live my life for myself and not for other people."

"That's just not true."

"Why?"

"Because humans are selfish, they're cruel, they break one another's hearts for fun. They let their emotions dictate their actions, they think too deeply with their hearts and not their brains, and that only applies to the humans that actually get out of their own way to allow themselves to experience happiness. You're not meant to be a human, Jude. And I can't see how you'd choose that life for yourself."

"Because then I'd have an inch of freedom!" I tell her. "I'd get to love the person I want."

"Only because of where we live. That's not true of all places in this world."

As if I don't know that already.

"The life of a human is not an easy one to live," Leah continues. "It might seem easier from the outside, but they live in pain, in misery. Anxiety and worry. It only seems grander because of where you stand. Do you know how many humans would want to be in the position that you're in?"

She makes so much sense, and that only makes me feel worse.

Because this life is safe, it's guaranteed. I will always have a place, I will always be taken care of.

"But I'm not happy," I tell her.

Her shoulders slump.

"I'm not." It feels so odd to have the words out of me, finally. To verbalize how I've been feeling. "Living this life, it's shown me what I've missed. The experiences. Maybe I'd have my heart broken, maybe I'd be miserable, wish that I'd never done what I had. But maybe I'd be happier, maybe I'd be the happiest I've ever been. I could love Huy for a month, for a year, for the rest of my life. I could find someone else, or be alone."

I hesitate, my breath shaky. I'm proud of myself for not crying.

"But that's what being human means," I spit out. "It means taking risks, it means giving your heart away, it means being sad and your friends helping you out of it, it means falling so hard for someone that it hurts even if you've never exchanged a single word with them. It means being messy, and ugly, and brutal. And it means being happy, finding the people that you love, that you belong with."

Leah turns away from me.

I tell her, "I know that you think that humans need us all the time, that they'd be lost without us. But I don't think that's true, not anymore."

"So you'd see us gone? Erase all Cupids?"

"No, I didn't say that." I don't know what I mean, really. "Just that maybe the world could do with one less Cupid."

"You're not going to go through with it," she tells me.

"I haven't made a decision."

"There's not a decision to make. Jude, this is your life. Once you're human, there's no going back, there's no undoing what you did."

"I don't know what I'm doing, Leah. That's the thing! I don't know what I want."

"You want to be a Cupid!"

"But is that what I want, or is that just what I've been told that I want?"

She pauses. "Have you really not been happy?"

"I *don't know*." I put my hands to my hair, pulling hard. "All I know is that I've never felt better than when I'm with him. That I feel . . ." At home, in a way that I never have before. When I think of Huy, I think of comfort, I think of warmth, I think of home. "Happiness. Not that it matters anymore. I turned him down, it's over. He probably never wants to see me ever again."

Leah stands, walking toward me. "You're young, you're confused. I've been in your shoes before. I've been sixteen, in love, wondering if I should give it up for everyone."

I don't know what to say to that, how I'm supposed to react.

"But I knew that it'd be a mistake, to leave behind everything that I'd worked for. And I've never regretted it for a single day. That girl, she doesn't mean anything to me now. I was just stupid and a teenager."

"You've never missed her?"

"Not once. And I know I would've regretted leaving everything behind for her. That much I'm confident in."

But she never would've remembered the life that she left behind. She'd have no recollection of being a Cupid. So how does she know that for a fact?

"I'm going to make some calls," she says. "Get some boxes."

"Boxes?"

"I told you—we can't stay in the Bay, not with two different boys in the area who have made you question things this badly."

"Wait! We can't just leave. What about Cal? Richard?"

"They'll understand why we have to do this. We'll put you under more training, we'll get you straightened out, and everything will be okay."

"Why can't it be okay now? Why is even the smallest hint of

**260**

me wanting to be human enough for you to throw our entire lives away?"

"Because you're a Cupid," she tells me again. "This is what you were meant to be, it's what you were meant to do. And getting out of the city will help you rediscover that. You'll be able to clear your head, get a sense of the bigger picture. You're more than just yourself, Jude. We serve a greater purpose than the humans will ever understand. That's a privilege."

"But what if I just want to be myself?"

Leah stares at me, crossing her arms. "I'm going to make some calls, get some boxes. Be prepared to pack your things, okay?"

There's no room for debate. Despite the request that comes at the end of her sentence, I know that it isn't one. This isn't my choice. I can't stay in the city. And maybe she's right; maybe moving somewhere else would clear my head, help me escape from this trap that I've tricked myself into falling for.

Maybe just being away from Huy would be enough for me to forget him.

Deep down, though, I know it'll never be enough.

# CHAPTER TWENTY-ONE

Leah isn't kidding about the boxes.

Not that I thought she was.

She drags me out of the apartment later that night to collect them from the delis and grocery stores on our block. And she orders some more online for our larger things. Then she goes into the dining room with her laptop and phone to call around to moving companies. I'm left in my bedroom to parse through what I'll need for the next few days, and what can wait.

It doesn't help that I don't even know where we're going.

And if the conversations I overhear are anything to go by, Leah doesn't know either.

We could still end up in California, or maybe we could head north to Washington? I like to think that I know Leah well enough to believe she'd choose somewhere we'd both be safe, that she'd ignore states like Texas or Florida or anywhere else that feels the need to tell trans people how they should identify.

I try to distract myself with music, listening to the soft sounds through my ears, but I have to close my door at one point, climbing into my closet and hiding my face in a jacket just to muffle the sobs. At first, I don't even realize that I'm not holding my jacket, not until something falls out of the pocket and clatters down to the floor.

I have to open my door to find it, but when I do, I see the cassette tape lying there, waiting for me to rediscover it.

It's new.

I know that because when I flip over the spine of the case, there's writing that I know I've never seen before.

Written in black pen, the words *For Jude*. rest there, almost as if they're taunting me. He had this in his pocket that entire night. With songs he'd chosen specifically for me.

My first instinct is to rip into the casing of the tape, to snap it in half, rip the roll apart in my hands just so it won't exist anymore.

But I don't.

I have to stop myself from destroying this one last good thing that I have.

This one last reminder of him.

If I can't have Huy, I guess I can at least have this music he wanted to give to me.

I step out into my room, grabbing the Walkman and the wired headphones that I've been using, swapping out the tape for the last mix of his that I was listening to.

I hit play.

The tape runs for a bit, the tread audible in my ears.

Then his voice comes in.

"Hey, Jude . . . I, uh . . . God, this is so awkward, I'm so sorry. But I wanted to make this for you. Just because, and also because I like you, and I don't know if you're going to listen to this before or after I tell you. I guess I should make sure it's after, or else that'd be awkward, huh? I'm also going to ask you to forgive me for the first song choice. I couldn't resist. Enjoy it."

There's more silence.

Then the song begins softly.

"'Hey, Jude, don't make it bad. Take a sad song, and make it better . . .'" The words come in a cool voice that's soothing to my ears. And it feels like such a Huy thing to do to pick a song like this. I hate him for it.

I hate him for stumbling into my life, for making things so much easier for me to understand, for showing me kindness when he didn't have to. I hate him for what he's done to me, for showing me his favorite movie, for staying up late with me, for making me donuts, for letting me borrow his clothes, for letting me into his heart when I couldn't do the same for him.

I hate him.

I hate him so much.

And as the chorus erupts, I let myself cry again.

I'm home alone when the doorbell rings on Tuesday. Leah's been busy all day, hunched in front of her laptop. When I went into the kitchen to grab a bite to eat, I could see her investigating various lists of "Best Places to Raise a Queer Teen" and Zillow listings. I made my peanut-butter sandwich, but I took one bite and my stomach twisted.

I don't want to leave the Bay. This is my home, it's the only place I've ever known.

But I guess I don't have a choice.

At least I can get away from Cal. He texted me exactly once to say he's sorry, but I didn't respond to him. I couldn't. I can't think of a single word that I want to say to him right now. And the worst part? I'm not even angry with him. How can I be? I don't blame him for his feelings; I can't. Because that's exactly what I've done to myself.

I know I'll have to talk to him before we leave, but right now, the wound is too fresh. I half expect it to be him at the bottom of the stairs, waiting for me with some grand gesture like the cue cards Andrew Lincoln somehow charms Keira Knightley with in *Love Actually* despite him being terrible for her and her husband literally being in the next room. Then I start to wonder if it'll be Huy, here to talk to me, to tell me his feelings one final time. Or to shout and yell at me like I deserve for playing with his heart the way that I did.

But it's neither of them.

Instead it's Neve and Alice, both with their backpacks slung over their shoulders.

Oh, right. School.

I forgot about that.

"Hey." I open the gate, letting it swing slowly. "What are you two doing here?"

"Brought your notes." Neve shows me. "And the homework that you missed."

"Oh, well, thanks." I take the short stack of papers, which includes Alice's algebra notebook, which I assume she's letting me borrow. "I can't take this," I tell her, handing it back.

Alice crosses her arms. "Why not? Just give it back tomorrow."

"I'm not coming back."

The shock registers on both their faces at the same time. "What?!"

"I'm not coming back. To Hearst," I clarify. "So I don't need these."

"Wait, Jude . . . what are you talking about?" Neve asks.

Then Alice drops, "Is this because of Huy? Because that's super dramatic."

At least Alice is being honest with me. Not that I'd expect any other kind of reaction.

"Alice!" Neve cuts into her with her elbow.

"He told you?" I ask.

"Yeahhhhhhhhh." Neve drags it out. "Sorry."

"We didn't ask or anything," Alice adds. "We just wondered where he went at hội chợ, and we called, and he was on the beach, and . . . welp. You can probably figure out the rest."

"How is he?"

"Do you want me to lie?" Alice offers.

"Please?"

"He's doing great, perfectly fine, actually."

*"Alice,"* Neve almost hisses.

"What! I'm doing what Jude told me to. I can't be blamed for that."

"It's called tact!" Neve argues. "Try and have some!"

"They asked, I answered. It's as simple as that."

"But you didn't have to be so *sanctimonious* about it!"

"Do you even know what that means?"

Suddenly, it feels like I'm third-wheeling this conversation.

"Wait." Neve holds her hands out, taking a deep breath. "We're missing the important part here. Jude, you're not coming back to school?"

"No, and it's not because of Huy." I don't know if I can handle both of them thinking I'm that pathetic. "We do this every so often. My sister's job takes her all over."

"But you said you'd lived in the Bay your whole life."

Crap. "Yeah, I mean . . . when she told them she was raising me . . . they, uh . . . she asked for a more permanent spot, but they need her . . . elsewhere."

"Where are you going? Is it nearby?"

"I don't know yet," I say. "We're just packing our things now."

"Well . . ." Neve's voice turns melancholic. "Do you want help packing?"

The last thing I should do is let these two into the apartment. Leah could be back at any moment, and the second she figures out that I haven't erased anyone's memories of me, she'll take matters into her own hands. I know I should've done it last night at the very latest. But I just couldn't. Not yet.

I'm not ready for a world where neither of these two girls in front of me know who I am, for a world where Huy doesn't know why he'd ever make a mixtape for someone named Jude.

Today might be my last day with them. And I want to let myself enjoy it, despite the guilt.

"Yeah, actually . . . that'd be nice."

I lead them up the stairs, showing them around for a bit before we go into the kitchen. I turn on the electric kettle to make the both of them tea before I lead them into my room, which has become a mess of unfolded boxes and piles of clothing that I've been attempting to sort through.

"You haven't packed much," Neve says to me as she falls onto my bed.

"I'm not sure what to keep out and what should go in a truck." Or even if we're using a moving company. "Like do I keep all of my makeup out, or should I throw it away?"

"I call that bronze palette," Neve says without thinking. "You know . . . if you're going to toss your stuff."

"Now who needs some tact?" Alice asks.

"Here." I know exactly what palette she's talking about. "Take it."

"Jude." Neve stares at me, not taking the palette from my hands. "I'm not taking that."

"Consider it a going-away present," I tell her. "Besides, I only ever used the glitter. The rest is brand-new."

"I'm supposed to get you a going-away present, not the other way around."

"I know, but . . . I don't know."

"You know, but you don't know," Alice snorts. "The human condition."

"Yeah."

Except I'm not human. And that's the source of the problem, isn't it? Well, the source of the problem is me. How I can't control myself, how I can't stop my feelings from escaping when I should be better at controlling them.

Neve finally takes the palette from my hands, but she sets it right back down on the nightstand. "Is there anything you can say to your sister?" she asks. "Could you . . . I don't know, stay with one of us? My parents have a spare bedroom."

"I can't do that, Neve. Besides, her job is the one forcing us out. She doesn't have a choice."

I hate lying to them, but what else can I do?

"Who's going to help me fix my makeup?" Neve asks me.

"Yeah! She's useless at that stuff." Alice just has to get a jab in, earning her a glare from Neve.

"No one asked you."

"I can send you videos," I tell Neve, laughing with her.

"It's not going to be the same, Jude. You know that." She reaches around my waist, pulling me in close so her head rests on my stomach as she hugs me. I put my hand against her braids, holding her close. If there's one thing humans have perfected, it's the act of affection. Something so simple as having another person wrapping their arms around you, holding you close enough so that you can hear their heart beating in their chest. That release in my brain, it eases me, even for just a moment. It helps me to forget about the life that I have coming for me, the fact that I'm leaving these two behind. That soon they won't remember me.

"We can call you," Alice says. "Do the Zoom thing or whatever."

"Yeah, totally," Neve chimes in. "And you can tell us all about your new school, and your classes. You'd better not make new friends, though."

"How could I?" I ask them. I don't tell them how badly the words sting my throat, and how I don't want to say them out loud. Because how could I replace these two in my heart?

"Jude?" Neve finally looks up at me. "Are you crying?"

Am I? I hadn't even noticed.

"Sorry." I grab at my shirt, using the hem to wipe my face. "I'm sorry."

"It's okay," she says. "It's my fault. I didn't mean to get all schmaltzy."

"Way to kill the mood, Neve," Alice tells her as she investigates my dresser, her eyes glossing over the makeup and nail polish that decorate it until she finds that familiar black box. "What's this?"

"Oh, uh . . ." I stare at the tape player in her hand, wondering how I should explain it, and why I feel so guilty for having it. "It's a Walkman."

"Huy gave this to you?" She looks down at it.

"How'd you know?"

"He's the only freak I know who still listens to cassette tapes." She taps a button, and the player pops open, the tape he made for me on full display. "He would make you a mixtape." She shakes her head. "Cheesy ass."

"It's sweet," I tell her.

"It is." Neve bites the inside of her cheek. "He's had his eyes on you since day one."

I turn to her. "What do you mean?"

"She means that it's a miracle that you didn't notice that he was drooling over you the second he saw you."

"Alice!"

"You beat around the bush too much," Alice tells her before she focuses back on me. "You had to be pretty obtuse to not notice, and Jude, my friend, you're sitting at a pretty firm 120 degrees."

I look at her in confusion.

"Like the angle? Jesus." She throws her head back.

"Oh, right . . . I get it," I tell her, even though I don't. "It's whatever. It doesn't matter."

"Why?" Neve asks, putting her hand to my back.

"Because I can't be who he wants me to be. It's impossible. And now I'm moving, and it's just not going to happen."

"I don't think he wants you to be anything, Jude," Alice says to me. "At least, he doesn't want anything other than you."

I shake my head. "It doesn't matter." And I know that they're trying to help me out here, convince me that this is a path worth going down. But it isn't. And they can't understand why.

"When are you leaving?" Alice asks.

"No idea."

"Well . . . I think at the very least, you should have a

conversation with him. So that you don't end this friendship with a bad taste in your mouth. Get some closure."

"Bold coming from the girl who ignored him for three years." Neve snorts.

"He ghosted me first!" Alice argues. "But Neve is right, kind of. I know what it feels like to let those feelings linger for too long. They're not kind; they'll make you hate a person when they don't deserve that. And yeah, Huy could've talked to me first, but I could've made the first move too."

Then she laughs.

"What?" I ask her.

"Nothing, it's just funny that it took you starting at Hearst for me to do anything about what happened between Huy and me. It's like you're our little guardian angel."

"Right . . ." I try to laugh along with her, but it's forced.

If only she knew how close she is to realizing the truth. It should be a relief that their friendship is fixed at the very least. Maybe I can sleep easier knowing that much.

There.

Some proof, finally, that I'm not a total fuckup.

# CHAPTER TWENTY-TWO

The girls hang around to help me pack, and by that, I mean they watch me as I fold the majority of my clothes, packing them away in a box before I go for the few books scattered around my room.

Eventually, though, they have to leave. And they promise to see me soon, even though this may very well be the last time they recognize me. I try not to cry, because my eyes hurt, and I've done enough crying for the rest of my life in a single seventy-two-hour period. I hug them both as tightly as I can before I have to let them go.

Because that's what this job requires.

Letting them go.

For a moment I think about doing the spell now, erasing their memories, leaving them both wondering just why they're so far away from their homes.

But I can't bring myself to do it.

Because I'm a coward.

I want to speak to Huy anyway. Maybe it's the wrong move, but Alice is right. I want the closure.

An hour later, I'm starving, and get to making ramen on the stove because the night has gotten cold, and I want something warm and easy to eat. I haven't been doing that enough. I just don't have an appetite right now. And it's probably something I should talk to Leah about.

She comes home just as I'm sitting in front of the couch.

"Oh, hey. You packed?" she asks.

"Yeah, a little. I wasn't sure what I should leave out."

"Well, Richard offered some advice," she says, leaving her bag in the dining room before she walks back through to the living room. "He's securing us a few options, and I'll probably make my decision at the end of the week."

"Okay." My ears perk up at the mention of Richard. I want to know what she told him, and at the same time, I can't imagine knowing what he thinks of me now. Failing him twice like I did, it's a mark on his pride, I'm sure. "What did he say?"

"Just that it's last minute, but he could help out."

"No, I mean about me. What did he say?"

Leah's shoulders slump. "I think it's best that I don't tell you. It's nothing that you need to know."

"Leah," I plead. "Please."

"Well . . . he didn't say anything, really. He just hummed, nodded."

"That's all?" Though coming from Richard, that should probably be considered a slap to the face.

"Mhmm." Leah makes her lips vanish in a straight line, and she avoids making eye contact. The telltale signs that she's lying to me.

"Leah."

"What?"

"Is that all he said?"

"Yes, Jude. That's all that he said."

"I don't believe you."

She scoffs at that. "What could I be hiding?"

"I don't know. That's why I asked you."

"You don't need to worry yourself with what he said."

"So, he did say something."

I hear her whisper "Shoot!" under her breath. "It was nothing important."

"Leah, please."

She sighs, leaning against the wall. "He asked me if you fell in love with the boy."

"That was it?"

She nods.

"What was your answer?"

"I didn't have one for him. What was I supposed to say, Jude? Yes? That you fell in love with *another* human?" Her voice goes higher. I've heard Leah be annoyed with me, frustrated. But never angry. Never at me. But there's so much behind her eyes right now. So much that I don't like.

"I'm sorry," I whisper. "I thought I was doing the right thing. By telling you."

Leah breathes out deeply. "You're right. You did do the right thing by telling me."

"I didn't mean to fall in love with him, Leah. I couldn't help it. Believe me, I tried." I cover my face with my hands. "I tried, and I tried, and I told myself that I'm not supposed to be in love with him, but I couldn't help it."

I hear her footsteps, feel her sink into the couch next to me, her arms stretching to pull me toward her. I feel her presence so firmly and yet all I want to do is disappear.

"I know, Jude. I know that you tried. I believe that." And I believe what she says. "But this is the duty of a Cupid. You overstepped a line, and now, as your guardian, I have to do what I can to protect you."

"I'm sorry," I say to her.

"For what?"

"Ruining your life." I should've known better. That every decision that ever led me to this moment would affect her just as badly as it affected me. She has a life here too, she has friends, she's lived here longer than I have. She has a history in this city that's being completely undone. I'm thrusting us both into new waters.

All for a stupid boy.

"Oh, Jude." She pulls me closer. "You didn't ruin my life, kiddo."

"Do you promise?" I sound so pathetic, but I need this right now.

"Of course. My life is so much better with you in it." She kisses my forehead. It's a foreign thing but comforting all at the same time. "I don't know what I'd do without you."

"I love you, Leah."

"I love you too."

Later that night, when I'm tucked into bed, I grab my phone, stretching the ten-foot charger for all it's worth.

I find Huy's name in my texts, reading over the very last messages we sent to each other.

> ME: are you on the way???
> HUY: I'm coming!
> HUY: let me rephrase that
> HUY: I'm almost at your place
> ME: oh my god
> HUY: 😄

Whoever coined the phrase *butterflies in my stomach* nailed it perfectly. It's this light feeling, and yet so heavy at the same time. I hate that I've let this boy take hold of me, and yet I don't think that I'd replay this any other way.

My fingers hover over my keyboard, and I type a message quickly.

> ME: I'm sorry.

I delete that.

> ME: can we talk?

I delete that one too.

> ME: I'm sorry for what I said
> ME: please know that I love you back, it just can't happen
> ME: I wish I could explain why
> ME: I can't love you because I'm a cupid, and that's not allowed. It's not you, it's me.
> ME: literally.

I delete all these messages, ready to bury my face in my pillow and scream before I see the little ellipses bubbles pop up on Huy's side of the text chain.

But then they disappear.

> ME: huy?

My finger stops just above the send button, wondering if I can actually do this, if that's allowed. Why would he want to hear from me, especially right now? But he was looking at his texts; he must've seen I was typing. Or maybe he just wanted one last chance to tell me off.

I close my eyes, take a breath, and hit send.

I turn my phone over and set it on my bed facedown so I won't focus on whether or not he's replied. A watched phone never gets that text back. But try as I might, I can't resist. Huy doesn't have his read receipts on, so I have no idea if he's seen the message. I can imagine him so easily, sitting in his bed, back against the wall as he watches the street below him, the soft glow of that lamp on his nightstand coloring the posters on the wall. Maybe he was doing homework or watching a movie or something.

I wonder what made him think of me.

The screen lights up, barely visible from where the phone lies facedown, but I can spot the glow. I'm not proud of the speed with which I grab it, my eyes glossing over the name as I read the words *can we talk?*

But as I register what I'm looking at, I see that it's not a reply from Huy.

It's from Cal.

I stare at the message, my heart picking up in my chest as I hold my breath.

I don't want to leave San Francisco with him thinking that I never want to see him ever again. As lost as I feel right now, I'll probably be even more lost without Cal around to talk to. Who knows, in a year, we could be laughing about that kiss, he'll have hopefully moved on, and I . . .

Well . . .

I'll be somewhere else, probably still hanging on to something that never could've been.

My answer to Cal is an easy one to type.

> ME: yes.
> CAL: tomorrow? at five?

My instinct is to tell him that it's technically tomorrow as the clock hits 12:10 in the morning, but now doesn't feel like the right time to crack jokes. And I hate that I don't have what I used to with Cal, that a single kiss changed everything, that an admission altered how I see him.

Who knew that so much could be undone with a single kiss?

Then again, I probably should've learned that lesson the first time.

# CHAPTER TWENTY-THREE

I ask Cal to meet at NaYa. Just to get one last mango bingsu in.

"Is this seat taken?"

I look up to see Cal standing there.

"Go ahead." I nod to the empty spot.

"Thanks." As he pulls the stool, it scratches the floor, both of us wincing. "So . . . I hear that you're moving?"

I nod again, licking my lips. "I told Leah the truth, and she thinks that it's best to leave the city, get away from everything."

"You told her?"

Isn't that what I just said?

No. Stop. I'm not mad at him. I just hate how it feels like I don't know how to talk to my best friend anymore.

"I didn't really see an alternative," I tell him. "She would've figured it out anyway."

"Right, I guess so."

That's when the waitress comes over, and Cal orders a yuzu soda.

"Is there anything I can do?" he offers.

"I don't see how there could be."

"You're right, sorry."

"No, I . . ." I hesitate. "I'm sorry." I put a hand to my forehead. "I'm just . . . I'm confused."

"About Huy?"

**279**

"About all of it. About Huy, about you, about . . ." Being a Cupid.

I can't verbalize that last part to him. Because I can't stand the idea of another person telling me what they want me to do. Besides, I'm not thinking about that anymore. This is where I belong, even if it no longer feels like it.

"Jude." Cal reaches across the table for my hands, but I pull away without even realizing it. "Right, I'm sorry, I didn't mean to—"

"No, I just . . . I'm sorry." I put my hands back on the table.

"Why are you apologizing to me? I'm the one who kissed you after you had your heart broken."

Something so tragic about the situation pulls a chuckle out of me. "I don't really know."

"I'm sorry I did that," he says. "That I had to pick that night, that I did it at all without asking you first. Especially when you were feeling so vulnerable."

"I don't hate you, Cal. I just have to learn how to be around you again. I'm just not sure how that happens now."

"That's fair." He blinks slowly. "I hope I can regain your trust."

I give him a soft smile. "I didn't realize that you felt that way about me."

"Seriously? There were some days where I felt like I was being *so obvious* about it."

"I guess the lines were blurred somewhere along the way. I'm sorry if I led you on."

"You didn't, I mean . . . I don't know, I guess you did, but I don't want to blame you. They're my feelings, and it was my responsibility to control them."

**280**

"No, I know, but . . . I guess I mean I can understand how you were feeling."

"Because of Huy?"

I nod.

"Do you really love him?" Cal asks. "I mean, you've only known him for a month."

"You and I both should know everything that can change over the course of a month," I say.

"True enough."

The waitress brings Cal his drink, and he can't keep himself from playing with the straw, slowly pulling and pushing it back through the hole in the lid. "So what are you going to do?"

I stare at him. "What do you mean?"

"I mean exactly that. What are you going to do? About Huy?"

"What choice is there?"

"Have you erased his memory yet?"

"No." I stare down at the melted shaved ice in my bowl. "Not yet. Leah doesn't even know yet."

"Can I ask you a question?"

"Didn't you just?" I can't resist, plus I need to break down whatever wall has come between Cal and me, and the sooner the better as far as I'm concerned.

"You're not funny," he says, pulling the straw free and chewing on the end for a bit. "But . . . why are you waiting? What does that gain you?"

I pause, because that is the last question I expected.

It's a fair one too, which makes it all that harder to answer. I don't know why I'm waiting. I don't know what I'm hoping for. No reply ever came from Huy. I don't know if he even read the message or if he deleted the entire thread just so the temptation to reply wouldn't be there anymore. And if I just erased his memory, we'd all be done with this. There'd be no going back, no undoing what I've done.

He'd be gone.

"I don't know if I can handle that," I finally say.

"Losing him?"

"Him losing me." And I know that's the most selfish thing I could possibly say. I'm actively making both our lives worse by not doing the one thing that's left to do. But I just can't, and I don't know when I'll be able to.

"Could it be because you're still hoping for something?"

"What is there to hope for?" I ask.

"Closure? Or maybe . . ."

"Maybe what?"

"Maybe you're hoping for a fix? A secret solution."

"Do you have one?"

Cal shakes his head. "No. I don't."

"I know that I have to do it," I tell him. "There's no other option. No matter what decision is made, he'll forget who I am. It's just a matter of whether or not it's kinder to let myself forget him, or if I want to hang on to what we had."

"You're considering becoming human?"

I can't lie to Cal. "Yeah. I did, at least. I thought about it for a bit."

"You know—"

"I know what it means, Cal. I know what I'd be giving up. Trust me, I've looked at this from all angles."

"Well, I guess there's nothing I can really say, then."

"You could lie to me."

He smiles. "I don't want to, though."

"Then call me stupid, or ignorant. To give up my entire life for a boy who won't even remember who I am. To give up everything when I'm not going to know who he is."

Cal stares down at my melted bingsu, and then back at me. "Have you paid yet?"

"Yeah," I say. "Before you got here."

Cal reaches for his wallet, leaving a twenty on the table for his drink because he's the only person I know who still carries cash around with him. "Come on."

"Where are we going?"

"Just for a walk."

The walk actually leads us farther west, and it's only a few blocks before we reach the seawall and the beach that stretches into the endless ocean. The sky is orange.

"Why'd we come here?" I ask.

"I thought the café was getting a little cramped," he tells me as he hoists himself up onto the seawall and turns to face the ocean, the wind blowing wildly through his hair.

"Okay." I join him, our hands touching for the briefest of moments.

"I don't think you're stupid, by the way," he says to me.

"What?"

"For giving everything up for him."

"What does that mean?"

"Well, I'm not sure how you could possibly misconstrue what I've just said, but . . . I was there. I saw the way you look at him, Jude. I noticed it because I remember thinking, *Why won't Jude look at me that way?*"

Ouch.

"You knew? Even then?"

"Not at first. I noticed his looks before I noticed yours."

"His looks?"

"He looked at you like you held every ounce of his attention. Like you were the moon and the rest of us were just stars."

"Wow, and *I'm* the melodramatic one," I tease. "Stars are plenty bright."

"But the moon is brighter from where we sit. You know what I love about what we do?"

"What?"

"The fact that we're never remembered," he says solemnly.

"That's exactly what I hate about it."

"It's a thing of beauty, though," Cal continues. "To float endlessly through other people's lives, to impact them the way that we do. There's no real reward, and most of the time we never see the benefits of what we've done. But that's not all."

"Oh?"

"I love how, even if we aren't there anymore, what we do is never forgotten. The people, they get to remember the feelings that we helped to inspire. They get to bear the fruit of the seeds that we help to plant. Those feelings linger, they last, even when we don't."

"What are you saying?"

He sighs deeply. "I'm saying that, even if you and Huy were to forget each other, even if you kissed him, if your memories of each other were stolen . . . who's to say those feelings wouldn't still be there? Who's to say that the universe—or maybe Cupid magic—didn't place the two of you together for a reason?"

"You think that's true?"

Cal laughs softly. "Who knows how our powers work? Richard's never given me a straight answer in my life."

"Well, Richard and straight don't exactly go together."

Cal ducks his head to hide a laugh. "Stop!"

"I hate that I don't know what to do," I tell him.

"I've got news for you. I don't think anyone anywhere actually knows what they're doing, Jude."

"What if I make the wrong decision?"

"Life is full of wrong decisions. It was wrong of me to admit my feelings to you, but I still made that choice. Because I felt like it was the right one to make, even if I knew in the moment that it was wrong," he says to me. And then he laughs. "Besides, you'll never remember the life you're leaving behind."

"I . . ." I pause. "I never said which choice I was talking about."

He looks at me. "I know."

Slowly but surely, his hand finds mine, resting on top.

"Do you think that I'm a bad person?" I ask him.

"No," Cal says quietly. "You're not."

There's more silence between us, and oddly enough, I don't want this moment to end, even though I know that it must.

"I love you, Jude." He says it quietly. "No matter what happens, I'm going to miss you."

"Cal . . ." I feel the tears well up in my eyes, and for the first time in days it feels like they're not because I'm sad. I'd almost forgotten you can cry from being happy. I still don't know what I'm going to do, what's going on in my head. I don't know how to heal the hurt in my heart. I don't know if I'm going to make the right decision for myself, or if there's some version of me out there who will regret the choice I make no matter what. But maybe that's life.

Regret.

Regret and happiness.

I've spent sixteen years living for someone else, for some order of people who live for others. No matter what I do, it's going to make someone angry. Leah might never want to speak to me ever again, and no matter what, I might never get to see Cal. Everything is crumbling around me, but maybe that's okay. With everything gone, there's the chance to build something new.

To start living for myself.

Maybe it's not the right decision. Maybe, in some way or another, I'll come to regret what I'm going to do.

But it's my decision to make. No matter what ends up happening, this is my life.

And no one else's.

"I'm in love with him, Cal." I say the words slowly, but I know that they're the truth.

I've never been more sure of anything in my life.

He smiles at me. "Good. I'm glad that he has you. Now the question becomes, what are you going to do about it?"

"I don't know," I tell him. "I just hope he can forgive me."

"Give him a little more credit than that."

"You think so?"

"You managed to break both of our hearts in the span of like an hour," Cal jokes. "If I can get over it, so can he."

I don't want to laugh about the moment, because despite Cal's words, I feel like he can't really be over it. It's only been a few days, and if there's one thing I've learned, it's that heartbreak is something that sticks with you. I guess without the pain, you can never appreciate the relief, that swell of emotions, the way your stomach flutters when your favorite person smiles at you and only you, the sound of their laughter in the hallways, the things that remind them of you.

It's a part of a life that I'm ready for.

Finally.

It feels painful to say goodbye to Cal.

Because this is it. This might be the last time I ever see him and remember who he is. I don't want to let him go, because letting go of him means letting go of . . . everything. All of it. Letting go of him means that I'm letting go of Leah and Richard, of being a Cupid, of this weird, promised future.

But I refuse to budge. I refuse to not think of myself any longer.

I hug Cal as tightly as I can.

"I have to go, Cal," I say softly.

"I know." He pulls me in close. I love Cal; I love him so much. And the idea of never seeing him ever again makes me want to scream, but I don't.

"I love you," I tell him.

"I love you too." He breathes slowly before his grip around me relaxes. "Now . . . go get him, tiger."

I twist, jumping off the seawall, and I start walking. And walking.

I peer over my shoulder at Cal, who sits there, watching me. He gives me a short wave, and I smile back at him.

And then . . .

I run.

# CHAPTER TWENTY-FOUR

I run down the street, to the nearest bus stop, my chest heaving, the air cold enough to make my throat hurt as it pours in and out of me like water. And when the bus comes by and I see the bright orange NOT IN SERVICE lights that gleam off the front, I start to run again.

I run, and I run, and I run.

I run until my ankles start to hurt and my thighs burn. I run until I'm doubled over in front of the combination KFC and Taco Bell on Sixteenth. I run past this elderly Korean couple, apologizing as I almost bump into both of them. I run past this crowd of people lined up outside Dragon Beaux. I run past the people getting drunk on the outdoor patio. I run past the bookstore that's closing for the night, past the dimmed lights of the dentist's office. I run past Park Presidio Boulevard, narrowly avoiding cars as they screech to a halt in the middle of the intersection, the drivers yelling at me as I try to apologize.

I run the entire way down Geary, past the smells of the seafood markets and the grocery stores, the dessert cafés and the Indian restaurants. I run and I run and I run until I feel like I'm about to pass out, until the sweat feels so cold and gross on my body as my systems try anything and everything to cool me down.

I run until I reach the lawn of Hearst, resisting the urge to fall onto the grass just to catch my breath.

I run until I have to climb each of the six steps that feel so impossibly daunting now that my thighs hurt more than they ever have before.

And now . . . I'm here.

I don't have to run anymore.

The school is alive, with some kids watching me as I enter through the front doors, having snuck away for a quick make-out or to try their best to get rid of the pot smell that lingers on their clothing.

Spoiler: You can still smell it.

But I'm not here for any of them. I'm here for one person. One person who—I'll admit, it never occurred to me—might not be here until I was already standing here, looking in the hallways for him.

When I walk through the doors to the gym, Neve is one of the first people I see, her arms wrapped around Alice, their heads on each other's shoulders as a soft song plays. The gym has been decorated to the nines, with streamers and balloons everywhere, a table filled with finger foods and drinks. Even the lights have these translucent pink filters wrapped around them, so the entire gym is painted this loving aura.

Neve's eyes meet mine, and she gets Alice's attention. Both of them are dressed nicely, Neve going for a more traditional look in a soft orange dress, Alice almost going for a deliberately tacky prom suit like she purposely overdressed for this occasion. I mean, it's not prom, after all, but they both still look amazing.

"He's not here," Neve tells me, her voice low.

"Where is he?" I ask.

Alice grimaces. "The bakery, if I had to guess."

"I'm going to find him." I'm already backing out the door that I just walked through.

"Wait! Jude!" Alice reaches for my hand, but I'm already in the hallway.

"Don't try to stop me."

"We're not trying to stop you," Neve says. "We're trying to help you! I have my dad's car!"

"What?"

"Come on, there was no way I was getting on the bus dressed like this!" Alice holds her arms out, giving me a full chance to appreciate her outfit, poofy sleeves and all.

I can't help but laugh. "Where'd you even get that?"

"What? You think it's not flattering?" Alice turns again, showing off her butt. "I think I look good."

Neve walks over slowly. "I can give you a ride. We'll barely make it before closing, but maybe you can catch him."

"Please?" I say.

"What are you going to say to him?" she asks.

"I don't know yet."

"Well, it'll take us like twenty minutes to get there, so you'll have plenty of time to think about it." Neve smiles at me. "Let me get my purse. I left it inside."

"We'll meet you at the car," Alice tells her, and we watch her dip back into the gym while Alice leads me out toward the street where Neve has parked her father's black Honda Civic. "It's kind of funny, if you think about it."

The words surprise me in the soft night, cars driving past us, pulling up to the red light before they're allowed to go.

"What?"

"Just . . . I don't know, that Huy fell for both of us. It's pretty funny."

"Yeah, I guess so." I try to laugh, but I can't really force it.

"Hey, umm, Jude." Alice leans against the car door. "Can I ask you something weird? You don't have to answer it, if you don't want to. And if it crosses a line, just forget I asked. But I'm curious."

"Well, how can I resist the intrigue?"

"Fair point." Alice sticks her tongue into her cheek. "Are you in love with Huy?"

Another surprise, this one far less expected than the first.

I don't hesitate, though. I know my answer.

"Yeah. I am. Maybe that's stupid to say, and maybe it's too early, but . . . the way that he makes me feel. About him, about myself. No other person has ever made me feel that way before."

"Really?"

"Yes. Why do you ask? If I love him?"

"I just wanted to make sure. He's a good guy, and I know his heart has been hurting these last few days."

"I know, and I'm going to apologize to him for that. Before anything."

"With the move . . . what are you going to do?"

"I don't know," I tell her. Another question that I don't have the answer to. "Go for broke?"

She laughs. "People have made stupider choices."

"Right."

Neve comes out of the school, waving her keys in the air as she waits for the light to give her permission to cross the intersection.

"So—" I say.

Alice cuts me off. "Shut up."

"The two of you . . ."

"Shut up."

"Are . . . dating?"

"Shut up."

"I'm just curious." I scoot up next to her.

"Yeah, well. I'll punch you."

"Violence is never the answer, Alice." I pause. "But for what it's worth, the two of you are cute together."

"You're five seconds from getting smacked."

"Okay, okay!" I throw my hands up defensively, climbing into the back seat as Neve unlocks the car. After we all pile in, Neve ignites the engine and Rico Nasty begins to pour from the speakers.

"Everyone buckled in?"

I yank on my seat belt to show her, and Alice does the same.

"Good, because we're in a hurry."

She speeds so fast out of the parking lot the tires literally squeal against the road as she narrowly catches a yellow light before it turns red. And just like that, we race off into the night.

Desperate to find a boy.

I'm going to be sick.

For one, riding in the back seat has never been my strong suit. There has to be a science behind it, the difference between riding passenger and riding in the back. Or maybe it's the way Neve is slamming on the brakes, whipping me back and forth as my head hits the headrest over and over again. Geary is slower than ever, and we manage to get caught in front of a bus that *really* lays on the horn, Neve waving apologetically in the mirror before she turns onto Blake and then Spruce, doing her best to floor it where she can.

But the city is made of four-way intersections.

I only have eyes for the clock on the dashboard, counting down those precious seconds that remain between now and when the donut shop closes. We'll make it. Even with how close we'll be cutting it, we'll make it.

I'm sure of it.

"Jesus." Alice holds her stomach. I can only assume she's as carsick as I am as Neve's car lurches during gear shifts.

"Sorry!"

"It's okay, we're making great time," Neve tells us as she fails to slow down for a speed bump, nearly earning me and Alice concussions.

We're only halfway to the Sunset, and hardly any of the lanes are moving. And even when we do manage to merge, we only seem to get a few feet ahead at a time. And even as we *finally* get off of Geary, as I think we *might* just be in the clear and we can make it straight down to the donut shop, Neve has to pull into Golden Gate Park.

And traffic hits an absolute standstill.

"I should've known better." She smacks the steering wheel, accidentally honking at the car in front of her.

"It's either take this way, or go all the way around. And who knows how long that would've taken," Alice tries to reassure her with a calm hand on Neve's thigh.

I sink back into my seat.

Maybe this is a sign. The universe telling me that this is a mistake.

"Hey." Alice leans into the back seat. "It's okay, Jude. We'll get there."

"Yeah."

"And even if we don't, we can go to his house. Traffic is clear the other way."

"Yeah . . . maybe." With each passing minute, I can feel myself getting worse, my anxiety spiking. This was a mistake, obviously. It was stupid to plan this grand gesture, to think that I could show up at the dance and he'd want to see me. To come to his work and interrupt his night in an effort to convince him of . . . what, exactly? That I deserve him; that despite everything, I think that we belong together, even when it could never possibly work?

I'm thrown back into my seat as Neve floors it, nearly colliding with the car in front of us as she switches lanes like she's a character in *The Fast and the Furious*.

"What are you doing?" Alice shouts.

"Getting Jude to Trinh's Donuts." The car she's cut off blasts its horn at us.

"You're going to get us killed!"

"Pfft, please. I know how to drive," Neve says as she nearly merges into another car, which honks at her. She just winces and gives them an apologetic wave.

"Neve, it's okay, you don't—" I try to tell her. But she stops me.

"No, I do. I'm tired of the two of you bouncing around your feelings. It's so annoying. You're going to apologize to him, and then tell him how you feel."

I don't know how she does it, but Neve pulls through, she turns the corner on nearly two wheels, hitting the brakes so suddenly that both Alice and I are nearly launched into the windshield.

In the darkness, it's hard to see the face of the figure by the front door. The guy who *was* locking up the shop, but now stands there with a hand on his chest after Neve's antics nearly gave him a heart attack.

It's him.

I step out of the car, leaving the door open as I face him.

It's funny. Every single word that I ever thought I might say to him is gone from my brain.

There's only him.

"Jude?" Huy breathes, the cloud of breath forming in front of his mouth. "What are you . . ."

"I'm sorry," I spit out.

"What?"

"I'm sorry for what I said. The other night at the festival. I'm sorry. I'm sorry that I said that I can't love you back. I'm sorry for that."

"Jude, you don't have to—"

"I'm not done," I say. And he pauses, nodding to let me continue. "I'm sorry for making you feel like I was dragging you along, and I'm sorry for not being able to tell you the whole truth. I'm sorry that there are things that I can't tell you. I'm sorry that I'm leaving soon. And I'm sorry that I fell asleep during the movie, I really wanted to watch it. I'm sorry for making you stay up late to talk to me, and I'm sorry for all the times I asked you for a ride home. I'm sorry . . ." I breathe, my hands shaky. "I'm sorry for a lot of things, Huy Trinh. All of that and more. But one thing I'm not sorry for is falling in love with you."

He doesn't say anything.

"And maybe it's too late, maybe this is messed up of me to do, and if it is then all you have to do is tell me and I'll apologize again. But there was no way I was leaving this city, leaving you, without telling you the truth. At least the version of it that I can tell you. Because you deserve that. I'm in love with you, Huy, and I think some part of me has been ever since I met you, when I noticed that you chew on your fingernails when you're nervous, and that mole on the back of your neck, and those flecks of gold in your eye, and how excited you get when you talk about your favorite things." It feels like the words stumble out in a single breath. Because they do. Because I have to get this out now or I don't think I ever will.

In fact, I know.

Because I have minutes left with Huy, if I'm lucky.

There will come a time when those eyes don't recognize me, a time that will arrive very soon. And I need to appreciate every precious second between then and now.

"Did you three come from the dance?" he asks, peering into the car to see Neve's and Alice's outfits.

"Not the point, Trinh!" Alice shouts.

"Yes," I tell him.

"You went to the dance?" he asks.

"To find you."

"You . . . you're in love with me?"

I nod.

"I didn't mean to make you feel bad about yourself," he says. "I just . . . I needed some time away after what happened. I didn't want to pressure you into saying anything, or making you think you had to feel a certain way, Jude."

"You didn't," I promise him. "I've felt this way for a while."

"But we can't be together. That's what you said."

I step closer to him, because I only want him to hear this. "Because that's true. No matter what happens here tonight, we can't be together, Huy. I wish that we could, and I wish I was wrong more than anything in the world. But that's the truth."

"Why?"

"I am asking you to trust me here, because I can't tell you."

I could. I could spill the entire truth here and now, because he'd just forget it anyway. But I don't want to waste what time we do have together.

"I'm asking you to forget that," I tell him. "To just spend these minutes with me."

"You're scaring me, Jude."

"It'll all be okay." I take his hand. "I need you to know that. It'll all be okay."

"You sound like you're dying." He lets out an awkward laugh before it vanishes in an instant. "Wait, you're not, right?"

"No. There are just things that I can't tell you. Please just know that you met me at a very weird time in my life, and it's only going to get weirder."

Huy hesitates for a moment, before his hand wraps around mine. "Okay."

"Why didn't you go to the dance?" I ask him.

"I was afraid that you'd show up."

"Well . . . that didn't work out very well for you, did it?"

He smiles, shaking his head.

"Can I have this dance, Huy Trinh?"

"Of course you can, Jude Ricci."

Neve must realize what's happening, because she turns up

the volume on her radio before she and Alice step out of the car, taking each other's hands. Huy's hand tightens around mine, and he pulls me in close to him. For a moment, I think about kissing him. But I want this moment in front of me to last for as long as it can, until I'm tired and my body aches and my bones are brittle and I'm old. I want to be with him for as long as he'll allow me to, because I don't know how to be something he's forgotten about; I don't know how to be around anymore without Huy Trinh in my life.

I don't want to forget him.

But I have to.

If only so that I can find him all over again.

I can't stop the tears from spilling out, a sob escaping my lips as I turn away from him, and he smiles down at me.

"Look at me." His hand cups my cheek, wiping away the tears. "What's wrong?"

"I'm just really happy right now," I tell him.

"I'm happy too, Jude." His hand finds my hair, and he pulls me close to his chest. "Everything's going to be okay."

Except it isn't. No matter what we do, it'll never be okay.

But that has to be okay.

Even if I don't want it to be.

"I'm glad that I met you," I tell him.

"Me too."

I finally dare to look at him again. Because this is it. The moment that I've wanted and dreaded all at the same time. I want this, and I want him to know just how much I love him, just how much he means to me. I have to stand on my tiptoes, my hands on his chest as the song continues from the speakers.

When my lips meet Huy's, I hang on to him for every carefully precious second, because when this ends, he won't know who I am. He'll be so confused by this stranger in the middle of the street in front of his parents' donut shop where they make square-shaped donuts, this stranger locking lips with him. And me . . . who knows what'll happen to me. If I'll have a few minutes to get on the bus or BART to get home before I wonder just what I'm doing. If I'll be totally lost, unaware of just where to go.

It's why I hang on to him for all that I have. Because our first kiss could very well be our last.

His lips are soft against mine, his hair soft in my hands. I want to giggle at the way he grips my hips and my butt, and just how protected I feel in his arms. But my mind can't fathom any of that right now. Because this is it.

It is.

It's done.

My fate is sealed, and by extension, so is his.

I made this choice for us. And maybe that's unfair of me, to make this decision without consulting him, without knowing what he'd want. But the tragedy is that it doesn't matter. One way or another, this decision would've been made for the both of us. At least this way, I can be the one.

His eyes open when we separate. And for a moment, I wait to see the unfamiliarity in his eyes, his confusion, wondering just why he's dancing in a parking lot with a stranger.

"Jude?"

He says my name softly, and my heart breaks.

"Huy."

"How was that?"

I press my forehead against his chest, and I can't stop the

crying, the swing in his step carrying both of us to the song as he comforts me, pulling me in so tight I can't breathe for a moment.

"It's okay," he promises me. "It'll all be okay."

It will be.

I have to believe that.

"Hey," he says. I feel his hand on my chin, pulling me back up. "It's going to be okay."

"I know." And I kiss him again.

And again.

And again.

I kiss him for as many times as I can spare because for some reason he hasn't forgotten about me, and I've been gifted these extra seconds that I won't waste.

"Huy." I pause when I say his name. "Please, do something for me."

"Whatever you want."

"Please don't forget me," I beg him. "Okay?"

He smiles. "How could I ever forget someone like you, Jude Ricci?"

Huy leans down one final time. Not that we know it's the last one. Our lips meet, and I taste that sweet vanilla on his tongue before everything shifts, the world around us moving from beneath our feet.

And everything goes white.

# CHAPTER TWENTY-FIVE

I've never understood why it's so hard to pack up an air mattress. It literally comes in a box, but no matter how many times I try to fold it, I can't manage to make it fit, and the stupid little box on the side with all the inflation controls gets in the way and the power cord slips out of the case that's literally made for it.

"God, please! I don't know if you're up there, but please . . . enough is enough." I sit on top of the mattress, trying to squish it down to fit properly, but there's no way to maneuver the box.

"Everything okay in there?" Leah calls from the kitchen.

"It's fine!" I lie, but I can already hear her shoes on the wood floor.

"Here." She squats down. "Hold the box, help me guide it in." She squeezes the mattress tightly, forcing it into the box as hard as she can before she gives me a chance to close the box. "Did you actually break a sweat doing that?" she asks, standing up with her hands on her hips.

"Listen . . . it's hard with just one person."

"Sure, kiddo." She laughs, brushing the hair that's slipped free of her baseball cap away from her face. "Are you all ready?"

I nod. "My bags with my stuff are already in the car."

"Okay. The moving truck is already across the bridge, so we're running late."

"I know." I'll admit that part of it was my fault. I've been dreading this day for weeks now, but I knew it'd come. Leah got a new job that's carrying her up to Washington, which means goodbye, San Francisco. For the first time in my life, I'll be somewhere that isn't the Bay, and I don't like thinking about that. I'm sure Washington is great—I mean, we'll be right in the heart of Seattle, but . . . this has been our home since I was a kid, since Mom and Dad disappeared and Leah took me in. No more walking down to NaYa for nightly desserts, or Gordo's for the best burritos in the city. And sure, it's foggy and wet and cold in the Richmond, but it's a different foggy, wet, and cold from the northwest.

We packed my bed frame earlier this week, which is why I've been sleeping on this uncomfortable headache in front of me. All my posters and music and most of my clothes are all packed in a truck that's headed north now.

Leah's excited. She's been looking up the best scenic route for us to take so we'll get those perfect views, plenty of photo opportunities, and some nice motels. At thirteen hours, we could make it in a single day if I had a license, or if Leah trusted me with her car. But since she's the sole driver, it'll take us today and tomorrow to get there.

Quite the road trip.

I hoist the box for the air mattress, carrying it to the stairs, where the rest of our stuff we're taking with us in the car is sitting. A bag of snacks and drinks, phone chargers, pillows and blankets, Leah's work laptop that she allowed me to load with a few choice rom-coms for the trip.

"Are you ready?" she asks from the living room, taping the last box.

"Yeah, all my stuff is here."

"Good, I'm leaving the keys with the in-law tenants downstairs, so we don't have to wait for Mrs. Anderson to come by for them."

"Sounds good."

That's when the doorbell rings, and Leah looks at the stairs, confused. "Weird, I didn't order anything."

"I'll get it."

It'll suck to say goodbye to this place, this home. Then again, it's not like I had many friends that I'll be saying bye to. Or any friends at all. It's never been my strong suit to get to know people. The homeschooling didn't help. Leah says that Mom and Dad really did a number on me with that one. Most of the time I just have to trust her judgment, because I don't remember many of the years that we had with them. There are blips where I can picture Mom's face, and Leah promises me that I have her smile, and she even admitted that seeing me happy makes her sad sometimes.

I let the door swing open, expecting someone to be on the other side of the gate, but instead of the postal guy waiting to give us any late mail that came before the change of address took effect, or an Uber Eats delivery person ringing the wrong doorbell, no one's there.

There is, however, a manila envelope on the ground.

An envelope with the words *For Jude* written in black Sharpie.

I take it and close the door, opening it as I walk up the stairs slowly.

"What is it?" Leah asks.

"An envelope."

"Probably just some delayed mail or something," she tells me. "I'm going to go take things down to the car."

"Okay, sure." I wait until she's out of sight to open the envelope, spilling the contents out onto the kitchen counter. All that falls out is a piece of paper taped to a cassette tape.

All right, definitely leaning into the serial-killer vibes.

Like this tape will have some confession on it with the voice of the killer.

I take the paper first, reading it quickly because there are only a few words.

> Go to Marx Meadow, at the bench in front of the big oak tree. And listen to this tape on your way down.
>
> —your friend

"Okay . . . right." Like I'm going to do that.

I ball up the paper, prepared to toss that and the tape away before I remember our trash cans are packed in the moving truck. So I have to go out the back door in the kitchen and down the precarious wooden stairs that lead out to the backyard to toss them both into the recycling bin.

But before I do that, I pause, looking at the tape again.

It's a mix of some kind, with my name written on the spine.

*For Jude.*

Then I remember!

I have a Walkman. I race up the stairs, going through my backpack and nearly spilling out all the contents on the floor before I find the small black box. I think Leah gave this to me as a gag gift or something. I don't even own any tapes to play on it, so I'm not sure why I hung on to the thing.

Maybe because it was a gift.

There was just something about it, something that made me feel guilty any time I thought about tossing it.

I open the compartment, slip the tape in, put the headphones on, and press play.

"Hey, Jude . . . I, uh . . . God, this is so awkward, I'm so sorry. But I wanted to make this for you. Just because, and also because I like you, and I don't know if you're going to listen to this before or after I tell you. I guess I should make sure it's after, or else that'd be awkward, huh? I'm also going to ask you to forgive me for the first song choice. I couldn't resist. Enjoy it."

It's an unfamiliar voice, one that I don't recognize at all.

And yet . . .

There's something there.

Something more than the weirdness that I feel from having someone mail me a confession tape with a note asking to meet. All that, and the audacity to make me listen to the Beatles.

"What's that?" Leah asks, seemingly appearing out of nowhere.

"Oh, it's um . . . nothing."

"Okayyyyy. Are you ready?"

"I, uh . . ." Marx Meadow isn't that far from here. A three-block walk, plus a short jog in the park. I think I know which oak tree that letter was talking about. It's a big area for people on the weekends, where lots of families will come for cookouts or people will just chill on the grass. "I've got to go and grab something."

"Grab something? All of your stuff is packed." Leah looks at me, confused again.

"I know, I just forgot something."

"Jude, what are you talking about?"

I'm already halfway down the stairs, though. "I'll be right back! I swear!"

"Jude!" She calls out at me from the top of the stairs just as I'm out the front door, coordinating myself to walk south toward Golden Gate Park. The voice on the tape seems so . . . not familiar, I don't recognize it at all. But I also do? That doesn't make any sense. There's just . . . there's something about it. Something warm, comforting almost? Is that possible?

I finally get to the park, walking down a few blocks to find the right entrance that'll lead me to Marx Meadow, to this tree.

It's down a long path, and I narrowly avoid the Frisbee from a disc golf tournament going on just a few yards away. For a moment, I wonder if one of the disc golfers sent the envelope. But I don't recognize any of them, and they all look like grown men, which . . . ew. Then again, if I'm murdered, I'm the one who followed a random tape that was left on my doorstep. Not that I'm victim blaming, but I could've played it safer.

I peer up and down the path, and . . . there's no one.

A couple walks by with a baby in a stroller, and an old man walks his dog.

That's it.

Great.

I sigh, walking over to the nearest bench on the side of the trail, ignoring my phone with the missed calls from Leah.

That's when I pull the Walkman out of my jacket pocket. I hit play, letting the Beatles finish before Omar Apollo begins to play, and then Mac DeMarco. They're all soft, sad songs. But they're also love songs. Soft kisses and hands touching. It's sweet.

And someone made this for me?

But who? And why?

I hear the shuffle of the gravel in front of me, daring to look up, where a few yards away a boy walks by, staring up and down the trail. Our eyes meet for the briefest moment before he looks away, pacing back and forth before he settles on a bench a few yards away. He might look away, but I don't, sneaking glances in his direction.

He's cute. Bold black hair trimmed short, with an oversized sweatshirt and gym shorts. A terrible, lazy outfit that he somehow makes work. The only "odd" thing about him might be the way his arm is covered in a cast decorated in dozens of signatures and drawings of dicks.

Maybe I know him from the neighborhood or something?

Maybe he's been my barista?

And if he's the one who sent the letter and the tape, he'd say something, right? Which means we've both been fooled by someone. I don't want to sit here much longer, not if I'm going to be ghosted by some idiot I don't even know. Plus it's getting colder, and with every passing minute of ignoring Leah's calls, I'm sure she's getting more annoyed with me. We're already late.

Which means I need to go.

For a moment, I think about talking to the cute boy, but what's the point? By the end of today, I won't be in the state anymore. So . . . I listen to the crack of the gravel under my feet as I walk toward him, back along the trail, my phone in hand, ready to text Leah my apology. I guess I'll never figure out who sent that weirdo letter.

"Hey!" The voice surprises me, and for a moment I think it

can't possibly be for me. I mean, there are a few people nearby; maybe it's the disc golf people shouting a warning.

But no, it's not.

It's the cute boy. He's standing up, his hands awkward at his sides as he walks up to me.

"Hey, sorry . . . I, uh, didn't mean to shout." He rubs the back of his neck. He's even cuter up close. His nose sharp and angular, lips full. The haircut could use a little time to grow out, but it's not bad.

"You're fine," I tell him.

"I was just wondering . . . are you here because of a letter?"

"Yeah. Are you?"

"Yeah. I got one like an hour ago. It told me to come here."

"And you didn't write it?"

"No. Did you write mine?"

I shake my head as well.

"Well, that's . . ."

"Weird."

"Yeah." He smiles softly, and it's almost like he glows. This is the kind of boy that breaks hearts, I've seen enough rom-coms to be able to tell. "Sorry, I just . . . I feel like I know you? What school do you go to?"

"I'm homeschooled," I tell him. "But I, uh . . . I'm leaving, today actually. Moving."

"Where to?"

"Seattle."

"Yeesh . . . that's far."

"Yeah." I step forward, and he follows my stride. "My sister got a new job."

"Dang, that sucks."

"Yeah, not looking forward to it."

"You've lived in the Bay for a while?"

"My whole life. You?"

"A long time now, but I'm from Atlanta. And Vietnam a bit before that."

"International boy."

"Right, yeah." He laughs awkwardly. "So I guess we're never going to know who sent these letters?"

"I guess we can only hope it's not someone who wants to wear our skin."

"Well, not if we solve the case first. I think we should start by analyzing the handwriting on the letters. That'll give us our first clue."

"We could, but I threw mine away."

"Damn, same."

"There must be other leads, though. I got a tape."

"A tape?"

I nod. "With a voice on it. Which, now that I'm thinking about it, sounded a *lot* like yours."

"Okay, well . . . that certainly feels like serial-killer behavior."

"Would you know?"

"About being a serial killer?" He smiles. "Or tapes?"

Any potential awkwardness of the moment isn't enough to hide my soft laugh. "The tapes."

"Well, I've made tapes for friends."

"And you expect me to believe that you didn't send this letter? Your story isn't adding up anymore." I laugh with him.

"I've never written a letter, and that you can trust me on."

"Never writing letters seems like a weird brag," I tell him. "I don't even know your name."

"And I don't know yours. So we're even." He smiles again, showing off his dimples. Of course, it's just my luck that I'd meet a nice, very cute boy the day that I'm leaving the city. Fuck my life.

"Unless you are the letter sender?"

"I could say the same thing about you."

"Right, right." I look up at him. The height difference is a lot, and . . . kind of hot. I've always loved a boy who's taller than me. But what am I getting myself into here? "Well . . . I guess I should probably get going. My sister is waiting for me."

"Oh, right. You know, you could do that."

"I could."

"Or . . ."

"Or."

"Do you think that you have time for a coffee?"

"Coffee?"

"A quick one, I swear."

I bounce on my heels. I shouldn't. This will only end badly. What's the hope here? Best-case scenario is that we agree that long-distance suddenly works for brand-new relationships and we see each other once a year. What am I talking about, relationships? I hardly know this boy, and he might still very well be a letter- and tape-sending murderer.

But when I look in his eyes, I don't know, there's something trustworthy about him. Like I've known him for a long time. It's a big what-if, I guess. And it's not like anything has to happen.

It's just coffee, after all.

"Sure." I smile at him. "I'd love a coffee."

"Great." He leads the way, giving me a chance to catch up to him. "I'm Huy, by the way. Huy Trinh."

He holds out his hand for me to take, which is awkward as we're both walking along the trail, but I still take it, his palm wrapping around mine. His hand is warm, like this boy has his own personal space heater in his coat. Maybe that's why he's fine in shorts.

"I'm Jude Ricci."

He smiles at me, and suddenly there's something even brighter than the sun. "It's nice to meet you, Jude."

I smile back at him, and let his touch linger for a moment longer than it should, because it's nice. I like this.

"It's nice to meet you too."

# ACKNOWLEDGMENTS

A book is a village, no matter how solitary of an activity it is to write one. First and foremost, I must thank my agent, Lauren Abramo. Without you, none of this would've been possible, and knowing that you're in my corner maybe doesn't make things less scary, but it makes them easier to manage.

David Levithan, my all-star editor, who helped to shape this book into something that I'm so proud of. You chose Jude's story at a time when I was *desperate* for you not to. This idea had haunted me for years, and I'd never been able to figure it out, to get the pieces to fit together in my head in a way that satisfied me. But you issued me a challenge, even if you weren't aware of it. And I accepted. I'm so proud of what we were able to create together.

For Jeffrey West, who first believed in me and my stories. For Maeve Norton, who wows me with her cover design every single time. And to the team at Scholastic and IReadYA for always championing my stories and bringing them to readers everywhere.

Of course, there are my best friends. Corey and Nguyen, who make me smile like no one else. And Hương, there was a time during the editing of this book when I had to grapple with the possibility of a world without you in it. Nothing scared me more, but my theory that you're too stubborn to die proved to be correct, and I've never been happier to be right in all my life.

Then there are the friends that make the lonely art of writing feel so much less lonely: Becky Albertalli, Camryn Garret, Jason June, Sophie Gonzales, Alice Oseman, Sabina Khan, Jay Coles, Adib Khorram, Misha Osherovich, Sina Grace, Adam

Silvera, Rachel Lippincott, Alicia Thompson, Page Powars, Aiden Thomas, and Tracy Deonn.

And an extra special thank-you to Leah Johnson, for listening to my whining, for helping me through far too much, and for being there when I needed you most.

Thank you, Mark Oshiro, Kacen Callender, Claudia Gray, Preeti Chhibber, and Jackson Bird. I'm not sure if the five of you remember sitting in a greenroom in Boston back in 2019 and listening to me first explain this idea, but those conversations came to me so many times during drafting when I wanted to give up, write something else. I started writing this book on the flight back home and got a very odd stare from the man in the seat next to me as I opened up a book with a too-detailed making-out scene. Thankfully, the book evolved from there.

To my mother, who believes in me at every step of the way, who always encourages me and buys extra copies of my books for her friends.

And lastly, to my readers, who make this all worth it. Thank you, for everything.

I hope it's enough.

# ABOUT THE AUTHOR

**Mason Deaver** is the acclaimed author of the YA novels *I Wish You All the Best*, *The Ghosts We Keep*, and *The Feeling of Falling in Love*. They were born and raised in a small town in North Carolina and currently call San Francisco home. You can find them online at masondeaverwrites.com.